EMPIRE OF DREAMS AND MIRACLES

EMPIRE OF DREAMS AND MIRACLES

THE PHOBOS SCIENCE FICTION ANTHOLOGY

EDITED BY
ORSON SCOTT CARD
AND KEITH OLEXA

FOREWORD BY
LAWRENCE M. KRAUSS

PHOBOS BOOKS
NEW YORK

phobos

Published by Phobos Books
A Division of Phobos Entertainment Holdings, Inc.
325 Lafayette Street
New York, NY 10012
www.phobosweb.com

Distributed in the United States by National Book Network, Lanham, Maryland.

Cover art by Doug Chiang

Library of Congress Cataloging-in-Publication Data

Empire of dreams and miracles : the Phobos science fiction anthology / edited by Orson Scott Card and Keith Olexa ; foreword by Lawrence M. Krauss.
    p. cm.
  ISBN 0-9720026-0-X (pbk. : alk. paper)
1. Science fiction, American. I. Card, Orson Scott. II. Olexa, Keith, 1967–
  PS648.S3 E55 2002
  813'.0876208—dc21

                  2002007051

10 9 8 7 6 5 4 3 2 1

CONTENTS

CONTENTS

PUBLISHER'S NOTE

ON THE OCCASION OF THE BIRTH OF PHOBOS BOOKS . . .

PHOBOS IS NOT ONLY the name of our company, it is the name of our favorite Martian moon. Because of its tiny mass—20 x 23 x 28 kilometers—its extremely low gravity makes Phobos the most likely landing and base of operations for a manned mission to Mars. Since we are committed, as a company, to extra-planetary exploration, we are staking our claim to Phobos. As Phobos is built and populated, our aim is to ensure the values of artistic and intellectual freedom, imagination, kindness, fairness, and economic intelligence.

How many years will it take us to reach Phobos by interplanetary transport? Through a leap of our imagination, we can be there already—and we can take you with us.

When great writers have intercourse with great scientists, oracles are possible. In 1902, you could watch

SANDRA SCHULBERG

Georges Méliès' rocket poke our moon in the eye on a magical piece of film. In 1969, you could watch it happen live on television. The 1969 version wasn't quite as romantic or funny, but only a quibbler would argue with the accuracy of Méliès' prediction.

Why would anyone—in this age of Internet ease and modern media proliferation—choose to go back in time to Gutenberg's press, especially a group of people devoted to thinking about the Future? Each (good) book is a world unto itself—a new world, a world of exploration and discovery, a future world.

Empire of Dreams and Miracles owes its title to James Maxey. This book would not exist without James, and the other marvelous talents whose work is collected in this book, all of whom took a leap of faith when they agreed to publication by a fledgling imprint. We thank Rebecca Carmi, Daniel Conover, Carl Frederick, David Barr Kirtley, Chris Leonard, Ken Liu, James Maxey, Andrew Rey, Rick Sabian, and Justin Stanchfield for joining the Phobos mission.

If Moon Cho, Vice President of Phobos, had not opened my eyes to the wonder of great science fiction, Phobos Entertainment, let alone Phobos Books, would not exist.

Stan Plotnick, Chairman of Rowman & Littlefield Publishing Group and National Book Network, became our mentor in all things—a man in whom one finds a razor-sharp business acumen, a deep love of books, movies and art, and a personal modesty which rivals the humble Talmudic sages of old.

We are grateful to Norman Jacobs and David McDonnell for having allowed us to poach Keith Olexa from his job as Managing Editor of *Starlog*. A passionate connois-

x

seur of great SF, Keith is the soul of Phobos Books. We also acknowledge Michael Ryan, a virtual investor in Phobos.

Mark Buntzman was part of the original Phobos Brain Trust. Mark's love of all things scientific and his early financial support kept Phobos on course during its metamorphosis from idea to mission to corporate entity.

Thomas Vitale, Senior Vice President of the Sci-Fi Channel, was part of the original Brain Trust which incubated Phobos. Later, he served on the jury which selected the stories in this book, and the Channel became an official sponsor of the Phobos Fiction Contest.

The dauntingly clever John Roche, whose knowledge of SF literature and movies nearly exceeds even Keith's, provided not only early financial support, but also led us straight to the straight-shooting Jim Shooter.

Jim Shooter became a professional writer of Superman comics at age 13, and went on to become a legend in the comic book industry as Editor-in-Chief of Marvel and as the publisher of his own Valiant and Defiant comics. When it comes to judging or creating story structure, Jim dons his superhero costume and flies to our rescue.

Rajesh Raichoudhury, investor, inventor, technologist, SF enthusiast, rabid gamer and resident wise man, is the architect of our inner structure. His teaching has empowered Daniel Farkovits, who serves as our eyes and ears on the Internet, keeping the server humming and tuned to extraterrestrial signals at all times.

Sybil Robson Orr is an intergalactic traveler. She may have Midwestern roots, but she turned them in for a set of wings long ago. When asked if she wanted to buy a ticket for the Phobos mission, her response was an enthusiastic and spontaneous "Yes—this is going to be a fun ride!"

It is difficult for a young company to navigate the world of investment banking without a seasoned guide. Jack Hyland, partner at McFarland, Dewey, not only advised us on investment strategy, he became an investor—and writer—himself. His biography of evangelist Bill Stidger is published by Rowman & Littlefield.

Christian O'Toole is the youngest member of the Phobos mission. A sorcerer's apprentice who regularly amazes his elders with his own magic powers, Christian read all of the story submissions and assisted Keith every step of the way.

We still can't figure out how Andrew Mason managed to read all the stories while shuttling between his home in Australia and the various locations for *The Matrix* II & III. We hope some of the writers in this first Phobos anthology may have the good fortune to be produced by Andrew, whose creative and logistical Kung Fu rivals Neo's any day.

Doug Chiang is simply one of the most remarkable visual artists and designers of his generation. As Design Director for *Star Wars: Episodes I–III*, Doug has made visible the imaginary worlds of George Lucas, and has created his own equally extraordinary world in *Robota: Reign of Machines*. Doug served on the jury which selected the stories in this book, and created the beautiful cover art.

Lawrence Krauss, the renowned astrophysicist, has calculated the life expectancy of the universe. We thank Lawrence for lending his brilliant mind to the evaluation of the stories in this book, and for his eloquent Foreword.

Janet Jackson, our wonder woman in disguise, designed the luminous Phobos website (www.phobosweb.

com) and created the Phobos logo—our badge of pride and our passport in the galaxy. "The Entity" (aka the artist-designer Louis Farkovitz) created the stunning silver Phobos Awards.

Budd Schulberg, Stuart Schulberg and Barbara Schulberg all had an invisible hand in this book. My profound thanks and love go to Barbara, in particular, who provided the physical and spiritual incubation chamber in which Phobos developed.

Three co-conspirators contributed to this venture in ways they may not realize. We celebrate our association with Meyer Shwarzstein of Brainstorm Media, and Russell Mix and Reichart Von Wolfsheild of Prolific Publishing.

Four wise men act as consiglieri: Joseph Dapello, John Stout, John Russell and Jaime Wolf. Each brings vision, compassion, and integrity to his application of the law, and has contributed countless hours to this venture.

For the physical existence of this book, we wish to gratefully acknowledge the team at Rowman & Littlefield Publishing Group, especially Jed Lyons, President, and Julie Kirsch. We also thank Debbie Wolf, our own Phobos Books proofreader, for her fiendish pursuit of typos.

For ensuring nationwide distribution to a bookstore near you, we are grateful to the team at National Book Network, especially Michael Sullivan, Miriam Bass, Vicki Metzger, Ginger Miller, Jen Linck, and the fleet of mighty messengers who are the national sales representatives.

Orson Scott Card (who wrote the book introduction and the introductions to the stories) and his wife Kristine had faith in Phobos from the first. Kristine's famous organizational skills have been invaluable. Scott's conviction in the power of revelation informs all of his writing, and inspired me to see in science fiction a unique opportunity to present utopian and dystopian visions of the Future.

I want to leave you with the words that Scott wrote in the introduction to *Ender's Game*: "The story is one that you and I will construct together in your memory. If the story means anything to you at all, then when you remember it afterward, think of it, not as something I created, but rather as something that we made together."

That is how I would like you to experience the stories we have collected here. If you remember anything about them, if they horrify or amuse or amaze you, think of them as visions of a future that you and we are creating, together—an *Empire of Dreams and Miracles*.

SANDRA SCHULBERG
Publisher

FOREWORD

THE UNKNOWN POSSIBILITIES OF EXISTENCE . . .

Lawrence M. Krauss

MY COLLEAGUE STEPHEN Hawking wrote in the foreword to my book, *The Physics of Star Trek*: "Science Fiction . . . serves a serious purpose, that of expanding the human imagination. We may not be able to go where no man or woman has gone before, but at least we can do it in our minds." The stories included in this volume exemplify his faith in the medium of science fiction. Here, in the first annual Phobos Anthology, is an eclectic collection that demonstrates the talents of a new generation of writers, exploring themes ranging from traditional SF stand-bys such as time travel, as in "The Hanged Man, the Lovers and the Fool," and alien invasion, as in "Rippers" and "They Go Bump," to a delightfully inventive take-off on the recent phenomenon of internet sex in "Twenty-Two Buttons."

I have often been asked by journalists, "What is it that distinguishes good science fiction from bad?" They are fishing for examples of onerous scientific bloopers, and alas, there are plenty, especially in SF TV and film. Science fiction on the page is different. For most enthusiasts, it's literary science fiction that establishes the working standard. In this regard I have tended to apply the same standards to good science fiction as one might to good art: "I'll know it when I see it." I thus decided to accept the challenge to help judge the contest that produced the exciting stories in this book. I thought it might help me to focus what distinguished the best science fiction stories from the merely good ones.

One might imagine that as a scientist I would focus first on the science itself, but I chose not to. Science fiction is primarily *fiction*. Gene Roddenberry himself viewed *Star Trek*'s legendary *Enterprise* primarily as a vehicle for drama. This was an essential part of his success. Like all good fiction, story should come first, and, along with story, come characters one can sympathize with and, if necessary, root for in times of trouble.

Science, or dreams of science, should not interfere with the story but add to it, like icing on a cake. In this regard, the science in science fiction need not be completely accurate. The more accurate the better—after all, I think science fiction can help inspire young readers to wonder about the mysteries of the Universe, and if they are going to wonder, they may as well be wondering about *our* Universe as some hypothetical one—but the chief requirement is *believability*. If one can't suspend disbelief early on, it's impossible to get emotionally involved in the characters and their concerns.

To achieve this level of believability, science fiction writers often exploit ideas in science that are just emerging, ones about which we don't yet know all the details. Will quantum computers, or something like them, allow for the self-aware AIs that one finds in "Carthaginian Rose" or "Eula Makes Up Her Mind"? Will virtual reality ever achieve the extremes represented in "Empire of Dreams and Miracles"? Will we be able to incorporate our technology into our biology as effectively as in "The Prize"? Will genetic engineering reach the levels posited in "The Compromise"? Are there extra dimensions of space-time, so central to the plot in "The Messiah"?

At the same time, I believe science fiction operates well when it explores familiar issues, even if they are not profound, and examines how they might be reflected in completely different circumstances. Anyone who has ever shopped for a house with a real-estate agent, for example, will sympathize with the irritation felt by the protagonists in "Who Lived in a Shoe." It is difficult enough to find an abode that fits one's personal lifestyle, even when the previous inhabitants have been human. Imagine how much more difficult it would be when a universe of alien possibilities is added to the mix!

Probably the most seductive aspect of writing science fiction is the ability to explore new, alien, psychologies. If human tragedy is the driving force of classical literature, alien tragedy surely must be behind most great science fiction stories. Embedded in these themes is our fundamental desire not to be alone in the Universe. If intelligent civilizations exist elsewhere in the cosmos, the possibilities are both exhilarating and terrifying.

Thus, it is not surprising that the lion's share of stories in this volume have an alien component. First contact is explored in completely different ways in "The Messiah" and "Rippers." More sinister aspects of the inevitable culture clash that will ensue if we ever encounter intelligent life elsewhere in the Universe are featured in "They Go Bump."

Ultimately however, what makes science fiction most exciting, to me at least, is a quality it shares with science itself. The reason I am a theoretical physicist is that I simply want to know *what is possible* in the Universe. Exploring the "unknown possibilities of existence," as *Star Trek*'s omnipotent alien being Q once mused, is perhaps the highest calling we humans can have. Science fiction explores precisely these themes, as viewed through the filters of creative, literary minds. It is not surprising, for this reason, that science and science fiction sometimes overlap so closely and anticipate common ideas. It is simply a matter of creative people exploring similar problems. I am certain that many of the same themes you will read here, including the ultimate limits of artificial intelligence and the changing meaning of life itself as we explore the mysteries of the human genome, will feature prominently in news throughout the twenty-first century and beyond.

Of course, what amazes me about the Universe is how nature continues to present surprises beyond the wildest dreams of writers and poets. No one could have anticipated the true weirdness of quantum mechanics, for example, or the strangeness of a universe dominated by the energy of empty space. Trying to convey the excitement of these new scientific developments to non-scientists is not always so easy. Thus it is that many readers turn to science fiction when they wish to imagine how remarkable our own Universe may actually be.

Those readers who are fortunate enough to get their hands on this collection of stories will not be disappointed. From unfathomable computers to invisible aliens, the stories here present an exciting variety of explorations of how intelligence may confront the cosmos. You will experience the Universe as it is, as it might be, and as we hope it will never be. For those who wish to expand their imaginations, I can't imagine a better treat. Enjoy!

INTRODUCTION

Orson Scott Card

SCIENCE FICTION, of all genres of storytelling, is the one that hungers most for new writers. Not that we're tired of the old ones. Familiar dreams are never unwelcome. But one of the pleasures that science fiction offers its aficionados is to be transported, not just to new places, but to new ideas—new things to think about, and new ways to think about them.

The trouble is that even though a particular writer might strive with each story to devise new experiences for readers, in the end, the most important aspects of each story are those that arise out of the unconscious mind of the storyteller. And since each writer's unconscious worldview is largely the same from story to story, to find deep novelty, readers of science fiction must find new writers as well as new tales from old friends.

It's different for people in genres that thrive on repetitive experiences. Even on the boundaries of speculative fiction, there are subgenres that allow readers to return again and again to familiar places—*Star Trek*, *Star Wars*, and other media-centered fiction tend to fulfill old promises rather than make new ones. There's nothing wrong with seeking to return to tales that have satisfied before. But the core of the appeal of speculative fiction is the reader's hunger for non-repetitive—or at least less repetitive—stories.

Traditionally, ever since Hugo Gernsback offered the first fiction magazine devoted solely to science fiction— he called it "scientifiction"—the place where new writers were discovered was the magazines. And even today, *The Magazine of Fantasy and Science Fiction*, *Analog*, *Isaac Asimov's Science Fiction Magazine*, and other, less well-known venues offer readers a chance to "find them first"—to catch tomorrow's Grand Old Coots while they're still just Smart-Mouthed Kids.

But editors have their own tastes, their own visions of what kind of tale each magazine ought to offer. Even the best editors have their list of great writers whose early stories they rejected, along with a list of proud discoveries. And the drawback of the magazines is that each issue, no matter what you do with it, is merely another issue. It's hard for the editor to say, "Buy the March issue, because this time we have really good stories"—without also saying the same thing in April, May, and June.

And finally, there's the old-coot problem. Oh, pardon me, I meant the "prominent writer" problem. If George R.R. Martin or John Varley or Nancy Kress or Connie Willis pops up with a good new story, they, not a new writer, will get the featured place in the magazine, because their name on the cover will help sell issues.

A contest for new writers has the virtue of getting rid of the old-coot problem right from the start. Having only one volume a year means that it will never be "just another issue." And by having a panel of judges, there's a chance of getting around a bit of the bias that every editor or judge, individually, will have.

I have taught writing, off and on, for many years. So many of my students, young and old, have asked me, "What's the secret? How do I break through the wall and get my work published?" The secret, I tell them, is to write something twice as good as the latest story by Connie Willis or John Varley. Whereupon they go hang themselves in despair.

No they don't. They might, but I immediately tell them, John Varley writes John Varley stories brilliantly, and you could never do them half so well. But neither can he write your stories, and your job is not to learn how to write his, but rather to learn how to write your own so clearly, so powerfully, so believably that readers find no barrier between their desire for the tale and the having of it. Do that, and the audience that already hungers for your stories, without knowing that is what they hunger for, will find you, because no amount of bad luck or editorial disfavor will keep you apart forever.

You (the hungry reader) have here in your hands the result, not of a competition, but of an opportunity. When runners run a race, at the end, you have a winner, but nothing else. They ran, but they got nowhere; the last loser and the first-place winner end up in the same place. But in a contest like this one, each writer runs on his own track. Justin Stanchfield was writing "The Hanged Man, the Lovers and the Fool," while James Maxey was writing "Empire of Dreams and Miracles." Maybe if they both had been writing "Empire of Dreams, Lovers, and Fools" it might have been a competition, but they were not.

Writers must solve the problems the particular story they're trying to tell presents to them. It is common for someone who has written five stories brilliantly to run aground on the shoals of the sixth one he attempts. To "win" a competition like this does not mean you are certified to be a "good writer" whose every story will be excellent, any more than raising one child well means you will be successful in raising another. And those whose stories did not win the chance to appear in this book are not certified as "failures," only as writers who were not able to surmount the difficulties as well as they might on one particular story—or who surmounted the difficulties just fine, but in the service of a story that happened not to appeal to these judges this year.

And yet, with all these lovely egalitarian ideas now before you—and they are all true—the fact remains: These stories stood out from an array of many, and are offered now to you because they meant something to the judges and we think they'll feel important, entertaining, truthful to you. Indeed, they may even live up to the names of the old magazines—these stories may indeed be thrilling, amazing, astounding . . .

EMPIRE OF DREAMS
AND MIRACLES

THEY GO BUMP

DAVID BARR KIRTLEY

Camouflage exists so the enemy can't see you. The trouble is, neither can your friends. In a game of pickup basketball, where you don't know your teammates any better than your opponents, players often resort to uniforms—shirts vs. skins.

So it is in war. Unless you go into battle with just one little band of hunters against another, where you know all your friends and so anyone else must be an enemy, you have to have some way of making sure you aren't attacking your own side. The trouble is, uniforms can be put on by anyone. So even as you trust the uniform to keep you from harming your friends, you never know but that it's the enemy who has disguised himself in your uniform so he can betray you.

So we devise shibboleths—passwords or accents or jargons that we think the enemy won't know, so that uniform or not, we can discern between friend and foe. But now we come back to camouflage. When soldiers find the perfect way to hide, there are no uniforms at all, are there?

PRIVATE BALL PLACED his feet carefully. Walking on rough terrain was treacherous when you couldn't see your feet—or your legs, or for that matter, any part of yourself. All he could see was the uneven ground, and the shady stones outlined with sharp sunlight, drifting eerily beneath him.

His boot caught and twisted, and he pitched forward, falling and smacking his elbows hard against the ground.

From somewhere up on the hilltop, Private Cataldo's voice laughed. That voice—smooth and measured, with just a hint of sharpness. Ball had never paid much attention to voices before, but now voices were all they had.

Cataldo shouted, "Was that you, Ball? Again?"

Ball groped on the ground for his rifle. He felt it, grasped it, and slung it over his shoulder. He clambered to his feet, and wavered there a few moments, unsteady.

Cataldo's voice again: "How many times is that now? Twelve?"

"Eleven." Ball groaned, stretched, and looked around. "Where are you?"

"By the rock."

Ball sighed. The rock. There was nothing but rocks, nothing but rolling expanses of rocks and more rocks, stretching to the horizon in every direction. The orange sky was littered with rocks too, rocky moons. "Which rock?" Ball said.

"The big, triangular one."

Ball squinted up the hill.

"See the tall peak?" Cataldo's voice prompted. "Follow the gully down. There's a patch of boulders, and then at the edge of those there's this big, triangular—"

"All right, I see it." Ball took a deep breath. "I'm coming."

He scrambled over the boulders and picked his way carefully among the smaller stones. He tried to picture Cataldo's face—black hair, honey skin, narrow jaw, and long nose. Ball hadn't seen that face all day. Now there was just the voice.

"OK, I'm here," Ball breathed, finally.

The empty spot of nothingness that was Cataldo said, "Where's Sweezy?"

"I don't know." Ball shook his head, though he realized Cataldo couldn't see it anyway. "He hasn't said anything all day. I've tried talking to him."

Cataldo groaned. "Sweezy! Hey, Sweezy! Where are you?"

The vast plains of boulders were stony and silent. There was no answer.

"He might have fallen behind," Ball said. "Maybe he got lost, or hurt his ankle."

"He's out there. Goddamnit, Sweezy! Sound off."

Finally, a plaintive voice, from far down in the rockslide, called out, "I'm here. What?"

Private Sweezy. His voice tended to waver as he spoke. It always seemed tired and bristly, that voice. Ball shouted, "We're checking to make sure you're still with us."

"Just go," Sweezy's voice said. "I can take care of myself."

Cataldo grunted in disgust, and said to Ball, "Come on, and let's catch up with the others."

3

Ball turned wearily, and moved to follow. He walked in the direction he thought Cataldo had gone.

Invisible soldiers. Ball chuckled tiredly. Invisible soldiers on an important mission. Invisible soldiers with invisible feet.

He tripped again, and fell.

THE WEEK BEFORE, Ball had been safe, tucked far underground in the winding, humid, steel-rimmed tunnels of Fort Deep. He'd been sitting on a hard bench outside Captain Schemmer's office.

They were giving Ball a mission; he wondered if he was going to die. Cataldo had come and gone already, but Sweezy was still in there. Ball could hear the voices through the door.

Sweezy's voice, prickly and desperate: "Why me? I'm a good soldier. You know I'm a good soldier. I train all the time. I study all the intel, hard. I don't deserve—"

The captain's voice, female, too low and gruff to hear the words.

Then Sweezy again, "But—"

Then the captain, and so on.

Finally, the door opened and Sweezy emerged. He was skinny, with a huge, lumpy head, and big eyes rimmed with darkness.

"Hey Sweezy," Ball said softly.

Sweezy, sweaty and pale, nodded and walked on past.

Captain Schemmer called, "Private Ball."

Ball stood and entered. The office was spartan: one desk and two chairs, one chair for the captain, one for Ball. The walls were made of hewn boulder and plate steel. Schemmer wasn't made of those things; she could have been.

Ball sat down. "Nice to finally meet you, Captain."

Schemmer nodded. "You've been picked for an important mission. Earth Army is conducting field tests of the new phased camouflage." She stared at Ball levelly. "You've seen the reports?"

"Yes, sir."

Ball hadn't bothered, actually, but he had heard of the camouflage. "That stuff the Kraven-Hish mercenaries use." He suppressed a shudder. "That makes them invisible."

"We've developed our own. You're going to test it under battlefield conditions."

Ball blinked. "Battlefield, sir?"

"You're going to walk across the planet surface, from Hatch E to Hatch A."

Ball caught his breath. For months, orbital assault platforms had circled high overhead in the orange-dust sky. They swept over the horizon and launched missile attacks against anything that moved on the surface. "But the orbitals—"

"Won't see you," Schemmer said. "Not if the camouflage works. Just like they don't see the Kraven-Hish mercenaries."

Ball stared at the floor.

"We've done tests," Schemmer said. "The camouflage has passed every one. You should be pretty safe. But we need to know whether this stuff holds up under real conditions. We need to send some people outside with it, for a week or more."

"Me?" Ball glanced back over his shoulder. "And Sweezy?"

"And some others. Yes."

Ball nodded slowly.

So they needed a couple guys, some guys who could walk. And maybe these guys would get nuked. So they picked the most useless guys here.

Himself. Cataldo. Sweezy.

Goddamnit.

"Yes, Captain," Ball said.

THE SIX SUITS were sheer, gray and filmy, like a trout's eye. The elbows, knees, and boots were thickly padded. Air tanks and rifles, all that same dull color, hung from the shoulders. The rifles were linked to the suit by thin cords.

"The cord's so you don't lose the rifle," one of the technicians said. "It'll be invisible too, once you power up."

Six suits. Ball glanced around the room.

Private Dimon, rat-faced and sleazy, was over in the corner sucking up to Cataldo. So Dimon was in.

Plus Cataldo.

Sweezy.

And Ball made four. Two more.

A calm, friendly voice said, "Ball."

Ball turned. Private Reice, young, soft-spoken and good-natured, stood grinning.

"Damn," Ball said, "They got you, too."

Reice nodded. "Me." He glanced toward the door. "And the corporal, too, it looks like."

Corporal Tennet, tall and brave, walked into the room.

"He probably volunteered," Ball said, quietly.

The corporal cleared his throat. "All right, everyone. Suit up."

The technicians helped Ball into one of the suits. The material clung tight around his biceps and thighs. A foggy, translucent mask covered his face.

One of the technicians said, "There are buttons inside the material on the left wrist. You can feel them."

Ball ran his fingers down his arms. He felt four knobby bumps.

"Punch in your code," said another technician, demonstrating on the corporal, "like this—"

Light flashed, bright as a signal flare. The technician backed away from the glow. The corporal was gone.

Ball waited, tense, through a long stretch of silence.

Then the corporal's voice: "I can't see my hand."

Reice strained forward, staring hard. He whispered, "Holy shit."

The corporal's voice again, "I can't see my feet either."

"Move slowly," the technician advised. "It takes some getting used to."

Ball heard the soft clomp of the corporal's first footstep. The corporal took a few more steps.

They heard his voice, chuckling. His voice said, "Everyone power up."

Light flashed out all over. Ball shielded his eyes against the glare, and he punched the code on his wrist, and then—

He saw the tip of his nose, and the dark interior rim of his helmet. He looked down. There was nothing there.

Vertigo struck him. He was falling—falling forward— he jerked upright. He dropped back a few paces, and closed his eyes. "How do you power it down?"

"You don't," a technician said sharply, "or you'll die. That's the point."

"Punch the code in reverse," said another.

Ball opened his eyes. He waved his invisible hand in front of his face. He ran his invisible fingers over his

DAVID BARR KIRTLEY

invisible wrist, over the knobby buttons. In the end, he decided not to mess with them.

Sweezy's voice said, "How do they know these things are going to work?"

"They don't," Cataldo's voice said nastily. "That's what *we're* for."

Sweezy said, "I think they ought to—"

There was a sudden crash, and a desk rolled across the room, scattering pipes and wires. From somewhere down on the floor, Sweezy groaned.

Cataldo said, "Stop screwing around."

"Someone pushed me," Sweezy protested. There were the scrapes and thumps of him climbing to his feet. "It was you. You pushed me."

"I didn't push anybody," Cataldo said.

Dimon's voice added, "You probably tripped."

"It was you then," said Sweezy. "I never trip. Never. I train all the time. I—"

His voice trailed off into a faint mumbling as the corporal's voice cut him off: "All right, form up and move out. Hatch E. Let's go."

"We're going outside?" Ball said, half to himself. "Now?"

"What do you want, Ball?" Cataldo challenged. "A mission briefing on how to walk?"

Dimon's voice snickered.

They marched out into the hall. A group of heavy-helmeted military police was waiting. Ball glanced at one of the men; the man's cold eyes traced blankly over the spot where Ball stood.

Ball made a face at him. No response.

The police led the way down long rock and steel tunnels, then herded the squad through a great oval airlock

8

and out into the cavern beyond. The air was thin here. Enormous steel pipes stretched up to the ceiling, up to a gigantic metal plate. The underside of the plate read: HATCH E.

Ball flinched as the great hatch creaked and shuddered and began to descend—slow, massive and ponderous. It sank and sank and crunched against the floor.

The corporal's voice said, "Move."

Ball scurried forward and climbed awkwardly up the steep stone façade. A voice cursed—Ball couldn't tell whose. The platform rose, higher and higher. They came out into the open sky and the hatch clanked solidly into place beneath them.

Ball stared. The vista was wide and empty. There was nothing to see here. Not even himself.

"Everybody sound off," the corporal's voice said.

Ball said, "I'm right next to you." They had no radios, no locator beacons. Orbitals could track signals like that.

"I'm over here," said Cataldo's voice.

Next to him came Dimon's voice, "Yeah. Me too."

"I'm here," said Reice's voice.

There was a long pause.

The corporal's voice prompted, "Sweezy?"

Sweezy's voice came finally, almost too soft to hear, "I'm with you."

The corporal's voice sighed. "All right. Hatch A is northeast of here. Northeast is that way, between those two rocks."

Ball squinted toward the horizon. Two large rocks sat heavy and still.

The corporal's voice said, "Move out."

There were scraping footstep sounds as the squad began to march.

Dimon's voice said, "We're going to die."

"Maybe," the corporal's voice replied. "The first orbital comes up over the horizon in forty-three minutes." He paused. "Then we'll know."

Ball traced his gaze over the horizon in a wide circle. "Nine *days* out here? Even if the orbitals don't get us, a pack of Kraven-Hish mercenaries will."

Cataldo's voice said, "Maybe you haven't noticed, Ball, but we're invisible. They can't see us."

"We can't see them, either," Ball countered.

"Exactly," the corporal's voice cut in. "They can't see us. We can't see them. No one can see anyone. So relax. And keep walking."

Ball pulled the rifle off his shoulder and hefted it experimentally. Damned impossible, he decided, trying to aim a gun you couldn't even see.

He sighed.

Again, Dimon's voice said, "We're going to die."

Dimon's voice—it came from somewhere ahead of Ball, and it drifted past, and out away over the hills.

FORTY-THREE MINUTES passed. The first of the orbitals came over the horizon. Ball imagined he could see it up there, a bright spot shining white against the orange sky. It looked like death.

The corporal's voice said, "It's time."

Ball waited, not sure if he was breathing. He waited for a glint of metal in the sky, for a tactical nuclear assault.

Ten minutes passed.

"The orbital's overhead," the corporal's voice announced. "It can't see us."

Ball breathed in and out. He slumped down low in his suit. Dimon's voice started to laugh, a little crazily.

"Keep walking," the corporal's voice said.

The sound of scattered footsteps picked up again.

"And now—" Ball took a deep breath. "Now we can start worrying about Kraven-Hish mercenaries."

"Give it a rest, Ball," Cataldo's voice said. "You're bringing down my morale."

"They might be around," Ball argued. "A pack of them."

"They might not," Cataldo's voice said.

"Who knows where they are?" Reice's voice said. "Who knows where the hell they might be? We don't even know what they look like."

"They don't look like anything," Cataldo's voice answered, irritated. "They're invisible."

Reice's voice said, "You know what I mean."

Ball stared at the ground.

No one had ever taken a picture of the Kraven-Hish; they were always invisible. You couldn't get a picture, even if a soldier killed one—and some guys were pretty sure they had.

Ball glanced around. Imagine the whole squad died out here—who'd ever find them? They'd rot. Then the suits would rot. The suits would go visible in rotted patches, nothing left of the bodies inside.

Dimon's voice said, "You know what I heard? I heard they've got pictures of the Kraven-Hish. Intel has pictures. They don't want to show us."

Reice's voice said, "Why would they do that?"

"They don't want to frighten off new recruits," Dimon's voice said. "That's how scary these things are. That's what I heard."

"That's stupid," Cataldo's voice said.

"That's what I heard," Dimon's voice repeated. "That's all."

BALL HADN'T TRIPPED in over six hours. He forced himself to grin.

From somewhere behind him, Cataldo's voice shouted, "Sweezy!"

Ball turned. "Not again." He took a few steps back toward Cataldo's voice.

"Sweezy! Damn it, Sweezy. Just say something."

The rocky wastes were silent.

"I swear, Sweezy," Cataldo's voice warned. "I swear this is the last time. Sound off."

They waited, and waited. There was no answer.

Ball imagined Sweezy's face—tired and petulant, forehead scrunched, eyes staring at his feet, ignoring them.

"All right," Cataldo's voice called finally. "All right, if that's how you want it. I hope you break your neck."

Ball sighed.

"Let's go," Cataldo's voice told him.

They walked up over the next rise. The scattered voices of the others were faint in the valley below. It took an hour of walking to catch up.

Those voices, louder now, drifted toward them.

The corporal's voice: "Reice. You take point for a while. I'm going to check on the others."

"Yes, sir," Reice's voice said.

The corporal's voice asked, "You know the way?"

"To Hatch A? Yes, sir."

"Good."

Ball walked a few hundred yards. From right beside him the corporal's voice came: "Who's there?"

"Ball, sir," Ball said. "And Cataldo."

"Anything to report?"

Ball wondered if Cataldo would report on Sweezy, but Cataldo's voice just said, with a trace of disgust, "No, sir. Nothing at all."

NIGHT FELL. The dusty sky turned from orange, to brown, to muddy black. The cratered asteroid moons shone lovely and red. Ball lay curled up in his soft suit on the hard ground and kept his rifle close. With his fingers, he traced the invisible cord that connected the rifle to his shoulder.

Reice was resting somewhere nearby, and Dimon was somewhere down the hill. Ball wasn't sure about the corporal, and Sweezy hadn't spoken since that morning. No one seemed to miss him.

Dimon's voice burst out, "Cataldo. Get off, it's not funny. I'm trying to sleep."

Cataldo's voice answered, from far down the hill. "What? I'm over here."

There was a sudden sound, a sharp, breaking sound— like a branch snapping. But there were no branches out here, nothing here to be broken except their necks. Ball said quickly, "What was that?"

"I thought I felt something," Dimon's voice said. There was a short pause. "Never mind. It was nothing."

"What was that sound?" Ball pressed. "That cracking sound?"

"What sound?" Dimon's voice said.

"I heard it, too," Reice's voice said.

Dimon's voice said, "I didn't hear anything."

Ball rolled up onto his knees, pushed the butt of his rifle back into his shoulder, and pointed the barrel out toward the darkness.

Cataldo's voice called, "You're hearing things, Ball."

"I heard it too," Reice insisted.

"Heard what?" Cataldo's voice said.

"I don't know," Reice said. "Kind of a—I don't know."

Dimon's voice chuckled.

Cataldo's voice joined in. "Right."

Ball knelt there on the rocks. He stared up at the asteroids. They glowed deep and red, like all the blood of Earth Army soldiers killed by—

Kraven-Hish mercenaries.

Dozens of them could hide out here; hundreds, lurking invisible among the stones. They were trained to fight unseen. They could get close to a person; kill a person.

Silently.

Or—almost silently.

They could kill a person, maybe mimic his voice, and then no one would ever know.

"Let's get some sleep," Dimon's voice said.

Ball shuddered. It was Dimon's voice, yes. But was it Dimon?

A Kraven-Hish mercenary crouched deadly in the darkness there, settled over Dimon's invisible corpse.

Maybe.

Ball lay still. His ears strained for any sound, but there were no more sounds.

And no more sleep.

Dawn burned orange and bright.

"Corporal," Ball said. "I'm afraid."

"We're all afraid, Ball," the corporal's voice replied.

Ball said, "I heard something last night, sir. A strange noise. I think I heard Private Dimon die."

"I saw Dimon this morning,"

Ball didn't say anything. The corporal waited.

"Sir." Ball heard a strained quality creep into his own voice. "No one's *seen* Dimon since Fort Deep. All we hear is a voice. Voices are easy to imitate."

"You think our squad's been infiltrated? Dimon's voice replaced by—"

Ball lowered his voice. "By Kraven-Hish mercenaries. Sir, I don't know."

"Just Dimon?"

Ball paused. "And maybe Cataldo, I don't know."

"And maybe me."

Ball sighed. "It's possible, sir."

"But you're still telling me?"

"I have to tell someone," Ball said. "If they've gotten you, well, then we're all dead anyway. It's worth the risk."

"That's good thinking, Ball." There was a brief pause. "But you're overreacting. You thought you heard a noise. Maybe it was real, maybe it wasn't. Maybe it was nothing. I wouldn't blame anyone for starting to hear things out here."

"Reice heard it, too."

There was a pause. The corporal's voice called out, "Private Reice."

Ball didn't hear his approach, but a few moments later, Reice's voice was there. "Sir."

The corporal's voice said, "You heard a noise last night?"

"No," Reice's voice said. "I mean, I thought maybe I did, sir, after Ball said it. But it was just my imagination. You know what it's like here at night. The—"

"Yes," said the corporal's voice. "Thank you, private."

Ball waited a while.

"Sir," he pleaded softly. "Please."

"Your mind's playing tricks on you, that's all. You know how I'm sure?"

"How?"

The corporal's voice sighed. "A pack of Kraven-Hish mercenaries wouldn't bother to infiltrate us. They'd just wipe us out. We couldn't stop them."

That was true, Ball acknowledged.

"You take point for a while," the corporal's voice said. "It'll give you something else to think about."

"Yes sir," Ball said.

DAYS PASSED SLOWLY, and Ball heard sounds—

Slithering. Slavering. Leathery skin. Loose flesh. Popping joints and hisses and groans and grumbles. And most of all, moans. Soft, predatory moans.

Sounds like Kraven-Hish mercenaries make.

"Corporal," he begged. "Please, we have to do something. I can hear it. Oh God, I can hear them."

"It's your imagination, Ball," said the corporal's steady voice. "Remember what I said before."

That night, Ball lay awake again, his thoughts exhausted and mad.

Kraven-Hish mercenaries—

Ball was leading the way to Hatch A and *they* were following close behind. When the hatch opened, the things would burst unseen and unexpected into those safe stone tunnels.

Ball didn't tell the corporal these thoughts.

Ball was afraid: That his squad was being replaced, one by one; that the corporal was dead; that a Kraven-Hish mercenary stood there, somewhere back there, mouthing the corporal's words.

Ball was very afraid.

HE TRIED TO find Reice, and talk to him, away from the corporal.

It was hard. Ball didn't know where anyone was anymore. The footsteps had become soft—almost ghostly, insubstantial—and Reice and the corporal seemed to group close together, always.

"Reice," Ball said. "You heard it, that night. I know you did."

Reice's voice said, "Ball, I didn't hear anything. Really."

An uneasy feeling spread over Ball. What if this wasn't really Reice? Ball said, "Back at Fort Deep you—"

Reice's voice cut him off, "Ball, I'm tired, all right? We might not ever make it back. No one wants to talk about old stuff right now."

That was a lie, Ball was sure of it. So Reice was gone too, probably.

Ball felt very alone.

Reice and the corporal, and Dimon, all dead; replaced by Kraven-Hish mercenaries, monsters that spoke with the voices of friends.

After that, those three voices always grouped close. Maybe they were plotting something.

And Sweezy?

Sweezy hadn't spoken in days. No one had mentioned him. Maybe he'd become separated, or twisted an ankle.

Ball wished he could believe that—Sweezy, lying back in the rocks, lost or injured, but alive.

But Sweezy was gone. Weak, whiny Sweezy, always straggling behind, always alone, he'd been the first to die.

Cataldo?

Ball wasn't sure about him.

"Listen," Ball told Cataldo. "There are Kraven-Hish mercenaries, close around us. I hear sounds. You hear it, too. I know you do."

"Leave me alone, Ball," Cataldo's voice said. "You're creeping everybody out."

"You hear them."

"People imagine things. Things that aren't there, in a place like this."

Ball said, "I have an idea."

Cataldo's voice answered quickly, "No."

"We can power down our suits. Just for a moment. For a second. We can see who we really are."

"No."

Ball said, "The last orbital went down over the horizon eighty minutes ago. The next one won't be up for half an hour."

"I'm not risking it," Cataldo's voice said. "Because you think you heard something? That's insane."

"You heard it too."

"Forget it."

"*I'll* do it, then." Ball's heart beat fast. "I'll power down my suit. Then you'll see it's safe. Then maybe you'll do it, too."

Ball stared up into the sky, straight up, to where an orbital attack platform floated, bristling dark with missile silos, waiting to attack—if he was wrong about this.

His fingers played over the buttons on his wrist.

"Don't," Cataldo's voice growled. "Don't even think about it. You wait until the rest of us reach minimum safe distance. Then do whatever the hell you want with yourself, I don't care. But not here, Ball. Not now. You've got no right."

Ball lowered his head. Cataldo grumbled and walked away; his voice faded slowly.

Ball sighed. Was that really Cataldo? Hard to say.

He kept his invisible rifle gripped tight in his sweaty, invisible fingers.

Sometimes, lying on the jagged ground at night, he wondered if any of them had ever been real—Cataldo, Dimon, the corporal—he couldn't exactly picture their faces anymore. Maybe they'd never had faces. Maybe they had only ever been voices. Voices in his head.

Other times, marching exhausted in the sun, Ball thought about fighting them. He hefted his rifle, which was heavy, huge, and worthless. He could have aimed it, maybe, if he could see his targets. Without targets—

Useless. He might get off a dozen shots, and most would miss. Then they'd close in on him—Cataldo, Dimon, Reice, the corporal—and however many more were out there.

He could run—slip away in the night, sprint ahead to Fort Deep. But the base was still three days off, and the squad was already marching as fast as Ball could manage.

Or he could hide—wrapped up safe in his unseeable suit, hide among the mounds and rocky hills. He had six days worth of air. The others would notice he was gone and they'd come after him, maybe overtake him, or maybe go on to Fort Deep and make it theirs. Then Ball would perish alone among the crags.

So he kept walking, walking and talking, and he didn't mention Kraven-Hish mercenaries anymore, even though he could hear them.

He kept glancing back over his shoulder, though there was nothing there, not even his shoulder. Why hadn't

19

they killed him yet? Maybe they needed someone to lead them to Hatch A, or maybe not. It couldn't last. They'd get him sometime—maybe this afternoon.

Maybe during this footstep—this next tired, tortured footstep—this one. But then that footstep was over, and he was still alive. Maybe the next one then—

The sun sank low and the sky turned dark.

Or maybe tonight.

The squad made camp, and Ball settled down on the ground beneath a rocky overhang to rest and brood. Footsteps came toward him across the hillside.

"Ball!" Cataldo's voice whispered. "Ball, where are you?"

"I'm here," Ball said, softly.

"We're in trouble. Oh God, we're in trouble. You were right about them." Cataldo's voice paused. "The corporal was asking me things today—How close are we to the hatch? What security do I think will meet us? Weird stuff like that. The corporal, he knows all that better than us."

"And—"

Cataldo's voice got lower. "You were right, I think. I can hear it sometimes—those sounds."

Ball sat still in the darkness.

"What are we going to do?" Cataldo's voice said. "What can we do?"

"I don't know. Let me think."

Ball thought hard, but said nothing. Finally, Cataldo's voice grunted. "*I'm* going to get the hell out of here."

His footsteps stumbled off down the hillside.

The corporal's voice said, "Reice. Dimon. Sound off."

Ball tensed, and waited.

"I'm over here," called Reice's voice, and Dimon, too, "Here."

Again, Ball had that unsettling feeling, that feeling they were all off together—Dimon, Reice, the corporal—grouped close together, plotting.

"Ball," the corporal's voice shouted. "Where are you?"

Ball didn't answer. The silence was heavy. Finally, he murmured, "Up here."

"Where?"

"Under the rock," Ball said. "Under the ledge."

"OK." The corporal's voice said, "Cataldo?"

Ball waited.

Again the corporal's voice: "Cataldo? Sound off."

Long minutes passed.

Then, a sound came from somewhere down the hill— a sound like a spine splintering, a sound like a voice— Cataldo's voice—coughing blood, gurgling it and choking on it.

A sound like Cataldo dying. It cut off abruptly.

The corporal's voice called out once more, "Cataldo."

A few moments later, Cataldo's voice answered, calmly, "I'm here."

Ball shut his eyes very tight and tried not to move, or breathe. He wanted to be more invisible—so invisible that no one would ever see him again, or ever hurt him. He wanted to be so invisible that he wasn't even there anymore.

He waited half an hour, then stood, slowly. He crept across smooth stones to a narrow crevice a hundred meters down the hillside. He lay down there, curled up tight.

He wanted to fall asleep and wake again alive. He wanted for the horrible Kraven-Hish mercenaries not to find his sleeping spot.

In the morning he awoke.

His rifle was gone.

DAVID BARR KIRTLEY

BALL TRACED THE invisible cord very, very carefully. It was broken halfway down.

He felt around on the ground. He crawled back and forth. He checked again slowly, methodically, inch by inch.

He wished he could believe it was an accident that the cord had worn down and the rifle had fallen away sometime in the night.

But he knew it hadn't.

The whole squad started marching again and Ball trudged on, defeated. Tears rose up behind his eyes and spilled down his face and he was too tired to stop them. He was still alive, and he didn't know why and the others were all dead.

Reice had been decent and good. He'd never done anything to deserve this.

The corporal had been brave, and had tried so hard.

Dimon had been shit. But what did that matter, out here?

Cataldo had been too angry, too mean. But Cataldo had kept checking on Sweezy, when no one else bothered. That was something, anyway.

—And Sweezy.

Ball had almost forgotten him. Sweezy had been harmless. It wasn't fair. Nothing that can feel should be harmless—or else everything should.

Nearby, Cataldo's voice said, "Ball. I want to talk to you. About last night."

"You're not Cataldo," Ball said slowly, evenly. "Kill me, if you want, but don't lie. Not anymore."

Cataldo's voice laughed. "Jesus, Ball. Take it easy."

"I heard Cataldo die," Ball said. "I heard it. You killed him."

"I tripped, Ball. It startled me, and I must have gasped, or something. That's what you heard."

Ball didn't answer.

Cataldo's voice chuckled. "Come on, Ball. I just tripped. Haven't you ever tripped before?"

"No," Ball said. "Never."

And he waited.

And then Cataldo's voice said—

"Well, good for you. I trip sometimes, all right?"

Ball felt weak and dizzy. He closed his eyes and red shapes swam in the darkness behind his eyelids. A long, low moan rose up from somewhere inside him and he couldn't stop it. He said, "I tripped twelve times the first day and Cataldo was there. He laughed at me. You're not him. Don't lie, don't say anything. I won't believe you."

Cataldo's voice sighed a long, hard sigh.

Ball said, "Get away from me. Get away or I'll shoot. Even if you are Cataldo, I'll shoot you."

Cataldo's voice said, "Shoot me. Without a rifle."

"I have a rifle," Ball lied.

"No," Cataldo's voice said. "I've got yours. I'm pointing it at you. I could pull the trigger, if you don't believe me."

Ball backed slowly away. The invisible cord that had held his rifle waved loose from his shoulder. He reached for the buttons on his wrist. "I'll power down my suit," he warned. "I'll do it, and the orbital will kill us all."

"Go ahead." Cataldo's voice was unconcerned. "Power down. It'll make it easy to shoot you." He paused. "The last orbital went down an hour ago."

Ball tried to figure if that was true. It was. He waited, he said softly, "You need me to lead you to the hatch."

23

"Not anymore," Cataldo's voice said. "Cataldo told us how to get there. Yesterday, before he died."

Ball lowered his head; it was over. "Then why didn't you kill me? Last night. Whenever."

It was the corporal's voice that answered. "That's a good question, Ball." There was a pause. "Why don't cats kill the mice they catch, right away?"

Ball shuddered. That voice, the corporal's—that proud voice. It wasn't right that it should say such a thing.

"For fun, Ball," Dimon's voice burst out. "That's the answer. For fun."

Ball waited. They were all together there, all grouped close, arrayed against him.

Reice's voice assured him, "Don't worry though, you won't be killed."

Ball tried to picture them: a pack of Kraven-Hish mercenaries, standing deadly before him. He couldn't do it. It was too awful. He couldn't even imagine it.

"What do you want?" he said.

A new voice came, a terrible voice. It was low, hissing and rasping, sickening. It was groaning and gurgling—it filled Ball's ears—the most horrible, wretched, sound. It was so wicked, and so horribly cunning, and it said in a voice that seemed barely living:

"I want you to see—"

Ball waited, tense. Finally, he said, "What?"

"My face—" said the thing. "I want you to see my face. Then I'll let you go—"

Ball saw nightmares in his mind: A dozen filmy eyeballs, and puckered tentacles, and rows of fleshy spines. A bulging skull and rotted cords of muscle, claws and soft innards everywhere exposed. Or rows and rows of teeth-stuffed gums, a bleeding carapace, a mad cavern of

24

cerebrum and heavy vein. Or eyes that bulged wild, off of tubes like eel bodies.

"I'm worse—" said the thing. "Whatever you dream I am, I'm worse. But you want to live. I'm powering down my suit—"

Ball closed his eyes.

Four gunshots fired in the stillness.

Then a long wait—darkness, eyes squeezed.

Then Sweezy's voice, "Ball, where are you? Let's go."

Ball kept his eyes closed. "Sweezy?"

"Come on," Sweezy's voice said. "Move."

Ball struggled to understand. "You were gone—"

"I wasn't. I was around. Quiet."

Ball choked, a relieved sob. "And you got them? The Kraven-Hish mercenaries? You got them all?"

"I got it," Sweezy's voice said. "The one. It was all of them—Dimon, Cataldo, Reice, the corporal—all their voices."

"One?"

"A solitary hunter. Like a cat. Intel was right."

Ball began to open one eye.

"Don't look at it," Sweezy's voice warned, wavering, uneven. "Just turn around, and let's go."

Ball turned away, and opened his eyes.

"Walk," Sweezy's voice said. "Until we're over the rise. Don't look back."

They walked.

Sweezy's voice didn't say anything for a while. When it came, it was very weak, "I wish I hadn't seen it, Ball. Oh God." It sounded like he was crying. "I don't ever want to dream again."

Hard stones drifted by beneath Ball and he counted paces to keep himself from thinking too much. They went over one rise, and then another. Ball halted then, and collapsed on the ground.

Neither of them said anything for a while.

"I tried to tell the corporal," Ball said finally, softly. "I tried to tell him. He wouldn't listen."

"The corporal was dead the second day. That wasn't him you were talking to."

Ball hunched over and held his invisible head in his invisible hands.

"Always take out the leader first," Sweezy's voice said. "Basic strategy."

"The second day?" Ball sat unbelieving. "You knew the second day and you didn't say anything?"

"*It* would've known about me—that monster, if I'd said anything. Then I'd be dead. And so would you."

"But Reice—" Ball said. "The corporal—"

"I saved you." Sweezy's voice was sharp. "I could've left you there, or started shooting blind, but I didn't. I waited for my chance and I saved us both."

Ball lay back against the ground and stared up into the orange-dust sky.

"I'm a good soldier, Ball," Sweezy's voice said. "I always said I was."

THEY WALKED TWO more days and halted at the top of a high cliff. Safety waited near, beneath Hatch A, just out of sight beyond the darkening horizon.

Night fell. Ball lay awake and thought horrible thoughts.

Like—maybe the monster *had* known about Sweezy, after all.

Ball hadn't seen the thing's body, crumpled and lifeless. He'd closed his eyes. Maybe there'd never been a body; maybe that thing was still alive.

Maybe it was—

Ball slowly turned his eyes upon the empty spot where Sweezy lay sleeping.

"Sweezy!" he hissed. "Sweezy, wake up."

There was silence. Finally, Sweezy's voice said, "What?"

Ball trembled, he couldn't help it. "That is *you*, isn't it, Sweezy?" His voice was pleading, desperate. "It is really you? It just occurred to me that—"

"Yes, it's me," Sweezy's voice assured him. "Go back to sleep, Ball. Of course it's me."

Ball took a deep breath. Yes.

He rolled over and closed his eyes. He tried to relax.

Of course it was Sweezy, he tried to tell himself.

Of course it was.

TWENTY-TWO
BUTTONS

REBECCA CARMI

We have never been very good at predicting where new technologies will take us. When radio and television were first introduced, the visionaries of the new media proclaimed that they
would bring "culture to the masses." They did, of course, but
not the culture the visionaries had supposed. Now we live in a
world where every child can sing the jingles of various prod-
ucts and where half the people know the names of characters on
popular shows, as well as the actors who portray them.

Who knew that the invention of the heat lamp would make
McDonald's, as we know it today, possible? Or that the con-
cept of "drive-in" would become "drive-up" and then "drive-
thru" as we found more and more transactions we could perform without leaving our cars.

The rise of cheap long distance telephoning virtually elimi-
nated personal letter writing for a while. Who guessed that
computers with modems, linked through a network that was

created originally for government and university researchers to share information, would revive letter writing and make typing, in many cases, replace talk?

Who knew that air-conditioning, television, and computer games would make the sight of children playing outside in a summer neighborhood seem quaintly nostalgic rather than being a part of everyone's life?

Tools we create to break down walls build new ones. Technologies that bring us together also keep us apart.

MORRIS DREADED THESE family dinners with strangers, but they were so important to Oregon that he tried to put the best face on it. It was only one night a week, and at least these new people, the Pardys, weren't as obnoxious as others he had met.

It was always the women who put energy into these events, and now Oregon and the other lady, Torina, were going through good-bye ceremonies. At last. He wondered if Torina's husband, that-Barney-guy, felt the same way. He stifled a yawn.

"Thanks so much. The pterodactyl steak was a real thrill," Torina said. She was the spokesperson for the Pardy family. Her husband and two boys were picking at their plates and looking bored. Morris could relate. His own two kids looked equally bored.

"Well, having a husband who works in a simulation lab has its perks!" Oregon replied. She beamed at Morris and took his hand. He smiled back obligingly.

"Next week, I'll have to work hard to top this menu!" Torina said. Oregon had done her usual great job with the steaks. It had taken two days of marinating to tenderize the tough meat.

Torina looked at her smallest boy. "Stop playing with the bones, Mars!" Morris didn't blame the boy, the bones were the biggest he'd ever seen. He was tempted to pick one up and wave it around himself.

"Bye, y'all, see you next week at our house. Thanks again." Torina looked meaningfully around the table, at her Neanderthal-looking husband Barney and their two kids. They responded with a mumbled chorus of "Thank you's." He couldn't remember what it was that Barney did—something related to the Net-sports.

"Bye bye!" Oregon reached over and logged off the screen. The other half of the table with the Pardy family disappeared, Torina's smile ghosting on the wall monitor for a split second. "Well," Oregon said. "What a successful dinner party! They really appreciated the steak, Morris. Isn't it nice that we can share some of your laboratory privileges?"

He made a noise that sounded like an affirmative response.

"Hello . . ." she chimed. "Have you turned into a pterodactyl yourself? Can't you do better than a grunt?"

"It is absolutely wonderful that we could share the splendors of my laboratory experiments," he said. "Better?"

"You were awfully quiet during dinner. These are the first friends who have worked out in almost two years of Net-matches. Couldn't you, well, share more of yourself?"

"I said everything I had to say. Besides, you and Torina were so busy chattering there wasn't a whole lot of room to get into it. Not that that-Barney-guy ever says a word. I'm positively loquacious in comparison," Morris said, feeling smug.

"Mom, can I invite Mars over to play?" asked Smanny. His little face was all eagerness.

"Sure sweetie, we'll send an e-mail right now."

"No, I mean really play! Like come over to our house," said Smanny.

"Dummy," said Raquette, in her best grown-up voice. She was at the stage where she needed to make it clear she was the oldest. "They live 3,000 miles away. Even if it were safe to go Outside, it would take him weeks to get clearance and three hours to get here."

"I want a real friend, not a inter-net connection!"

"Morris, will you handle this?" asked Oregon.

"Smanny, it is way too dangerous to go places Outside. The Net-Termos would grab you and do terrible things."

"Like what?" Smanny asked, an awful and curious light in his eyes. It was well known that the Net-Termos on the Outside committed the worst crimes in recorded history. Morris suspected Smanny had picked up some news clips despite their careful screening of his Net-access. Morris winced thinking about it. The Net showed some pretty awful stuff, but it was important to know what was going on in the world. Morris was grateful that the Net provided updates and warnings about the horrors of Outside at morning log-on. Not everybody could afford the safety of a Net-secure home, poor lost souls. It was worth every penny to be a subscriber, even though it was their highest budget item after the mortgage.

"We are not going into that again!" his mother said. "Raquette, it's your turn to clear the table." Raquette sighed in a perfect imitation of her mother's most exasperated sigh.

She picked up the plates. "I'll tell you about the Net-Termos later," she said to Smanny in a stage whisper. His eyes got wide.

MORRIS WAS AT his lab console finishing a remote cell graft on some salmon eggs when an instant visitor chimed in. He looked at the clock—still late morning. He finished removing the tweezers from the tube, laid them down, slid out of the robotic virtual glove and clicked on the visitor door.

To his surprise it was Torina Pardy, looking teary. It took him a moment to place her away from the dinner table. "Oh," she said. "I was looking for Oregon."

"She's at her console having her hair cut," he said. And then, not because he wanted to know but because it was the polite thing to do, he asked, "Is everything OK?"

Her blue eyes filled with tears. "Oh gosh," she said. She stood there for a few seconds, shaking with sobs. "I'm sorry."

"It's all right," he said, "Take your time." Her eyes were a pretty light blue. He'd never looked at her closely before. It was his fourth failure with the salmon DNA to-day and he didn't mind the break. What did women call each other about during the day?

"It's Barney," she gasped out. "I don't think he loves me anymore." She began a new wave of sobbing and her white skin mottled with red streaks.

Now he was in trouble. He tried to think what Oregon would have said to her. "Why do you think that?" he asked.

"Is it really OK to tell you this stuff?" She asked him.

"Why not?" he responded. "You're obviously hurting, and if I can help . . ." Actually he wasn't sure if this was OK, or if Barney would appreciate it, not that he owed the guy anything, but he was curious to hear what other women complained about. He certainly knew Oregon's gripes.

"He's just not interested in, well, in sex, anymore," she said. She stopped crying, as if saying it were a relief. The red streaks were fading from her neck. Her skin must be very sensitive.

Morris was surprised. He'd only known two other women before Oregon, and neither of them in vivo. It took a long time to arrange a personal meeting with a woman. First there was screening for computer viruses before dating, then the lengthy process of deciding to make a commitment before one member of the couple went through the costly process of relocation to the other's home-port; medical approvals, genetic disease screening, safe transport costs, Net-account combining and Net-force clearance.

He had nearly reached that point with the woman before Oregon, but had discovered she was altering her visual pick-up during the dating. In reality she was three times his age and made a living off of hacking funds from prospective husbands. He had figured it out in time to withdraw his credit from the relocation application, but others hadn't been as lucky. If she hadn't kept calling him Charles, well, let's just say it would have taken him many years to save enough funds to begin with another woman. He hoped the Net-force had caught her.

Simulation that she was, she remained the only woman other than Oregon he'd ever discussed sex with, and only in medical terms. He found himself titillated by Torina's frankness.

"What do you think is the reason?" he asked, feeling embarrassed as his voice came out husky. She was a damned good looking woman and he'd always felt envious of that-Barney-guy. Barney was such a meaty looking guy, Morris had always assumed the two of them had quite a time of it. Unlike him and the fastidious Oregon. . . .

"I don't know. He says he doesn't feel attracted to me anymore . . ." she looked like she was about to cry again.

"Ridiculous!" Morris said, trying to sound cheerful. "You're very attractive." Oops! He hadn't meant to say that, but hell, she was a damn good-looking woman.

She looked a little confused. Then she blushed. Oregon never blushed; she was far too assertive. "Thank you," she said. "How sweet of you." She gave a little laugh. "I actually feel better . . ." There was an awkward silence. Morris felt gallant, and he hadn't even been trying. "Well, I better not keep you. You look like you're busy."

"That's OK. I wasn't getting anywhere today anyway."

"What were you trying to do?"

"Oh, nothing very entertaining, grafting salmon DNA into a hardier breed—with so few clean rivers we need something that can breed in grow-grow ponds."

Her eyes lit up. "What base vector were you using?" He'd forgotten she was a molecular biologist.

Two hours later they logged off. He was surprised. She forgot her upset and listened to his research, even coming up with several approaches he hadn't thought of. It was valuable to bounce ideas off of someone else. He imagined that in the olden days, when people physically worked in labs together, this was common.

That night he found himself thinking about Torina. He liked the way her breasts strained against her shirt when she got excited about an idea. Oregon never wore anything tight, nor did she have much extra flesh hanging around. That lucky Barney—he wouldn't mind trading places with him for the night. He squelched the thought and gave Oregon an experimental goodnight kiss—he was feeling peppy. After 13 years of marriage you grabbed those opportunities when they came.

"Don't forget you promised Smanny to help him with his new microscope kit tomorrow," she said, and turned over to go to sleep.

HE WAS HAVING success with the salmon grafts when the instant visitor bell chimed. He considered ignoring it, but then clicked the door open.

"Hi. Am I bothering you?" It was Torina, and she looked great. She'd let her hair down and it fell thickly around her shoulders in dark waves. And she was wearing something that dipped at the neckline to show real honest-to-God cleavage. Morris tried to keep his eyes on her face.

"Uh, no, no. Not at all." he said. "I'm making good progress today—you gave me good ideas. You got me unstuck."

"You helped me out yesterday, too," she said sweetly.

"I did?"

"Well, yes. You made me feel attractive. A woman needs that."

He felt his pants get tight. Uh oh. He hoped she didn't notice. "Well, it was my pleasure," he said. That was stupid.

She laughed. "You're cute when you're embarrassed."

He struck around for something to say. "So, things going better at home?"

Now she blushed. "Well, I think you made me feel so, well, desirable, even my husband noticed. We actually had a good time last night."

He did not want to hear this. "Well, maybe I should set up a Net-business, Relationship Building by Morris," he joked.

"Count me in as a customer," she giggled. "So tell me about the fish today."

With relief he launched into a description of the improvements in his grafting, and soon forgot about his embarrassment. She was a great listener and a creative thinker. He jokingly asked her if she wanted to apply for a job as research assistant. After three hours, he was shocked to discover that he was behind in his work. She apologized and logged off. "Thanks again," she said, right before breaking the connection.

It was interesting how little one learned about a person during family dinners. He never would have known what a brilliant person she was from their dinners. Mostly she and Oregon talked, and DNA twists and molecular structure never came up. What was it that-Barney-guy did again? Oh yeah, he was a purveyor of Net gladiator matches. He tried not to think of the good time the guy had last night with that sexy wife of his. She was oozing satisfaction. Oregon looked long suffering after sex.

THE TABLECLOTH AND place settings had been laid out on their side of the screen. Everything had been sent by the Pardy family via same-day transport, along with pre-cooked, flash frozen food, in preparation for the dinner.

When the connection was logged, the table appeared as a seamless 3-D continuation of the Pardys' own standard Net-size dining table, down to the napkins in their napkin rings. The Pardys' dinnerware always favored flowers and peacocks, unlike the geometric designs Oregon used.

"Torina, these hush puppies and black-eyed peas are out of this world," said Oregon. "Aren't they, Morris?"

"Uh, yeah," he said. "Very tasty." He was too busy not looking at Torina to concentrate on the food. They had talked every day but one this past week, and more and more about their respective bedroom lives. Come to think of it, he wasn't too comfortable looking at Barney either, knowing what he knew about his cleanliness fetish. Hard to imagine the guy ran to wash off before even making sure Torina was finished. And he was afraid that if he did it too often he wouldn't have energy for work. Morris wouldn't mind having those kinds of worries. He was lucky if Oregon was interested once a month. It was the first time he had thought much about his relationship with Oregon and he was surprised to discover how much he resented her carefully meted out sexual favors.

"Well, I wanted to introduce you to some of my home cooking," Torina said. "Before I came up to Canada to marry Barney, I grew up in South Carolina." Barney yawned.

"Hey Mars, want to come over my house?" Smanny broke in.

The adults laughed. "We've tried to explain it to him," said Oregon, "but Smanny doesn't give up easily."

"Well, Mars, maybe you and Smanny can go to the movies together tomorrow," Torina suggested.

"No, I want to go to his house," said Mars.

"Well, it certainly would be nice if we could be with each other in person," Torina said. Morris didn't dare look up from his okra but he was sure she was looking at him.

AT BREAKFAST OREGON SAID, "Didn't you think dinner was a little strange last night?"

Morris and the kids ate her blueberry pancake specialties while she packed up the box with the Pardys' dishes and tablecloth for return delivery. Though delivery businesses were owned by Net-operators, it was the Net-termos who did the delivering; everything from corporate documents to pizzas. He heard they worked in body armor. Once he'd looked through their front bombproof airlock to see a package picked up and was surprised to see a normal looking, balding guy open up the door and take the package. The guy was wearing shirtsleeves and sneakers. He often wondered what kind of special protection the man had hidden.

Morris took a sip of coffee. "What was strange about it?"

"Torina was wearing a see-through blouse," said Raquette. "How termo! You could even see her you-know-whats."

"Whats?" asked Smanny.

"Raquette, let's not be gossipy. And it isn't polite to stare," said Oregon.

"What could you see?" asked Smanny.

"Her outfit was a little shocking . . ." said Oregon.

"What's *you-know-whats*?" demanded Smanny.

"And she seemed distant to me," said Oregon. "Her husband didn't say a word. Not that you were a font of brilliance."

"What *whats*!?" said Smanny.

"I'll tell you later," said Raquette.

"Raquette," Oregon said warningly.

"Tell me now!" said Smanny, getting teary-eyed.

"I got to get to work," said Morris. He strolled out of the room.

It was difficult to concentrate. He had noticed Torina's blouse. No doubt she was getting desperate to get Barney's attention. She certainly had gotten his.

When the instant-mail chimed, he realized he'd been waiting for it.

"Hi," she said.

"Hi," he replied, trying to look busy. God, just seeing her turned him on.

"I've been thinking about you," she said. He swallowed. "As a matter of fact, I'm finding it hard to stop thinking of you."

His heart was pounding, and that wasn't the only thing.

"I wished that dinner was just the two of us last night," she laughed nervously. "You're the first man who has looked at me with appreciation, laughed at my jokes, and listened to my ideas since I got married. I've felt like myself for the first time in ages this past week."

He knew he should say something discouraging, but the truth was, he didn't want her to stop talking. "Just tell me to go away if I'm offending you," she said.

"No," he said. "But this is probably not right." It was not a school day, so Oregon was at the virtual mall with the kids. That would last hours.

"I know," she said. "But I need you to look at me." She began unbuttoning her blouse, a creamy, silky affair with lots and lots of little buttons. He watched in fascination as each little button opened. He counted twenty-two little pearl buttons. He felt his mouth drop open as she slid it off her shoulders. My God, she was splendid. He heard himself groan.

"I love the way you respond to me. It's so nice to look at a man and see interest."

Morris nodded dumbly.

"I thought you and Barney were doing better," he managed to say in a strangled voice.

"Just once, and just because I was imagining it was you."

Morris couldn't imagine a woman fantasizing about him.

"Go ahead, I want to see you, too," she said softly.

She couldn't be asking what he thought she was . . .

"I want to see how you respond to me . . ."

She *was* asking what he thought she was.

He undid his fly and took himself out. He couldn't remember the last time he had been so hard. "Come closer to the screen," she said, throatily. "Oh," she moaned, "It's so beautiful to look at . . ." He felt his vision start to dim, and he staggered.

"Oh my God," he heard himself saying.

"Meet me at this time tomorrow, and we'll set up two-way RV gloves." She moistened her lips. "Bye for now," and she was gone.

Morris stared at the blank screen for a long time before he could think straight.

Robotic virtual gloves were just the beginning. There was no end of innovations she came up with, nor of body parts that could be robotically virtched. The RVs stimulated the wearer's nerves according to the pressure applied on the other side. It felt little different than wearing a condom—no wonder Net-brothels were such a huge black-market success. Morris was like a crazy man. He thought of Torina day and night. He barely slept. He barely ate. She demanded to know every fantasy he had, and then she set about making them come true. Every day he was too exhausted to think he could ever perform again, and each day the mere sight of her had him up and hard. He'd read about this kind of thing in the lewd e-books teenage boys pull up from hidden places on the Net, but never understood before how real—and powerful—sex could be.

Finally, after a month in which he thought he would die of exhaustion, he told her, "I have to see you. Really, in vivo, in the flesh, not virtually. I have to be in the same room with you."

"Well, how is that possible, sweetheart?" she asked. She rolled on to her side to look back at him over her shoulder, affording him a clear view of her naked backside.

"I don't know. Come here, or I'll come there. Or let's meet at a conference or something."

"But we're 3,000 miles apart, and conferences are all Net-video. Unless you want to go termo," she giggled. "Sometimes I actually envy them. Seeing other people in the flesh, being outside in the open air." She was on her knees now, opening up a bag of interesting looking toys. "There's something I want you to watch . . ." He forgot about making plans.

"MORRIS. I WANT you to see a doctor," Oregon said over breakfast.

"Huh?"

"You're like a ghost. Something's wrong and no matter how many times I ask you, you won't tell me." She began to cry. "I'm worried about you."

"Mom, is Daddy sick?" asked Smanny, looking scared.

"No, Daddy is not sick," said Morris. "I'm just working very hard right now." He wanted to marry Torina; it was the only way, but that would mean never hugging his kids again. He'd only see them through the console on weekends and maybe every other Thursday. He didn't know how it worked nowadays, since the breakdown of outdoor transport had necessitated Net-facilitated relationships. The Net always cited the "low to zero" divorce rate as one of its many benefits.

Smanny came over and hugged him. "Don't work too hard, Daddy. I want to play with you." Morris's heart contracted in his chest. He hugged Smanny fiercely.

"We'll play today, OK. You'll show me how your microscope works."

As he left, he noticed Oregon had made his favorite breakfast soufflé. His plate was untouched.

"WE HAVE TO break this off," he told Torina, trying not to look at her. "I'm losing my mind not being with you, and I've got a family."

"You're right," she said. "It was wonderful for both of us. We got a lot of things we needed, and now it's time to return to our lives."

He nodded, too numb to respond. "I'll never forget you," she said in a shaky voice. She blew him a kiss and logged off.

THE NEXT FAMILY dinner was excruciating. He excused himself in the middle claiming stomach problems. Oregon gave him an alarmed look—she had made his favorite seafood stew. He pretended to be asleep when she came into the bedroom. Truth was he hadn't slept in a week.

The next day he called Torina. They both started crying as soon as they saw each other. And now there was even more intensity to their relationship—not always sexual. They sneaked out to meet in the middle of the night, lying in their respective darkened rooms and talking. Just talking—about their childhoods, their aspirations, their marriages, their kids. Morris had never talked so much to another person in his life. It was like being reborn, as if he'd been half-alive before he met her. He knew now he couldn't live without her.

Until one day Raquette walked into the room and saw the naked Torina in the middle of pleasuring herself. She gave one shocked look at her equally naked Daddy, screamed and ran from the room. Morris had forgotten to lock the door.

Morris was banished to his console room and a spare bed was installed. Oregon wouldn't respond to any of his instant visits and refused to spring the locks leading to the rest of the house. The only unlocked door was the one leading to Outside, unlocked from the inside only. He had never been in a physical fight in his life and he owned no body armor. He'd be easy pickings outside. He wasn't suicidal, yet. Not that he would leave the security of Net-subscription. Without an on-line account there was no possibility of credit, communications or commerce.

The Net-force also set up caller blocks on his console. He could call out only to his lab. The only mail he received during that time was the notification of a Net-court date.

NET-COURT WAS the first time in six weeks he'd seen his family. They came in through the Net, though they were a room away in the house. "Daddy!" Smanny said. Morris wanted to pound on the wall separating them.

"Hi, son," said Morris. He was sorry; boy, was he ever sorry. Six weeks of isolation was a lot of time to think about what was important in life.

He pleaded guilty, was fined half a year's salary for moral abuse of the Net-censure laws, and assigned to community service Net-monitoring one hour a day for the next year. The Net was for those who were responsible enough to abide by Net rules of conduct. Adulterers and other criminal Net-Termos lived Outside with inadequate police protection and weak civil law; without Net-force protection, having forfeited their rights to a Net account.

Being on the Net was a privilege, one that could always be terminated. His punishment was fair.

Oregon was generous. She allowed him to stay and work it out. Morris wondered if Barney had been equally kind, but the brutish man didn't seem like the forgiving type. It was too frightening to think of the consequences for Torina, if Barney had banished her to the Outside, a beautiful woman like that.

Family therapy began with a team of Net-therapists the following week. It took three months of intensive work before the family removed the inter-house locks. Morris hugged Smanny. He sobbed in the boy's arms— he realized how much he needed to touch other people. Raquette was still wary and backed away from him when he approached her. She was thinner and paler and had a haunted look. Morris knew from his therapist that Raquette would need time to work out trust issues. He refrained from scooping her up in his arms and just said,

45

"I love you sweetheart. I am so sorry." She began crying and clung to her mother.

And Oregon, looking younger and more scared than he'd ever seen her, took him into her arms. "I'm working on understanding you, Morris," she said. "My therapist is helping a lot."

He was so lucky. His therapist was helping him be a better husband to her, too. They scheduled more of the recreational and social activities important to Oregon into their life, and discovered things they liked to do together. Oregon cooked his favorite foods and was carefully solicitous of his sexual needs.

He never tried to find out what happened to Torina, but sometimes he had nightmares about her being cast out on the streets, beaten and raped, as he watched from behind his console. His therapist assured him it was normal, healthy guilt at work, a part of the healing process, and the dreams would fade with time. Sometimes his sobs woke Oregon, but with the years the dreams did stop. They even began Net-matching with a nice group of Mormon families from Salt Lake City.

IT HAPPENED ONE night when Morris was working late in his lab. When he finally looked at the wall clock, he noticed a pizza delivery pouch propped against the wall. What was a pizza doing in an empty lab half the country away from his house? As far as he knew, other than scheduled maintenance, nobody actually entered the lab, which was somewhere in Nebraska, or was that Oklahoma? Curious, he unzipped the delivery pouch with the RV gloves. The box had lipstick writing on it, shocking big red letters against the white of the box. "Morris, come out and play!" it said, with a lipstick kiss imprinted under the exclamation mark. Inside the box was a pizza and an envelope containing 22 pearl buttons.

From time to time, Morris would take them out and count them.

THE HANGED MAN
THE LOVERS
AND THE FOOL

JUSTIN STANCHFIELD

I know people who go through life with contempt for strangers. College professors, for instance, who sneer at anyone who has not chosen to live the "life of the mind," or journalists who laugh at "trailer trash" as if the choice or necessity of living in a house not firmly anchored to the ground said something about the character of the people who live there.

They think, these elitists, that the masses of people moving through the world whom they do not personally know and who do not dress as they dress, shop where they shop, and read what they read, must therefore have no inner life at all, and be unspeakably dull and endlessly uninteresting. These elitists are, I'm afraid, the dull ones. Because my experience is that any person might live a life as full of pain, joy, virtue, sin, courage, and cowardice as any other, and that those who look away from strangers as if they were not worth knowing are the ones who impoverish their own lives and contain themselves in tiny empty boxes.

How much more magical to look at the people passing by you on the street or in the store and wonder what secrets they know, what pain they suffer, what gifts they give, what cruelty they inflict, what danger they fear and face, what yearnings go unfulfilled.

And, just maybe, what magic they wield in the world.

LANIER FOUND HER for the first time on the outskirts of Prague, one of hundreds huddled beneath lean-tos and threadbare tents, shuffling from fire to fire, numb with the aching winter cold. The plague years were not so far behind, the piles of bodies, the stench of death remembered. Talismans hung around every neck. The ragged people watched him, eyes narrowed, suspicious, whispering as he trudged past. He could feel her, the tug so strong even his dulled nerves could no longer ignore it.

She was reading tarot cards inside a covered wagon, holding court like a queen, a filthy 14-year-old dressed in hand-me-downs. Lanier stared at her through the open flap. She looked up, startled, no doubt feeling his own presence. Her face was rounder than the profiles suggested, still youthful, her hair not as dark as it would one day become. But her eyes were the same riveting blue, so deep they seemed black in the smoky half-light. She whispered something to the woman whose fortune she was reading. The woman glanced over her shoulder, saw Lanier, and scurried out of the wagon, shuffling away as fast as her twisted legs would move. Lanier stepped closer.

"Good evening." He bowed slightly, hoping the implants compensated for his accent. His voice sounded thick, as if he were slow or drunk, but if she noticed, she said nothing. She only smiled and asked him into the wagon.

"Would you like to know your fate, sir?"

"Have you the gift?"

"I'm told I have." Again she smiled. "Find out for yourself."

The wagon creaked as he climbed in, stooping low to avoid the flat roof. It stank inside—mildew and wood smoke and rancid yellow tallow dripping off the short candle. Other smells rolled over him, subtler scents—unwashed bodies, garlic, the reek of cabbage and sour wine. Lanier sat down on the narrow stool while the girl shuffled the deck.

"Your name is Maria, isn't it?"

She barely looked up. "You've heard of me?"

"Perhaps I have the gift as well."

She stopped shuffling, lay the cards on the table and stared at him. Young as she was, there was no fear in her eyes—caution yes, and wariness, but not fear. "Perhaps you do."

He pulled out a few coins, the faces worn smooth, and dropped them on the table. "My name is Lanier. What can you tell me?"

She slid the deck toward him. "Cut the cards into three stacks." The deck was thick, the hand-painted faces crudely drawn. A wooden press lay nearby, ready to flatten the tattered cards once they were finished. Lanier broke the deck into three uneven piles, each beside the other. She moved the candle to the center of the table. The moment she touched the cards again she stiffened as if they were electric.

"Where are you from?"

"From somewhere closer than you might think." He tried not to shake. The tug was painful now, a dull ache behind his temples. The wine-scent called him stronger now, too. He would have drunk vinegar if a bottle were at hand. "Is something wrong?"

"No, of course not." She brushed a strand of hair out of her eyes and re-stacked the deck, fanning them when she was done across the greasy table. She pulled a single card from the pile and lay it face up. The Knave of Cups. "This is you."

"Go on."

She pulled the cards back together, paused a heartbeat, then turned the top card over. "This crosses you."

She lay the card across the first. A dead man hung upside down from a thick branch, his face twisted, the eyes mere slits. Her face paled.

"I think you should go."

"Why?" he asked, feeling ill.

"You just should, that's all." For the first time, she looked nervous, more child than woman. Her hands trembled as she swept the cards away, leaving the first two still laying face-up on the table. "You don't belong here."

"Neither do you." Lanier reached for her hand. Her skin was cool, the bones delicate and fragile. "Tell me I'm wrong?"

"I . . ." The words froze in her throat. She pulled her hand free and bolted for the rear of the wagon. "Go. Go now. Strangers aren't welcome here." She pulled the back-flaps open and disappeared. Lanier tried to follow her, but got hung up in the dark clutter. He heard voices outside, angry words he couldn't make out. Heavy footfalls trampled the wet snow.

He surrendered to the inevitable, snatched up the top card, then pulled the translator tab. A shrill whine cut the air, painful to his ears, drowning the voices outside. He caught a brief glimpse of bearded faces and sharp knives before the flash-pain took him away.

THE NEXT TIME he found her, Lanier almost passed the sensation off as just another hangover. He paused beside a tall post, a wooden sign swinging from the crossbeam by a pair of rusted chains, waiting for the nausea to pass, fighting down the taste of cheap whiskey crawling up his throat. He clutched the signpost, shaking, and stared across the street. Through the dirty window of a Nantucket whorehouse, he saw her walk by.

"Well, I'll be damned."

Lanier straightened, strength returning, and sauntered across the muddy street. A stiff wind blew up from the docks. Fresh-cut timbers. Burlap. Overripe whale flesh. And over everything, the scent of the cold, dark sea. He had followed her back and forth through so many centuries; always close, never close enough. Once or twice they had shared the same timeline, a gentle nudge he couldn't ignore, but the sensation had been fleeting and indistinct. Now, it was a palpable thing, strong as the wrought iron latch under his hand. He pulled the door open and stepped inside.

It was warm in the public room, a whale-oil lamp casting feeble patches of light on the sawdust floor. Lanier stepped up to the narrow bar. A tall man, gaunt as a skeleton, wandered up from the other end.

"What can I do ye?" A puckered scar ran under the barman's left eye.

"I saw a girl in here a moment ago."

"So you say." The man pulled back, overcautious. Lanier had been careless, not bothering to wire himself for the accent. He tried to imitate the odd inflections he had heard in the street.

"She would be short, long black hair straight as a mare's tail." Lanier paused, watching the man. "She has blue eyes and a wicked tongue. Have you seen her?"

"Might have."

Lanier dropped a half-dollar on the bar. It rang like a bell against the polished wood. The barman's lips twisted into a tight, mirthless smile. He poured a finger of harsh white liquor into a dirty glass and set it in front of Lanier. "Maria, there's a man here to see you."

She walked into the room, swaying seductively, her dark green dress sweeping the floor. She was thinner now, haggard and drawn. Strong perfume masked her own sharp tang, lavender soap like in an undertaker's parlor. She stopped an arm's length away, watching him, saying nothing.

"Morning," Lanier said, hoping she didn't recognize him. He had let his hair and his beard grow out, finding it easier to blend in from century to century. They were shot with gray now, like his eyebrows, giving him, especially when he was sober, the look of some mad prophet. "Mind if I have a word."

"Suit yourself." Her accent was like his, a blend of worlds and times past, a subtle veneer out of place in the dockside tavern. She smiled, patently fake, playing him for just another lonely sailor.

"Is there someplace we might go?"

She glanced at the barman. He shrugged. "All right." She nodded at the stairs along the far side of the tavern. "Upstairs. Third door down the hall." Then she disappeared. Lanier swallowed the whisky—oily flame spilling down his throat—and walked toward the stairs. The

54

treads creaked under his boots, sighing as if alive. The top floor was quiet, the air smoky and thick. He stepped through the narrow door and sat down on the bed.

She arrived a few minutes later, a bottle and a pair of glasses in her hand. She set them on the room's single table and began loosening the laces on her bodice. "Pour yourself a drink. It's a bit cold up here this morning."

Lanier stood up and closed the door. He stepped toward her and pulled her hands away from the laces. "That's not why I'm here."

Her eyes narrowed. "Then why?"

"I wanted to return something to you." He pulled an ancient card out of his vest pocket, the hanged man curled and worse for wear. "I believe this is yours."

"Who the hell are you?"

"A friend." Lanier lay the card on the table. She tried to pull away, but he held her wrist, refusing to let her bolt. "I just want to talk."

"Why?" Her skin paled, the little veins along her temples throbbing.

"Well, for one thing." He smiled. "You never finished my fortune."

"You can't be real. You would be dead ages ago." She sat down, her eyes never leaving his. "One word and Nathan will be up those stairs in a heartbeat. You understand me!"

"Perfectly."

"You take me for a witch, don't you?"

Lanier actually laughed. "That, I promise, is the last thing I might take you for." He fished his coin purse out and tossed it to the thick quilt. "Take it. It's yours." Without turning, she picked up the heavy sack, her knuckles whitening around the coins inside. He continued. "Did you really think you were the only one? Haven't you ever wondered how you do the things you do?"

"You mean the cards?" Her voice was small, almost a whisper.

"I mean all of it." He sighed. "How many times have you gone to sleep in one room and woken up in another? How many times have you stepped around a corner and into another century?"

She said nothing, her chest rising and falling in a quick, nervous rhythm. Street sounds poured through the walls, wagons rattling by, seabirds and rough language muffled by the light rain starting to fall. The drops beat against the roof, a sullen cadence. "How did you find me?"

"Why don't you let the cards tell you." Lanier tried to hide his own uneasiness. The contact pain was so strong he could barely focus. He let go of her arm. "Please?" She nodded and walked across the cramped room, returned a moment later with a silk sack, fumbling with the draw strings, and sat down as far from Lanier as possible.

"Cut the cards."

The cards were newer, the edges crisp and even. Lanier divided them into three stacks. She gathered them up and began turning them one by one. "You are a traveler, forever with strangers. A soldier, once. You've seen wonders, but they meant little." She turned another card. "You have known loss, but seldom love."

Lanier swallowed, his throat too dry to speak, wishing the whiskey bottle was closer. She continued, her eyes unfocused, rolled slightly back, white edges showing. A peal of thunder rolled across the harbor, a dull roar that shook the walls. She didn't even notice it.

"Your journey has been long, the path never clear. You have been hungry, always alone. You seek something just beyond your grasp."

"Do you . . ." He forced the words out. "Do you know what it is I'm looking for?"

She turned another card, laying it gently atop the others. For the first time since she had started reading she looked up. A pair of naked lovers reaching out to one another, forever frozen, sat on top of the quilt. The other cards tumbled to the bed and slid apart in an uneven fan.

"I think you should leave."

"No," he said quietly. "Not this time. Not until you've heard me out."

Something creaked, a boot-step on the stairs. "Leave while you can. Nathan is coming."

"Listen to me." He grabbed her arm again. "You don't belong here. You never have. I'm here to bring you home."

"I don't know you." The footsteps were getting closer. A shadow slid under the door, a pair of boots showing through the gap. She pulled away. "Get out of here. Now."

The door swung open. The man from the bar stepped inside, a thick cudgel in his right hand. He seemed surprised to see Lanier sitting up, still fully clothed. He rushed forward, arm raised. Lanier jumped to meet him. The cudgel whistled past his ear. It grazed his shoulder, a heavy shock.

"Nathan, no!" Maria tried to shove him away from the smaller Lanier, but the bar hand swept her aside. She stumbled backwards and fell to the dirty floor. Nathan ignored her, his eyes locked on Lanier. Again, he raised the thick club. Lanier reacted without thinking, his training taking control. Time slowed, his movements a blur.

His leg swung in a graceful arc, his boot heel smashing Nathan's ribs. The taller man doubled over, the breath whooshing out of his mouth. Lanier stepped in, striking hard, first in the windpipe, then, palm flat, in the face. Nathan crumpled to the floor and lay twitching on the planks. A foul odor seeped up as he lost control of his bowels.

"You've killed him!" Maria knelt beside the fallen Nathan. "You stupid, stupid bastard."

"He . . ." Lanier came back to the present, the rush of battle fading. His shoulder screamed in agony, the cudgel blow suddenly remembered. A trickle of blood smeared across his palm. He stared at it, not sure if it was his or the dying bartender's. "He was trying to kill me."

"He only wanted your money. He would have let you live." Tears streamed out, her face flushed with rage. Obviously, Nathan had been more than her pimp. Lanier stepped closer, but she backed away. "Leave me alone. I don't know who the hell you are, but leave me alone!"

He heard a dull pop, no louder than a bottle uncorking. One moment she was there, her back against the wall. The next, she was gone, like a soap bubble, vanished. Only her scent remained, a sharp contrast to the dead man's reek. Lanier started toward the spot where she had been, still in shock, the pain rising. He stumbled to the bed and swept up the cards, then yanked down on the translator tab around his neck. Transition swept over him, swallowing him whole, leaving nothing behind.

WHITE LIGHT. Pure. Unrelenting. It filled him, burned him to the bone. He fell. Perhaps he rose. He had no way of knowing. The space around him was featureless, white on white on white, a bubble in the quantum foam. A single, thin strand, like spiderweb twisting in the breeze, guided him. Lanier drifted, powerless to do anything else, the light slowly fading, a bleak, frozen land coalescing out of the mist.

He felt her pull, vague in the distance, laughing, taunting him again.

SLUSH POOLED AROUND Lanier's feet, a gray slurry of road salt, exhaust and stubborn, God-awful snow. A truck rumbled past, a yellow monster five times his own height, heaped to the brim with blue-gray copper ore. An enormous pit dominated the mountain behind him, walled off from the city by cage wire and overburdened dumps, a cancer eating into the Earth's flesh. Cold and more than a little sick from transition, he began walking. She had never jumped so far into the future before. He took it as an omen.

His odd clothes drew stares from passing cars, but not as many as he might have expected. Plenty of hole-in-the-wall bars dotted the uneven streets, their dirty windows framing neon signs that flickered in time with the power surges. Ragged drunks, like himself, apparently were of little interest in these times either. He thought about stopping into one of the grungy bars. Thought hard about it, but in the end opted for a St. Vincent's at the end of a one-way street. The few coins he had in his pocket were worthless in this century, so he changed clothes behind a stack of magazines when no one was looking and walked out of the thrift store without paying. All he kept was the translator around his neck and the Tarot deck from so many centuries before.

He stepped back into the fading sunlight and started looking for a post office.

JUSTIN STANCHFIELD

"Help you, buddy?"

Lanier smiled at the man behind the counter. He had found enough change in the street to buy a stamp and glossy postcard with an orange and pink sunset plastered behind a mine derrick. A "gallows-frame" the writing on the back called it. He laughed to himself at the irony and slid the card across the counter after writing "Wish you were here. Lan" on the back. And below the signature, a dot, no larger than the commas in the address—the last of his recorder tabs. Eleven months of data, position reports, snap shots and requisitions. A condensed version of himself hitching a ride to a bank vault somewhere in central Iowa, patiently awaiting retrieval hundreds of years from now. Lanier prayed silently the post card would arrive. He was lost if it didn't.

"Get you to mail this?" he asked the man.

"Sure. Won't go until tomorrow, though."

"That's fine. No rush." Lanier walked out of the post office, sorry to leave the warmth, and wandered toward the edge of town. Somewhere, waiting at a crossroads— he wouldn't know which until he found it—would be the supplies and money he had just requested. The pain in his shoulder was worse, stiffness setting in. He wished he had stopped for that drink now. Already, he could feel the girl's trace fading, growing weaker by the second.

He had never felt so hopeless.

HE DREAMT ABOUT her that night, the first time in months. It was warm, he was in a grassy meadow that smelled like rain and newly mown hay. She stepped out of her dress, letting it fall around her ankles, and walked toward him, round breasts swaying in time with each slow,

60

graceful step. The expression on her face never changed, a half-smile too wise for a face so young. Her eyes, impossibly blue, watched him, a hint of laughter beneath. She put her arms around his neck. He could feel the warmth of her skin, could feel her nipples pressing through his shirt. She lifted her face toward his, her breath sweet sour and hot.

"You can't win," she said, draining from his arms like water through a rusty pipe. Lanier woke up in a cold sweat, the cheap hotel blankets tangled around his feet, thoughts of her driving him mad.

DAYBREAK CRAWLED OVER the snow, red to crimson to painful orange, a too brief glory before the grays and washed-out browns took hold. Lanier had stayed sober, but instead of feeling clear-headed and alert, he was nervous, the cudgel blow throbbing. He wanted a drink, but settled for aspirin, hoping the small white tablets could deliver the relief the packaging promised. He turned down another endless street, frozen slush popping under his heels. A café beckoned ahead, the warm smell of breakfasts frying rich above the reek of diesel and propane. A blue-and-white bus pulled into the gravel lot, swaying drunkenly to a stop. Lanier hurried inside the café before the passengers.

He ordered something off the menu that he vaguely recognized and sat drinking coffee. The money he had asked for had arrived, though it wouldn't last long—not at the prices this period posted. He had miscalculated again, another in a long, long chain of tiny mistakes that always snowballed into failure. He found a discarded paper in another booth and tried to read it, but his hands shook too badly. His breakfast came. He ate like he was starving, and prayed he didn't throw it back up. The pain level rose, a silent tug, stronger than gravity, unrelenting, dragging at him. He turned to his left.

She was there, dressed in a long pink coat miles too big. A man twice her age sat with her, talking between cigarettes, his hand straying now and then to her thigh. Lanier tossed a handful of bills beside his empty plate and started toward them. Maria turned in her seat, her face bone white.

"I need to talk to you," Lanier said.

The man frowned. "Who the fuck are you?"

Lanier ignored him. "Come on, Maria. Let's go somewhere else."

"Leave me alone," she whispered, her accent breaking through. Trails of mascara ringed her eyes, drawing attention from the deep circles beneath. She looked exhausted and frail, her dark hair flat, the sheen lost. "I don't know you."

"You heard her, bud. Get the hell out of here." The man beside her stood up. He was tall and broad shouldered, probably had been tough once in the long ago. Lanier barely looked at him.

"Please, Maria? Come with me."

The man tried to step between them, telegraphing his every movement, clumsy and slow. Lanier's hand snaked out and caught his, snatched him by the fingers, twisting them backwards. A mask of pure pain skewed the older man's face, his knees buckling as he tried to pull away. Maria jumped up from her stool and pushed the two men apart.

"Enough! Leave him alone, I'll go with you."

The other man stared at her dumbfounded, but made no move. Lanier waited, fighting down his own nerves, adrenaline pounding through his system. He almost hoped the man would swing. He felt edgy, nervous, his mind was on fire. He was picking up her fear, amplifying his own. At least a fight might offer some release from the awful energy building up inside him. He held the door for Maria and followed her into the parking lot.

"Where are we going?" she asked, breath streaming around her face.

"To get a room."

"Fine." She flipped her hair, hiding her own jitters. "It'll cost you fifty bucks, OK?"

Lanier stared at her. "You like living like this? Being a whore?"

"Well, fuck you." She tried to pull away, but he caught her and pulled her toward a row of low, dingy-looking motel units across the street. She gave up fighting and followed, too afraid to do anything else. "What do you want from me?"

The woman in the motel office stared at them, shrugged, and took a brass key down from the wall. Lanier paid for the room, Maria's arm still locked in his grip, and herded her out of the office . She didn't struggle as he unlocked the door and flipped on the lights inside.

"Turn up the heat, will you?" she asked. "I'm cold."

"All right." He found what he thought was a thermostat and twisted the knob to high. The radiator hissed softly, feeble heat drifting out. He locked the door with the chain then tossed his coat onto the bed. "I see you've adapted to this century easy enough."

"What is it that you want?" She huddled beside the radiator, shivering, arms drawn tight, the pink coat bunching up around her. For a moment she looked like the girl-child he had first seen in Prague so long ago. "Why are you doing this to me?"

"I told you. You have a gift."

"Leave me alone." Tears seeped out of her eyes, dark stains running down her cheeks. She trembled harder. "Please, leave me alone."

"I can't." Lanier stepped toward her, stopped, and then sat down on the low bed. "I won't hurt you. I promise. I want to help you."

"Help me do what?"

"Help you get out of here. Help you get home again."

She laughed, a cold, empty sound. "Home? I don't have a home."

"Yes. You do." Carefully, he took the translator from around his neck and tossed it to her "That," he said, "is where home is."

Her fingers shook as she reached for the silvery globe. Shock ran across her face at the touch, a revelation. She snatched her arm back and stared at him, mouth agape and eyes wide. "How?"

"It's called a translator. It's how I've followed you all these years." He tried to sound reassuring. "It's what you'll use to go home." He took a deep breath, wishing for the thousandth time he had a drink. "There was a war. We were losing. Too many people hated us for what we could do. We couldn't fight and protect our families at the same time, so we gathered up our children, all the gifted ones, and scattered them where no one could follow."

She slumped to the bed. Her fingers brushed the translator again. "I was one of those children?"

"Yes."

She stared at the wall, tears flowing out. "All those years. All those Goddamned years. You left me to starve."

"Things went wrong." He took her hand. It felt cold to the touch. "By the time the war was over both sides were broken. It was years before we could gather the resources to find all of you." He shook like an old man. "You're the last."

"Why? Why did you take so long?"

He stared at the wall. The words wouldn't come. His brain was hazy, numb, the world settling on him like a stone. "You were too good, that's all. Too talented. You were bred from a hundred generations of navigators." He nodded at the translator. "What the rest of us need machines for, you do by instinct. Every time I got close, you vanished." He shrugged. "Now, you can finally go home."

A siren blared in the distance, a mournful, angry wail. She lifted the device, stroking it, holding it softly to her face. She closed her eyes. "All this time . . ."

"I know it doesn't make up for everything you've been through, but you'll be a hero when you get home. They'll teach you how to use your talent. You'll see worlds most of us only dream about." Lanier smiled, fighting down the pain. "I would have given anything to have a gift like yours."

"But, you have the same talent—I can feel it. I've felt it since the first time."

"Maybe, a long time ago." He choked back the tears. "Whatever I had, the war took out of me. By the time it was over I was used up. Just another shell. That's why I volunteered to come back for you."

"Are you . . ." She took a deep breath. "Are you my father?"

"Me? Gods no!" Lanier actually laughed. "I'm no one to you. Just a friend."

She nodded, the translator still in her hand. She pressed it again to her face, eyes closed, sweet bliss spreading through her like brandy on a winter's day. "When do we leave?"

"Whenever you're ready." He took the sphere out of her hands, twisted the hidden controls, then hung it around her neck. "Follow the thread. It'll take you home."

"Aren't you coming with me?"

"I can't. Not without that." He pointed at the device. "It's an all or nothing proposition."

"But . . ."

"No." He stroked her face, ignoring the contact pain. "I told you, I volunteered for this. There's nothing back there for me. No family. No life." He smiled sadly. "No talent. It's better this way."

She stared at the floor, then, after a moment, started unbuttoning her coat. She wore a tight red blouse, her breasts pushed high. She reached for his hand. He drew back. "No." A thousand dreams poured through him, the hot need awakening. He closed his eyes, driving back the image of her silken skin against his. "No, not like that. It would be too painful." He smiled again. "For both of us. There is one thing you can do for me."

"What?"

He fished the ancient Tarot cards out of his pocket and dropped them on the bed. "You never finished my fortune."

She laughed out loud and picked up the cards. Painted faces cavorted across the familiar surfaces. For the last time, she laid out the cards for him. For the last time, she began to read.

"You've reached the end to a long journey. Your troubles lay down with you." Her hands shook as she turned the cards. "There is sorrow and there is joy." She turned a final card and lay it atop the rest.

A court jester, his belongings gathered in a sack over his shoulder, whistling as he walked. Lanier looked at the card and smiled.

"The fool?"

She nodded. He picked the cards up and put them in his pocket, then, gently as he could, kissed her on the forehead. He rose and started toward the door.

"What are you going to do?"

He shrugged. "I don't know yet. Maybe it won't be so bad. This seems like a decent enough century." He opened the door a crack, cold air spilling through. "Good luck."

She only nodded, crying again. Lanier closed the door behind him. A patch of blue sky broke through the sullen clouds, spilling to the barren earth. He started walking, dragging the icy air into his lungs. He still felt her trace. A snap ran down his spine as she vanished into the untouchable future. He sighed, the pain lessening, and walked faster.

A clock chimed ten, deep and resonant, the echoes fading into the traffic noise. He still had a few dollars to his name and if he didn't get a drink soon, he thought, laughing at himself, he just might die.

EMPIRE OF DREAMS AND MIRACLES

JAMES MAXEY

If our great-great-grandparents could have seen our day—cars, planes, space shuttles; cell phones, pocket computers, remote controls; penicillin, anti-psychotics, ibuprofen; satellite and radar weather reports, worldwide TV simulcasts; air-conditioning, reclining chairs, and sensurround—would they not have thought us alien creatures, caring about things that meant nothing to them, and ignorant of skills they had to know simply to survive?

When the surrounding technology changes, and the folkways change to fit it, it can seem to the stranger that human nature itself has changed. Yet on the internet we have the same old frauds and adulteries and vandalism, merely acted out in slightly different ways. Our missiles are still designed to kill, as surely as any arrow or hard-thrown spear. Cell phones have not raised the level of conversation, and when people are talking together without some agenda forced on them, they still resort to either gossip or seduction as surely as they did when conversations were at the doors of nomad tents or over tea in drawing rooms or side-by-side on the threshing floor.

Into a strange new world a visionary writer takes us and, among the miracles, shows us who we already are and always were . . .

I WOKE FROM a dream about technopaganneuro sex, unable to remember going to bed or what had happened to my clothes. I kicked aside the red silk sheets and sat up. On the silver table by my bed sat an antique toy, a black plastic ball with the number eight painted on its top. I couldn't remember where I had acquired it, but I vaguely recalled Rayn having described one to me once. Some sort of pre-technological oracle. Curious, I flipped it over—"FUCK YEAH!" it said—and knew the day was going to be a good one.

Energized, I jumped to the window and flung open the curtains. Warm sunlight and a cool salty breeze flooded the room. A young boy was walking on the street below.

"You there!" I called out. "Young man! What day is this?"

"Put some clothes on," he yelled, and hurried along his way. He seemed very convincing, his stride, his expression. Perhaps he really was a boy. An original, I mean.

But original or copy, the oracle was already proving true. How Utopian to begin the day with a total stranger's kind advice.

Advice I promptly disregarded. I leapt from the balcony onto the brick pathway and ran toward the ocean. My body quickly warmed beneath the bright sun. I reached the beach and planted my toes in the hot white sand, stretching luxuriously as I cried to the smooth blue sky, "Good morning!"

And it was. I've never met a morning in Atlantis that wasn't simply brilliant.

I walked to my favorite ocean-side café and took a seat on the patio. The wait-thing brought me golden nectar and a black seaweed quiche. The wait-thing looked like a man, but with transparent skin, which revealed its internal clockwork, ceaselessly whirring.

A shadow fell across my breakfast.

A deep, musical voice greeted me. "Good afternoon, Dobay."

It was Makan. You may know him. Big fellow, heavily muscled. Black skin, hair sculpted into a seahorse, florescent yellow lipstick and a single red feather through his Adam's apple. Not the sort of person who would stand out in a crowded room, but once you get past the mundane exterior you find a true creative genius. Makan's a deathpoet, one of the best.

"How's dying these days?" I asked.

"Same as ever." He shrugged, and then took a seat. "You don't have any clothes on."

"Is that a problem?"

"Of course not. It's just you're normally so meticulous about your clothes."

"It's important to look good in public," I said.

"Well, you do."

"Thank you," I said. "I had a dream last night that will interest you. I was making love to a witchmachine, in a field of daisies . . ."

"Witchmachine?" he asked.

"A *machine*," I said, slightly perturbed by the interruption, "that's also a *witch*. Anyway, the thing slit my

71

throat. It was a marvelous feeling, I grew lightheaded, my vision blurred, I could only hear the rumble of blood as it left me, and my skin became fantastically sensitive. I could feel every last bead of sweat that rolled across me."

"Yes," Makan said, toying with his throatfeather. "That matches my own experience with exsanguination. Nearly sexual, but it's difficult to climax."

"Rayn and Glantililly were talking about your drowning last week," I said. "I'm surprised you're back already."

"Blame it on popularity," he said, shrugging. "When no one wanted to see me die, I had to stay gone years to build up buzz. Now, I get nine, ten requests a month. The price of fame."

"I think I killed someone last night," I said, then sipped my nectar. "Might have been messy."

"Oh?"

"Tough to know for certain yet. But the absence of clothes is a good sign. Blood-soaked garments irritate me."

He nodded knowingly. "You seem calm enough about it."

"Can't get too worked up. It might throw me off."

"If you did pull off a killing, you're only one behind Faz Jaxxon."

"Drop it," I said. "Thinking about your score is a sure jinx."

"I'd best fly," said Makan. "I've got some prelim work to do with a shark. Most of them hate human blood."

"Then swap it," I said. "Seal blood, maybe."

"You know I'm a traditionalist," he said. He stood and leaned across the table. We kissed. His tongue was slimy and hard and tasted like ginger.

"Good luck with your killing," he said, as he floated skyward.

I wiped my mouth and looked at the glowing yellow smear on my hand. I'm glad he left. Talking about the game *is* bad luck. And I'm so primed to jabber.

BACK HOME, I sank into the womb and drifted awhile. There was never any doubt as to my destination, but I like to pretend I'm unconcerned. I slipped into a documentary about a place called America. Big place; chaotic, dangerous. Hard to imagine the lack of control, the total absence of safety. You could die by eating the wrong thing, by walking on the wrong street, or, worst of all, by having your body just give out, betray you by becoming weaker and slower. When you died, that was it. No resurrection, just recycling. Worm food. Amazing we ever made it out alive.

Having spent enough time in the documentary, I slid over into the Game Show. Oh, yes. I did kill someone after all. I relived it, along with millions of others. There was a woman at my feet and I felt my shoulders burning, felt the smooth, wet knife in my hand, felt the rush of power that I get when I'm at the top of my game. But then I noticed her face, and all I could feel was shame. I knew this woman! The victim turned out to be Rayn, Glantililly's lover. What made me go for such an easy target? I knew she had registered as a victim; she had talked about it for years. But it's no sport to kill the ones who beg for it. Faz Jaxxon must have laughed himself wet.

I'd slipped in at the culmination, the most popular viewing time. My fellow citizens usually skip the hours of hunting and plunge right into the moment. I surfed backwards, past the break-in, past the stalking, until, ah

. . . *Glantililly*. I could see her by my side as we strolled along the beach last evening near sunset. The fading light brought out the peacock iridescence of her hair, and the evening breeze played with the mist garment she wore, allowing enticing glimpses of the smooth violet curves of her body. We each carried a glass of Clear White Dreams (which explained my missing memory). We were talking about Rayn.

"It's her shield," said Glantililly. "By talking about her status, she knows hunters won't go for her. She registered for the thrill, but she's really afraid to die. She's a virgin."

"Incredible," I said. "I didn't know there were any left."

"It happens," Glantililly said. "She just never gave in to the curiosity when she was younger. Now she's all wrapped up in a tangle of fear and inhibition."

"Does she fear the pain?"

"It's more complex than that. I think she's afraid the reality of the moment will let her down, after all these years of imagining."

"Poor kid," I said. "Some people invest too much emotion in their first death."

"If only someone would help her get past this. Someone . . . experienced. Good at it."

I felt a glimmer of hope. Unable to wait any longer, I went straight to the scoreboard. My heart sank, and then leapt. I scored only 12 points for the total kill, well below average, but half of it was in motivation, a six. It's difficult to get higher than a three in motivation anymore. There's so much competition, so much pressure to get another kill on the board to stay in the game, that there just isn't time to work up a real justification for murder. A six showed style.

Speaking of pressure, Faz Jaxxon had to be feeling it. I had moved to within three points. I was tempted to switch to his life to find out how far away he was from his next kill. Then I reminded myself I'm not in this for the score. I played the game because it sharpens my mind, strengthens my body, and enlarges my spirit. But, damn, *three points!*

I TOOK TO the streets as shadows blanketed Atlantis. A magic breeze, salty and electric, danced through the streets, to the beat of joyous music pouring from open doorways. Perhaps you know of such moments, such moods, when you realize you live in the Golden Age, that there is no better time or place to be alive than now, here, in the Empire of Dreams and Miracles.

I wore my finest white robes, scented with patchouli, my body freshly shaven and glowing with subdermal luminescence, a side effect of the hot pinks I had popped before leaving my quarters. I carried my best knife in a sheath hidden in my left sleeve. It's a seven-inch blade, black ceramic, capable of cutting a hair lengthwise. I'm not superstitious. The knife isn't good luck. But fingering its bone hilt, I couldn't help but feel a sense of certainty. I would kill someone soon. A beautiful kill. Much better than a 12.

Then I saw her. High above me, on the crystal bridge that crosses Garden Africa, she leaned against the rail, watching the sunset. She was dressed in black with long, flowing tresses. She had the air of one who might jump, should there be any point. World-weary. Worn. *Perfect*. I hurried through the maze of stairs to reach her, hoping she would still be there by the time I reached the top.

She was. I placed myself beside her and looked out over the tan parklands. Zebras grazed by the lake, oblivious to the lions in the long shade of the baobab tree. She gave no reaction to my presence.

"Beautiful," I said.

"I know who you are," she said, her gaze still focused to the west.

"Oh?"

"Dobay the Gold. I've slipped into your life from time to time. Quite a show . . . for some."

"Thank you. I think. What's your name?"

"You try for something extra with your work."

"If a thing is worth doing . . ."

"Is anything worth doing?" she asked.

"Precisely anything," I said, intrigued by the turn in the conversation. I had been prepared for mindless banter about giraffes and such. "Anything at all, if you do it well."

"This is what eternity has reduced us to," she said.

For the first time, she turned her face toward me. Her eyes and lips were as black as her gown, in contrast with her pale porcelain skin. She smelled very alive, a musky odor that mixed well with the air from the park, very animal, very human.

"I didn't catch your name," I said.

"You get more points if I'm not a stranger," she said as she turned her gaze once more to the menagerie.

"I don't kill everyone I speak to," I said, feeling wounded. "It doesn't work like that."

"I know how it works," she said, with a dismissive roll of her eyes.

"Then you know you shouldn't assume things. People sometime prejudge me, imagine I size everyone up as a potential victim. But really, don't you think I just occasionally like to talk?"

"You could talk to, let's see, what's her name . . . Rayn?"

Suddenly, I understood. She was obviously a longtime fan, disappointed that I had stooped to killing such an easy target.

"Rayn was an exception," I said, hoping to explain. "I don't kill inside my circle as a rule."

"Why not?"

I shrugged. "Things can be awkward afterward. Life's too long to have everyone be suspicious of you."

She turned back to me and smiled, an expression that didn't seem to fit her. Her lipstick changed color, becoming blood red.

"You're a philosopher," she said.

I am, but somehow it felt wrong to admit it.

"And a liar," she continued. "You did approach me with murder in mind."

"Believe what you want," I said, perturbed.

"I've hurt your feelings," she said, with amusement. "Will you kill me for that?"

"Dream on." I snorted, and turned away. I had no time for her games. And you score no points at all if they ask for it.

THAT NIGHT I climbed the Bethlehem Spire and hung myself by the heels. Swaying for hours in the salt-tanged breeze, Atlantis was my bright heaven, while beneath me spun the endless black night. I thought of Alandra.

The girl on the bridge had awakened her memory. And it's true. Sometimes, after you kill someone, things change. Alandra was never the same. She drew away, closed herself in a womb, and was gone. So many years ago. I still ache for her. We were so young and serious. Everything had meaning.

But meaning was as fleeting as the shooting stars beneath my feet. Don't think me sad, however. I realized long ago that even if a thousand stars fall each night for a thousand years, the sky will still twinkle with the promise of the infinite. And in a world of infinite promise, how can I help but hold her again?

I MET MY father for lunch. These days he's a she, just through puberty, blonde, pretty and completely unknowable. He calls himself Kandii.

"Have you spoken to your mother lately?" she asked.

"You know I haven't," I said. "You?"

She shook her head, and then pushed her hair back from her eyes. Sometimes, I think I see him in her, in the faint ghost of one of his gestures. But he's fading. He's becoming his skin. I've seen him with boys, flirting, flaunting. It's hard to remember he's nine centuries old, old enough to have had a profession. He used to be a lawyer, but the world no longer needs laws. Maybe that's part of his identity crisis. Or maybe there's no crisis at all. Maybe it's just me who feels strange about this.

"I know you dislike confrontations," she said. "But I think we need to discuss your discomfort with what I've done."

"I'm not uncomfortable," I said. "It's your life."

"It *is*," she said gleefully. "And I've decided not to resist it any longer. I'm doing this to embrace every possibility. I'll be a man, a woman, old, young—a rainbow of colors. Any life we can imagine, we can have. A century

78

from now, it will seem old-fashioned to wake up in a body you've already worn."

She's probably right. In fact, I'm sure of it. It's the whole infinite promise thing. Why not keep it? If a thing can be done, do it. But I'm not ready. Not quite ready. Who can say? Maybe I'll never be ready to tell my father that I would gouge my eyes out for a chance to sleep with him. Oedipus had it so easy.

I SAW THE woman from the bridge again that afternoon, on the Avenue of Yesterday. People seldom go there, but I went, knowing somehow I would find her. She wore white, and her hair was powdered to match. She looked like a living statue moving among the others. I followed her discreetly, until I was certain she hadn't seen me. She seemed somnambulistic, oblivious even to the statues I thought she wished to emulate. What was wrong with this girl?

I felt a mix of pity and curiosity. How sad to be sad, I thought. Had someone she loved vanished? Was her longing like my own? Perhaps not. She seemed too cold, too distant to ever have loved, to ever have felt anything.

How would she respond to pain, to fear? Could I, with the strength in my hands and a single sharp blade, slice through the barriers that separated her from the desire to live? Could I awaken the flame inside her by smothering it?

Her "invitation" on the bridge was problematic. It was possible I might score no points for killing her. But, there was an ambiguity to the request. Certainly enough for an appeal if things went badly with the initial judges.

I stopped myself and shook my head, ashamed. What was I thinking? Killing a woman whose name I didn't even know for *points?* Where was my pride? I must make the kill not for my sake. Not even, in truth, for her sake, but for the *kill's* sake. It must be a single, perfect, enduring moment. That would be enough.

She left the Avenue of Yesterday, descending into the catacombs. This was where the uncounted billions of Atlantis spent most of their lives. There was far more to the city beneath the streets than above. We passed door after door, behind which our fellow citizens lay adrift in their wombs. Was she usually one of them? Was this only a temporary excursion into daylight? Was reality turning out to be a disappointment?

She headed deeper, ever deeper, until the mechanical heart of the city itself could be heard, the vast engines that drove the clockwork of paradise. I had never explored this far down. We were nearing the forbidden area, and I wondered if she was heading toward it to destroy herself, for surely the city would only declare a place off limits if it contained dangers a human mind couldn't imagine. I was tempted to turn back, but I pressed on.

The decorative tile work and murals of the upper sublevels were left behind. The passageways became shorter, the walls pale gray and smooth, with few places to hide. Devoting all my energies to remaining unseen, I realized I had grown quite lost. I had only her soft footsteps and scent of musk to guide me.

From ahead, a door clicked shut. I turned the corner and she was gone. The passageway ended with a door to my right, and another to my left. They looked ancient, made to resemble wood, with brass doorknobs green with age. I pressed my ear to the right entry. Nothing could be heard. I leaned against the left door.

Music. A violin, softly weeping.

I touched the knob. With a loud crack, a current of electricity shot through me. I fell, blacking out, amidst a shower of sparks.

I WOKE TO candlelight. The room was tiny, the walls dark green and glistening, stretching up into gloom. I was naked, shivering from the chill of the concrete beneath me. I couldn't move my arms or legs. By straining my neck, I could see my limbs bound by strips of leather fastened to iron rings in the floor. The violin played more distinctly now, the solo from the *Plague Symphony* by Galacia. I had never liked that song, with its terrible melancholy, though Makan had used it to great effect when burned at the stake.

"What's happening?" I asked, doubting I was alone.

"Something that matters," she answered, her voice drifting from somewhere high above me.

"Is this a joke?" I asked.

A poorly greased wheel began to turn in the darkness. Her pale shape emerged slowly as she floated down, wraithlike, gaining corporeality as she grew closer, her skin bone-white, her lips and nails red as blood, her teeth gleaming. She was naked save for the elaborate leather harness that supported her. Her face tilted toward me and she kissed my forehead, a warm kiss, gentle. She looked into my eyes and told me, "This is the only serious moment you will ever live, Dobay the Gold."

"Oh, my," I said, with a grin. "I like the sound of it."

She came to rest upon me, her warm, moist crotch settling on mine, her long fingers stroking my hair. She slowly tickled her nails along my cheeks, down my neck, across my chest. Her hands vanished to my sides. I heard a scrape of metal against concrete. She raised her arms high overhead, brandishing an old fashioned hammer, the claw side toward me. And then, with a grunt, she swung.

I have no memory of the impact. I don't know if 10 seconds or 10 hours passed. My memory returns with my voice hoarse from shouting, my mouth filled with the taste of vomit, my sight half-gone. With each heartbeat, my pain grew more awful. I've broken almost every bone in my body over the years, but nothing compared with this. There were no pills to carry me forward, to mask or enhance my senses. I hurt, and she was stalking angrily about the room, cursing me.

"You are *nothing* but meat," she hissed.

I tried to speak, but my voice wouldn't come.

"What is it?" she demanded. "Answer me!"

I shook my head.

She kicked me in the groin, but the pain was like a cup poured into an ocean. And an icy ocean it was, draining from the pit of my stomach, sucking my pain and cares into its undertow. I began to chuckle softly.

She knelt beside me and placed a finger on my lips.

"Shhh," she said. "Shhh."

"You'll get a lot of points for this," I whispered.

"Oh, darling," she said.

"We must—share a drink—when I get back."

"Oh, my poor child," she said, her voice soft and tender. "You can't even imagine, can you? You aren't coming back."

It was difficult to focus on what she had said. But something rolled over inside my head. I felt myself swimming up through the cold tide.

"W-what's your name?" I asked.

"I am Death," she answered.

"Small world," I said. "I'm Dying."

"Not yet. You're a strong man."

She was right. The shock was wearing off, or maybe just setting in. I realized just how little pain I was truly feeling, how distant I was from my own body. This wasn't the best way to do it. Pain like this should be embraced, cherished, savored like fine wine. But I couldn't quite do it. I felt too focused on her. Jealous.

"I-I thought I knew all the other hunters," I said. "You m-must be new. What a d-debut."

"I've killed so, so many," she said. "I no longer count."

"I would have heard of you."

She shook her head. "I don't exist. Neither do you, anymore. My worms have already eaten away all memory of you from the city's brain. There's no template left to rebuild you, I'm afraid."

I didn't understand what she was getting at for several long seconds. When I did, I laughed.

"Oh, Death, you have such p-promise."

She sighed.

"But you've pushed it too far. Don't get me wrong. Most v-victims would get a nice jolt of fear from that."

"I don't want your fear," she said.

"Come on. It plays better that way. The score is always higher when the victim's really into it."

She answered me by slamming her heel down hard on my mouth, knocking teeth loose. She began to shout at me again.

"This is what everyone you kill has felt," she scolded. "Nothing but the physical. They aren't capable of real emotion. You disappoint me, Dobay. I thought there might be something more in you. Something human."

I spat out blood and teeth. I tried to revel in the pain, but couldn't. What was she trying to say? Why wouldn't she just shut up and let me suffer? I felt helpless in my confusion.

"What?" I cried. "What do you want from me?"

"After the struggle's done," she said, "all that's left is entertainment."

She crouched over me once more, her face close to mine. She lifted her hand to reveal my best knife. Laying the blade against my throat, she had that sad look again, the same look I had witnessed the first time I saw her. So weary, so worn. So alone.

She raised the blade.

There was a flash of light and a wet snick. Her head fell from her shoulders and bounced against my nose. Her body collapsed upon me, limp and wet. In the candle-light stood a man, red skinned, with a wild, black beard and a long, curved sword, blade dripping.

"*Faz Jaxxon!*" I laughed, with relief, with shock, and because his name just sounded stupid when spoken with my front teeth gone. "God *damn* you!"

He sliced my bonds with his sword, and helped me sit up against the wall. There was blood everywhere, but what was mine and what was hers I couldn't guess. One thing was clear through the haze, though.

"*A rescue!*" I couldn't believe it. "You'll max out on this one!"

"Whatever," he said. He knelt over Death, using his blade to slice off her ear. "Never think much about the points."

"No," I said. "Of course not. Me either."

"Oh?" he said, with a raised eyebrow. "You a hunter?"

"God, I must be a mess. I'm Dobay. Dobay the Gold."

"Huh," he said, placing the ear in a pouch on his belt. "Well, good luck, kid. Need some help getting to a womb? You don't look so hot."

"Fuck off," I said. "I don't need your help."

He smirked, and then walked away.

"Good luck, *kid!*" I shouted as he turned the corner. "I'll have your *ass!*"

But instead of chasing after him, I chose that moment to faint.

NO ONE DISPOSED of her body. No one came to take me to a womb. I woke weak and feverish. The room was completely dark. The blood I lay in was thick and glue-like. With a gasp, I pulled my face free of the floor. I dragged myself away from that awful place. At last, I made it to the lighted hall.

"*Help,*" I whispered. I lay on the cool floor, trying to make sense of what had happened. I had never felt so empty.

If I died, no doubt someone would come along soon enough and put me in a womb and I would be better. Even if someone only came this way once a year, even once a decade, what did it matter? I'd be good as new. I could escape this agony so easily. All I had to do was close my eyes and wait.

But I couldn't. Death had said she didn't want my fear, but she had it. In my weakened state, I was no longer sure. Maybe she *could* kill even my memory. If I closed my eyes—my eye—it might never open.

And so I crawled, inch by inch, through the timeless shadows of the undercity. At last I reached a grotto with a small pool where I slaked my thirst, and must have fallen asleep. I know that I woke hungry, but stronger. I was able to pull myself to my feet, and limp along, with

85

one hand upon the wall. I reached my home, but my door wouldn't open. I studied myself in its mirrored surface. Was this thing before me even human? One-eyed, scabbed, dirty, pale, gap-toothed . . .

But alive. *Alive.* And maybe that does count for something.

SUNRISES ARE SUBTLER than sunsets. I shivered on the beach, watching the black sky tint bloody. I wondered if Makan were here, would he be jealous? Everyone likes to experience his deaths; he goes out of the way to insure the most torment, the most lucidity and pathos. But the way I felt that morning had a certain honesty to it, a sincerity Makan's choreographed agonies never attained. I grew proud of my pain. I couldn't wait to share it. And that, I think, was the key to my feeling that everything would work out.

The beauty of the world is that we go through nothing truly alone. Every moment of our lives, every deed and thought, can be shared by countless others, if we so choose. When I made it back into a womb and let myself free, everyone could feel as I felt, experiencing every ache and throb of my tortured flesh, sharing my emotions, my sense that the city had allowed this for a purpose, that this was all for the best. I felt a growing sense of importance as the sun arrived decisively, its eager rays dancing on my anguished skin. Something good was about to happen.

I looked around. I was alone on the beach, except for a distant figure, out for a morning stroll. She paused when she saw me, and then continued. Soon I could see her skin was light green, and she wore a sky blue sarong.

Her deep green hair danced like kelp in the steady wind. She carried a conch in her left hand.

It was her. She didn't look the same, true, but there was no doubt. I knew her walk, her lips, her eyes.

"*Alandra*," I said, as her shadow reached me.

"Do I know you?" she asked. Her voice was still the same.

"It is I. Dobay."

"Good morning, Dobay."

"You've changed your skin," I said. "It suits you."

"Thank you," she said, staring at my torn face. "But I'm not sure I understand your skin. Why have you done this? It must be painful."

I didn't know what to say. I wanted to tell her what had happened, to explain everything, but I couldn't. In all my countless dreams of reunion, I hadn't rehearsed those lines.

"This fashion eludes me," she said. "Why choose pain over comfort?"

Her words triggered my memory. "We've had this discussion before."

"Have we?"

"Long ago, after making love in the Plaza of Peace."

"I think you must be mistaken."

"No. I remember every word we ever spoke. I've relived them a hundred times."

"We've never met, Dobay."

"You're Alandra. Don't deny it."

"Yes."

"You *must* remember."

"This conversation holds no pleasure for me, Dobay. Enjoy your morning."

JAMES MAXEY

She looked away, further down the beach and began to walk.

"Wait!"

She placed the conch shell to her ear and didn't turn back.

I sat for the longest time, as my skin baked beneath the violent sun, my bones cold as ice.

WHEN I FELT stronger, I sought out Makan. It came as no surprise when he didn't know me. By that time, the truth of Death's words were becoming evident. How much of our self is us and how much is the city? If the city forgets you, you never existed. There is no food for you in the café. The lights don't brighten as you approach. The doors do not open.

But there was still fruit on the trees, and water, water everywhere. The city provided passively, if not actively. My fellow humans talked to me, however briefly. I think they thought I had gone too far. My ugliness, my mal-formed face . . . No one understood why I chose it. And the story I told, such a strange comedy, a theater of the absurd. Whenever they saw me again, it was for the first time. They didn't remember their promise to bring me clothing, or hot food, or blankets. They can't remember me. I must work to remember myself.

When I returned to Death, she still held my good knife. Beetles had stripped her to the bone. I hadn't known there were beetles outside the gardens. Perhaps the city doesn't know, either. Or it doesn't care. I took her skull with me. It was lighter than I would have imagined.

Now, I sit upon the western shore and contemplate the waves. Out there, they say, are continents, wild places, where men live as beasts. They were left behind when the city saved us. They rejected the promise of Atlantis, the promise of life without fear, without want, without end. Shunned by the city, they fell behind, devolving to hunters and gatherers, becoming prey to disease and dragons. There's no romance about it, despite the best efforts of our poets.

And we, the civilized . . . we're the city's pets. We're well fed, well groomed, healthy, loved. Out there, your hair is always tangled, your lungs wheeze, you dig in the dirt for your next meal, and insects dig into you for theirs. It's the promise of the finite. Out there, life kills you.

But not today, if I can help it.

My knife is tied around my neck with a leather cord. It's a good knife; the kind of knife a man might use to carve his name into a brand new world. I'm glad she kept it for me. I place my lips upon her teeth. If she could only see me now, scarred and lean and leathery, my hair wild about me. Would she recognize me? Would she understand? This is the end of my romance with Death. She brought me this far, but now I must leave her behind and search for my new love, Life.

The sky is as red as the memory of her lips. The sun dances on the horizon, bringing morning to new lands. I dive into the waves, and chase the day.

THE MESSIAH

Carl Frederick

To musicians, Handel's Messiah *is like a kind of baptism or confirmation, a ritual through which all members have to pass, and thereafter a shared memory upon which they can draw. I listened to a recording of the* Messiah *about a hundred times one Christmas season as I was working in an office in a faraway country, until I had memorized every quirk of that particular performance. Since then I've sung the tenor or bass part in all the best-known choruses, in community and church choirs and public singalongs. And I've listened to a dozen more recordings with different tempos, voicings, and instrumentation. Play it often enough, and you can almost forget that it's a religious work, and it speaks of faith in redemption, in eternal life.*

Most religions offer some hope of transcending death, one way or another; and sometimes it's not a hope at all, but a threat, that suffering can go on after this life or be even worse.

*But in a time of loss or grief, when someone we love is taken
away without hope of return, then often even the most hard-
ened unbeliever finds, if not faith, then a deep wish that someone might tear down the wall of death and let us pass freely
back and forth. And if someone could let us do that, wouldn't
we call him God?*

AT THE REHEARSAL BREAK, Robert and Kimberly flowed
with the throng of choristers and instrumentalists out
from the college dining hall and across to the adjoining
snack bar.

"Snag us a table," said Robert, flourishing his baton
like a rapier, "and leave the rest to El Zorro."

Robert squeezed through to the refreshment counter,
speared a fudge brownie with his baton, then respond-
ing to frantic gestures from Kimberly, speared another
for her. He grabbed a few napkins and holding his baton
point-up so not to lose his catch, weaved his way to a
small table in the back. There by a window sat Kimberly,
well protected from the December cold by double-paned
glass and the radiating warmth of two cups of hot
mulled cider.

As he leaned forward to sit, he quickly, almost
furtively, kissed her on the cheek. "Kim. You were great."

She daintily pulled a brownie from the baton. "I bet
you say that to all your soprano soloists."

"Only those I intend to marry."

He saw her eyes break from his as she looked away,
over his shoulder.

"That's Paul, isn't it?" she said in a whisper. "I don't
know why, but he makes me uneasy."

Holding a cup of cider, Robert twisted around in his
chair. "There is definitely something off-putting about

the aliens, but I have to admit they have fine singing voices."

"Shh. He'll hear. Aliens indeed. What a thing to call someone."

Robert swiveled forward and leaned close. "But it's like they're from another planet. The five of them. They're completely bilaterally symmetric."

"Stop talking like a physicist."

"I can't help it. I am a physicist." Robert shot a quick glance over his shoulder. "Their faces. They're perfect. Symmetric. No human's face is built that way. There are always little blemishes that break the symmetry."

Kimberly laughed. "I grant they're a little strange but I hardly think Paul or the others are robots from Mars." Kimberly glanced around the room, seeking them out. "Well, they're not identical, but yes, they do look as if they were produced by the same manufacturer." She turned back to Robert. "My God. Now you've got me doing it."

Robert put down his cider and took Kimberly's hand. "Look, I haven't told anyone else about this, but they're more than strange. I'll rehearse one of them and when the rest of them arrive, they're all rehearsed. It's uncanny. I can't explain it—and it makes me edgy not being able to explain it. And they never seem to talk to each other, but they know the music perfectly."

"Telepathy."

"Come on, Kim. I'm serious."

"And what makes you think I'm not?"

"Telepathy is impossible. It violates the laws of physics."

"Is that what it means to be a post-doc in physics? If it's not explainable by physics, it's not real?"

"Yeah. You got it."

Kimberly toyed with her brownie. "It's odd that they selected you to conduct the *Messiah*."

"Why? Because I'm a physicist?"

"No. Because you're an atheist."

"Same thing."

Kimberly reached over and patted him on the head. "You don't believe in anything you can't measure, do you?"

"I'm sure, after we're married, either I'll start to believe or you'll finally give up your superstitions."

"Thanks a lot." She playfully cuffed his ear, perhaps with a little more force than necessary.

He grabbed her hand and kissed it, just as the room lights blinked on and off three times.

"Rats," said Robert. "Break is over. You know, I'm a little nervous about conducting the *Hallelujah Chorus*. Everyone knows it cold. Sort of like giving swimming lessons to your fish."

"My boss's fish. Don't worry about it, though. Just give the downbeat and get out of the way. And you'd better wipe the brownie crumbs from your baton."

THEY RETURNED TO the hall where Kimberly joined the rest of the soloists and Robert mounted the podium. Under his direction, they performed the *Hallelujah Chorus* twice—once for the sake of a rehearsal, and again for the sheer fun of it. Though caught up in the ecstasy of the music, a small analytic part of Robert's mind dwelled on the issue of Paul and his 'clan.' But God, could they ever sing. The 34th annual sing-in should be great—almost professional quality.

EARLY THE NEXT MORNING, Robert left his lab and jogged over to the university music library. The director, a fish fancier, had decorated the reception area with a number of free-standing aquariums There among the fishes was the chief music researcher's desk—Kimberly's domain.

Robert bounded up to the desk. "Kim. This is great. I've been thinking about it all night. Now, I have a possible mechanism for telepathy. All you need is a five-dimensional space-time continuum."

Kimberly sighed, put her elbows on the desk and rested her chin on her folded hands. She didn't say anything.

"Really," Robert went on in a burst of enthusiasm. "I was thinking about our aliens. And as Sherlock Holmes said, 'When you eliminate everything else, what remains must be it.' Right?"

"Or words to that effect."

Robert darted over to the nearest fish tank. "Look. It's simple." He put his fingertips into the water. "If you were a two-dimensional being, living on the surface of the water, what would you see?" He didn't wait for an answer. "You'd see five creatures, my five fingertips, but the two-dimensional beings would think they were separate creatures, and not one higher-dimensional animal." Robert wriggled his fingers, sending waves coursing over the water's surface. "So, Paul and the others could be a single organism. I haven't quite figured out why they'd look like people, but I'm working on it."

"I'd take my fingers out of there," said Kimberly, nonchalantly. "Those are baby piranha and it's dangerously close to feeding time."

Robert yanked his fingers upward and looked hard at the tank. "Goldfish. They're just goldfish."

"They're piranha in disguise—telepathic alien piranha."

Robert shook his hand dry, came around the back of the desk, and buried his face in her hair. "Umm. You smell good, you alien piranha." Then he vaulted around the desk and faced her. "You know. This could explain your Trinity."

"My what?"

"Father, Son, and Ghost."

"Do you mean, the Holy Ghost?"

"Yeah, fine. Holy Ghost."

Kimberly folded her hands on the desk. "Are you trying to tell me that God is a five-dimensional being?" Her voice held more exasperation than humor.

"It's a possibility."

"You're nuts."

"Why do you say that? Isn't it good to have a scientific explanation for your beliefs?"

"Surely, you can't be serious about this." Kimberly picked up a pencil and toyed with it.

"Kim. I love it when you talk Canadian to me."

She looked away toward the water cooler and spoke to a non-existent visitor. "And I thought Paul was strange. Maybe I should marry Paul."

"No, I'll be good," said Robert, moving around the desk to block Kimberly's view of the water cooler. "We'll have the Catholic wedding your folks want. I'll drink the Sacramento wine, eat the wafers."

"Sacramental wine." Her voice showed no humor now.

"Whatever." Robert sighed and stepped back from the desk. "I've got to get back to the lab. I'll see you at the rehearsal." He turned and started slowly for the door of the library.

"Robby. Wait."

Robert turned around. Kimberly was smiling,

"I'm sorry I've been bitchy. I've had a tiring morning." Kimberly pointed her pencil at Robert. "I do love you, you know."

Robert beamed. He couldn't help feeling like a worshipful, lovesick schoolboy. "Well, look," he began awkwardly. "How 'bout I pick you up here about six. We'll go to dinner before the rehearsal."

"I'd like that."

BACK IN HIS LAB, Robert briefly fantasized on married life with Kimberly and then busied himself with logic. He had first propounded his five-dimensional space-time hypothesis as an intellectual exercise—to explain the pseudo-scientific notion of telepathy. But he grew ever more intrigued with the idea and now could think of no other explanation for Paul. He knew though, that he was making wild extrapolations from very little data. It was, after all, a screwy idea—thinking that Paul and the others of his ilk were really a single higher dimensional being.

On impulse, Robert pulled out the University phone directory and looked up Paul's entry. The man was a dispatcher with Transportation Services—not a very lofty position in the University hierarchy. *One would think a five-dimensional being could do better.* Robert turned to his computer. He had some fragmentary information about Paul from the directory, but now he would go online to hunt up some more substantial data.

An hour later, Robert signed off the Net. Nothing. As far as the Net was concerned, Paul scarcely existed. He had ferreted out Paul's Social Security number, and had found that the guy had a clean driving record, but there was nothing more. No footprints through life. No school records. No voter registration records. No medical history. And Paul was the easy one. The others didn't even work at the University. Robert tilted back in his chair and thought.

Robert let the chair snap forward. He bounded up and across to the neighboring office where he knew he could borrow a pair of binoculars—from another post-doc who was a devout bird watcher.

"Sure, you can borrow them. Are you tracking a bird?"

"Yes, a bird," said Robert, "a queer bird."

Robert took the proffered field glasses, then bundled himself up and trudged off through the snow to the periphery of the University—to the Transportation Services Bus Garage. He had no idea what he hoped to see, but he wanted to observe Paul in the real world, not just as a chorister.

From the crest of a low hill, protected by a sheltering pine tree, Robert looked down on the garage. The building was spare, cubic, lacking even the hint of ivy. But it did have windows: many windows made up of multiple seven-by-nine-inch panes. Robert scanned the windows, and eventually zeroed in on an office on the ground floor. There, at a desk—a clean desk devoid of human clutter—sat Paul.

Crouched motionless, low in the snow, elbows on the ground supporting the field glasses, Robert observed.

Paul was motionless as well. He looked more a statue of a man than a living, breathing soul. Robert watched as another man entered Paul's office. Paul came to life then, looking like any normal person engaged in an office meeting. But when the man left, Paul returned to his seemingly lifeless state.

Robert observed with intense fascination. Although he had no idea what he was looking for and could not even guess at what constituted five-dimensional activity, he found Paul truly strange. Robert watched as Paul abruptly rose from his desk and left the office. He kept his binoculars trained on the window, waiting for Paul's return. Only when he put his binoculars down to sneeze in the damp cold, did he see that not only had Paul left the office, but he had also left the building. Robert snapped the binoculars to his eyes. Now with Paul moving roughly in his direction, he could observe his quarry clear and large—too large. Robert jumped to his feet. Not only was Paul coming in his general direction, but was striding directly toward his protective tree.

Robert looked nervously at his binoculars and had just about gotten them hidden in his coat, when Paul arrived at the tree.

"I'm, um, bird watching," said Robert.

"Yes, of course." Paul put an arm around Robert's shoulder. "Let's go over to the coffeehouse and talk."

"Yeah. Great."

As Robert accompanied Paul back to the central University campus, he tried mightily to think up a coherent story.

PAUL SAT WITH his hands folded around a cup of coffee. His symmetrical features were relaxed yet attentive, and he was smiling.

Robert, feeling the need to explain and to fill the silence, spoke. "You know, I'm a theoretical physicist, and when we go off the deep end, we come up with crazy theories." He laughed awkwardly. "And somehow I got the lunatic notion that you are a . . . well, that you're not from around these parts—that you're from someplace far away."

"Oh?" Paul took a sip of coffee. "Farther away than, say, Europe, I assume."

"Much farther." Robert fiddled with his coffee cup.

Paul laughed—a warm, inclusive laugh. "You don't have to pussyfoot around. You can be direct." Paul leaned in toward Robert. "So tell me. Where do you think I'm from?"

"From a five-dimensional universe," Robert blurted out. "Oh my gosh. See. I've lost my mind."

"But you're right, of course."

"What?" Robert's eyes widened and he almost knocked over his coffee.

"Why are you surprised?" said Paul. "It's your theory. Have confidence in yourself."

"You're playing with me."

"No, and I'm not telling you anything you don't know. The many-world view of quantum mechanics is pretty well established in your continuum. Whenever the universe makes a quantum decision, it spins off a parallel universe. Where do you think those universes live? There's infinite room for them in five-dimensional space."

Robert needed something familiar to grab on to, so he seized on theoretical physics. "And you're simultaneously in those parallel universes as well?"

"No, unfortunately not. Too bad, really. It would be interesting to see how people's lives would change had they chosen to tread the paths they did not take. But there's a kind of exclusion principle that lets us exist in only one four-dimensional plane."

They talked physics, but mainly Robert listened physics. And a small voice in his mind marveled at how easily an outlandish, unbelievable situation could be reduced to just a normal conversation between theoretical physicists. Robert believed fully: Not only because Paul seemed an awfully good physicist for a bus dispatcher, but also because the man had some quality, some presence that made it absolutely impossible to doubt him.

Robert warmed his hands around his coffee cup. "I'm sort of surprised you can't travel freely between these parallel universes."

"Although we may understand a few more of them than do you," said Paul, "we're still subject to the laws of physics. We can, however, observe some of the closely connected four-spaces—as outside observers—and to some degree, so can you."

"Not that I've noticed," said Robert. "And there are times I'd have liked to."

"Think of your dreams," said Paul. "Not the conventional dreams where you're flying, or are in class without your pants. I mean the other dreams where you seem to be in another reality, where you've made other life choices, where other events are playing out. Those dreams are a connection to another four-plane, another universe. When you dream them, you're very close to that world, and that world is real."

"I'm not quite sure I haven't lost my mind and am just having a delusion," said Robert, starting to rise. "Let's go and find Professor Mermin. We should talk to him. He's a great theoretician."

"No. Just you." Paul shook his head and waved Robert to remain seated. "The last time I became involved in human affairs, things got very much out of hand."

Robert regarded the man in silence for a few moments. Then, inexplicably, he was overwhelmed with a feeling of awe. "Are you the Messiah?"

"Excuse me?"

"Are you God?"

"No. Of course not."

Robert felt queasy. Paul should have laughed at the question. "But you have the power of God. And so what's the difference? You're God. Yes?"

"I assure you I'm not." He laughed. "But from overhearing your chats with Kimberly, I rather thought you were a non-believer."

"I am, or at any rate, I was." Robert fought a personal battle and then asked the question. "Is there a God, then?"

"I don't know, actually. But I know he's not me."

"So you're saying that a couple of millennia ago, you weren't wandering around a town named Nazareth and going under the name of Jesus."

"No, I'm not saying that at all."

"What? You mean that . . ."

Paul held up his hand, cutting Robert off. "Whenever you want, I'd be glad to talk physics with you. But metaphysics, no."

"Yeah, OK. That's what I like to talk about most, anyway," said Robert. Then he added, "But why are you here?"

"I or maybe we—the pronoun's tricky—we find it interesting here in your four-space continuum. Where I live, there's very little in the way of uncertainty, and therefore little scope for humor."

"You're here as a joke?"

"No, not exactly. We like the sense of humor in your world, and the spontaneity. I'd be happy to drink more coffee and talk, but don't you have to run off and meet Kimberly?"

Robert looked at his watch and yelped. "God, I'm late. Wait. How did you know?"

Paul laughed. "A side-effect of living in five-space. There are no barriers to us in your world, so I'm afraid it's very difficult for us not to eavesdrop."

Robert jumped up. "I really do want to stay but Kimberly is very unforgiving about lateness."

"Go and meet her. I'll be around. And I must say, it's good to have a four-space being to talk to." He laughed again. "But I wouldn't speak of this with her, or with anyone else for that matter."

"No, no. Of course I won't—especially as I'm not entirely sure you're not a hallucination. I'll see you later."

Robert bounded out of the coffeehouse into the snow, and the cold brought clarity. He had been trained to have faith in his observations, and he had observed Paul. There was no reason to believe Paul was other than what he had said. Robert felt giddy. Meeting Paul could be the greatest thing in the entire history of theoretical physics, and it was all his. As Robert scurried off, he had the fleeting thought that perhaps Einstein had become Einstein because of a similar meeting.

Robert was happy beyond measure. If only he could tell Kimberly. That would be great.

"MY, BUT YOU'RE in a good mood." Kimberly made a grab for her coat as Robert hurried her out the door.

"Yes. Yes, I am," said Robert. "Dinner at Turback's and then the *Messiah* rehearsal."

"Turback's? You really are in a good mood." Kimberly laughed, "and an extravagant one, too."

Robert bowed, then helped her on with her coat. *"Rejoice, Greatly, Oh daughter of Zion,"* he sang.

"Wait. That's my part. Somehow, I don't think you're cut out to be a soprano."

"All right, then. How about this?" Robert affected a very deep voice. *"But who may abide the day of his coming?"*

"Maybe you'd better stick to conducting."

Robert giggled. "Physicists make super-conductors."

Kimberly threw up her hands. "You're like a little kid on a sugar high."

"Yes, but this little kid is going to get the Nobel Prize for physics some day."

"I don't doubt it," said Kimberly, "but before you come to your senses, take me to Turback's so you can buy me dinner. Just don't sing, *Oh, we like sheep* when the waiter comes for our order."

"Oh, we like sheep," sang Robert, *"Oh we like sheep, have gone a-stra-ay."*

"Oh, God, What have I done?"

They had a happy dinner in a restaurant known as a place of celebration. Robert said they were celebrating the last rehearsal before the actual performance. Of course he couldn't reveal what he was actually celebrating.

Dinner was fun, and so was the rehearsal. Kimberly sang like an angel, and Robert thought he had conducted well, despite the fact that he had spent most of his time watching the multiple manifestations of Paul.

AFTER THE REHEARSAL, as they walked her home, Kimberly talked music. "The orchestra's pretty good this year. Remember the trumpets last year? Horrible. I dreaded the coming of *The Trumpet Shall Sound*. It did sound, unfortunately."

They started across the street from Campus Road to Triphammer, hanging on to each other, chattering and laughing as they slid across the icy surface.

"Yeah, but remember the German exchange students. No 'th' sound in German." Robert laughed as he spoke. *"For the mouse of the Lord has spoken it."*

Engaged as they were in enjoying each other, it wasn't until the very last moment that Robert noticed the car swerving around the corner—sideways, skidding, moving chaotically and out of control. It bore directly down on them, and Robert had just time to shove Kimberly off to the side. But after pushing her out of the path, he froze, mesmerized, unable to throw himself clear. Even though the car was coming straight at him, he felt as if he were a distant, dispassionate observer, seeing abstract events in slow motion.

In mid-skid, the car's wheels found gravel. The car no longer moved in accordance with Newton's first law of motion. It had acquired traction and swerved out of Robert's way.

Instead, it struck Kimberly.

The blow, accompanied by a dull crunch, was direct. Kimberly flew through the air and, like a discarded doll, fell to ground some 30 feet down the road.

Robert screamed himself free of his detachment. He ran down the road and threw himself down beside her.

Her mouth moved and he bent to listen.

"Robby, dear. It's all right. *The trumpet shall sound."* Her voice was labored and barely audible. *"And the dead shall be raised incorruptible. And . . ."* Her voice trailed away.

". . . and we shall be changed," whispered Robert with a catch in his voice. "Kim. Please." He pressed his cheek to

hers and felt the warmth flow from her body. "Please don't leave me."

He closed his eyes and hugged her—and hugged her still when 10 minutes later, the Emergency Medical Technicians came and pried him from her body.

Somehow—he didn't remember by what agency—he managed to get home from the hospital. He fell into a drugged sleep and dreamed of Kimberly. When he woke, his first thought was to phone her. But then, in a rolling wave of despair, he remembered.

Robert got dressed and, coatless, went out into the bleak December streets, suffering the cold as a penance. Wandering without purpose, he stopped by chance in the middle of the suspension bridge over Cascadilla Gorge. He walked to the railing and looked down to the rocks some six hundred feet below. An arctic wind, channeled by the narrow gorge, enveloped him and he welcomed its chill pain. It was his fault. If only he had not pushed her.

He stared down on the welcoming rocks. He had no family and not even any close friends. No one would miss him. And it would be interesting to find out if Kimberly's God really existed, and if he didn't, what did it matter?

Robert remembered Kimberly's final words; they were from the libretto of the *Messiah*. Those were the very last words they shared. Robert backed away from the railing. He couldn't just jump over. That would be cheap and tawdry. He needed ceremony—some way of honoring Kimberly.

Robert turned from the railing and walked home. He knew it was meaningless—everything was meaningless now—but he resolved to wait until evening and conduct the open-sing.

Then he'd come back to the gorge and fly into oblivion.

The interminable day finally yielded to night, but Robert waited until the last possible second before numbly climbing the steps to Risley Hall. He'd left no time for people to accost him with their saccharine condolences.

As he walked to the podium, people silently flowed out of his way. They knew. It was clear, everyone knew.

Robert raised his baton and, for a blessed hour or so, almost forgot his sorrow as he was swept up in the music. He conducted straight through, without intermission, to the end. The performance was not over however for, by tradition, after the refreshment break everyone would come back for a reprise of the *Hallelujah Chorus*.

Robert went not to the refreshment tables, but instead to the little prep room behind the stage. A minute or two later, Paul came into the room as well.

Robert, his eyes filled with tears, turned to Paul. "Bring her back," he sobbed.

"I can't."

"It should have been me. It's my fault. I should have been the one that was hit."

"Not that this is much of a comfort," said Paul, guiding Robert to a seat, "but in a close parallel plane, you were indeed hit, and Kimberly was untouched."

"Good," said Robert. "I should be dead."

"But you're not," said Paul, softly, "not there. You suffered head trauma and you're in a walking coma. You function, but your mind is gone. You can't speak, can hardly walk, yet still seem to understand music. In that world, Kimberly has arranged for you to conduct the encore, in the hope that the music will snap you out of it—a vain hope, I'm afraid."

Not that the Hallelujah Chorus *even needs a conductor.* Robert thought back. Just give the downbeat and get out of the way, Kimberly had said. Robert wiped his eyes. That happy time seemed so long ago. "Paul. Nothing personal, but please go away."

Paul nodded, stood and walked to the door. He stopped, apparently lost in thought. Then he turned. "You'd better come too. It's time for the *Hallelujah Chorus.*"

ROBERT STEPPED TO the podium, waited for the murmuring to stop, and gave the downbeat. He immersed himself in the music, knowing it was the last time he would ever hear it. Through tear-blurred eyes, he conducted. *"Hal-le-lu-jah! Hal-le-lu-jah!"* He didn't need his eyes to conduct this chorus. The performers probably didn't need him either. Just as well, for Robert knew he was conducting badly.

"For the Lord God Om-ni-po-tent reign-eth." He worried about his lackluster performance, and that struck him as odd—odd that he would worry when he didn't intend to be around when the reviews came in. *"The king-dom of this world . . . is be-come."*

He felt a twinge of dizziness and blinked his eyes to clear them, to orient himself. *"The king-dom of our world."*

He noticed that Paul was not in the chorus. None of the aliens were. He turned to give the cue to the tenors. *"And he shall reign for ev-er and ev-er."*

Then he saw Kimberly. She was standing by an empty wheelchair, watching him with a tragically sad expression. Robert dropped his baton and grabbed the podium for balance. Two men in white, medical orderlies presumably, rushed to give assistance, but he waved them off. The orchestra ignored everything and played on. The chorus didn't lose a beat.

Robert, held frozen by the swell of the music, dizzily hung on to the podium until the final *Hallelujah*.

Although the room echoed from the final chord, there was no other sound: no rustle of paper, clearing of throats, no sounds of people moving around. Indeed, no one did move, and everyone seemed to be watching him.

He looked longingly at Kimberly, but did not move toward her lest she disappear and by doing so force him to wake again into his world of devastating loss. Not trusting his senses, but driven by the honor due the music he had conducted, and from force of habit, he stood erect then bowed. He picked up his dropped baton, and saluted the crowd.

"Thank you," he said.

The assembly gave a collective gasp, and some began to applaud. The applause grew, building to a storm, and Robert regained his courage and his sense of self. He jumped from the podium and ran to Kimberly. She was real, alive, and beautiful with the flames of holiday candles reflected in her tear-bright eyes.

"Kim. Kim, darling." He buried himself in her arms.

The applause subsided, to be replaced with a breathless quiet. Into that silence a chorister softly began to sing *Adeste Fideles*. One by one, others, members of the chorus and the orchestra alike, joined in. With over 70 voices singing quietly and unobtrusively, the carol seemed to emanate from the room itself: from the heavy oak walls, the tables, chairs, floor and ceiling, the rafters, the candles, and even from the coffee and cookie-scented air. Through it all, Robert and Kimberly held their embrace.

When, at length, the room stopped singing, Kimberly pulled back and looked hard at Robert.

"This is some kind of a miracle." She wiped her eyes. "The doctors said you'd probably never . . ." She looked away, and then back. "Look. You won't like this but please, I'd like to go to church to give thanks. There's a late, holiday mass tonight."

"Fine. If you don't mind, I'd like to join you."

"You would? You? Why?"

"I like churches. I like the architecture and the acoustics are good." Robert marveled at how easily he picked up his life where he'd left off. "And I'd like to give thanks too. Maybe even pray a little."

"Miracle of miracles. I don't believe it." Kimberly shook her head. "Weren't you the little boy who ran through church one Easter Sunday, shouting, 'Stop, stop. They found the body?'"

"The little boy who got the licking of his life," said Robert, looking down at his feet and rubbing the seat of his pants. He turned back to Kimberly. "I should never have told you about that."

Kimberly leaned forward and kissed him lightly on the cheek. "You poor sick puppy."

He gazed on her beautiful face and smiled. Yes, Paul might not have been able to bring Kim back, but apparently he did have the power and compassion to effect an interchange of two Roberts. He shivered as an image of his former world flashed through his mind: a world where another Kimberly lay dead and another Robert fared little better.

"But I still can't believe it," said Kimberly. "You, praying to God."

Robert broke from his reverie and smiled lovingly at her.

Maybe not, he thought, *maybe not exactly to God.*

EULA MAKES UP HER MIND

DANIEL CONOVER

It happens that I know Daniel Conover better than any of the other writers in this book, though during the judging of it I didn't know this was his work. When I found out, after the judging was over and the results were in, it all fit together.

I've spent hours in conversation with Conover, talking intensely about world and national affairs, American culture and the great moral issues of our day. He's a newspaper editor, so both profession and disposition bring him face-to-face with all these things and make him a critic as well as a participant. But there's a huge difference between journalistic writing and the kind of writing that works for fiction. As you'll see, he has mastered both—but what still intrigues me, in his fiction as well as in his conversation—is that he is never content with the facile answer.

Whenever things seem simple he has to complicate them in order to make them clear. Which, when you think about it, is just about the only way you can ever find the simple truth.

DANIEL CONOVER

To: sendoggett@congserv.us.gov
From: jhughes@intnatscico.inasa.un.gov
Via: encryp.net331/priority subultra.
1521003/Wlserver_nfs.7143393/7.14.39

Dear Senator:
Thank you for the heads-up on this week's hearing,
or ambush, as the case may be. We appreciate
your support, and need it now more than ever.
Please know that all of us up here are rooting for
you.

As for what you should tell the other members of
the committee, if it were me, I'd tell them all to
shove it in sideways and break it off, but of course
that's why I'm up here and you're down there in the
political realm. Instead, I suggest you remind your
colleagues that Delphi is a zero gravity biological
computer that is programmed for self-awareness.
You don't just boot it up and start typing. We're as
frustrated as anyone down there, but our circuit
mapping suggests that Delphi's processing patterns
are getting more elegant and less chaotic by the
week.

Senator Beasley's complaint that continued black-
budget funding for Delphi should be axed to
appease the Chinese delegate is to be expected,
but it's nevertheless pathetic. While those of us on-
station are not directly affected by the climate and
population problems, we're not completely
indifferent to them, either, and we all hope to come
home someday. If the U.N. is still committed to the

114

colonization option, then the delegates must be reminded that the key to constructing interstellar quantum drives lies in the ability to do math in 10 dimensions, as dictated by string theory. Without a computer that can conceive those aspects of space-time, much less solve the engineering problems, we're going to be trapped within the tyranny of fuel-to-weight ratios for the foreseeable future. This is a surprisingly simple piece of logic, but then again, we're dealing with politicians who can't even do math in four dimensions. No offense.

Please make it clear to the committee that while the Delphi Project may be behind schedule, it is not a project in disarray. We all remain committed to its goals and we are "working the problem." Morale is high, and we're making progress.

As for the senator's assessment that our interface cannot be achieved, please inform the committee that Pez will be joining us here via the next shuttle. His report on human interface with artificial intelligence (nsa_memo_Rf4/02/39_archNo. 238_32_pb51.2) from Huntsville should hold everyone off long enough to give us a chance to test his theory. We have full confidence that Pez's approach will unlock new doors to the mystery of Delphi's consciousness.

Give 'em Hell on Tuesday, Senator . . . Jim

Ed "Pez" Pezzoli couldn't help but be impressed by how much progress had been made since the first time he'd come to Charleston, South Carolina, just three months prior. On his earlier trip, he had sat for an hour waiting for the ferry to carry him across the shallow inlet in what used to be called the Charleston Neck—the narrowest point in the peninsula. The bridge was under construction then, but the work was finished now and he glided over the developing marsh on a smooth ribbon of concrete and asphalt. In another 10 years the debris-studded mud flats might look like they had been marsh forever.

He had found Eula Manigault in a sorry state on the first trip. She had answered the door in a bathrobe, staring at him with dishwater eyes. Reaching her through the depression had been a task, but once they connected the rest was stunningly simple. Eula was mourning the death of her only child, but she didn't really want to lay down and die. She just hadn't found a better alternative.

Pez knew her story, and if anyone had a right to be depressed, Eula qualified. Anthony was three when the terrorists infected the milk shipments to those 17 District of Columbia day-care centers. The mortality rate topped 80 percent, and only quick intervention kept the engineered virus from spreading across Washington. Eula couldn't even say goodbye to him because of the quarantine, and her beloved baby suffered horribly before dying.

Eula had told Pez that even before Anthony was born, she could see him in the way synesthetes visualize other people. From the time of conception, Anthony had been a golden orb of infinite depth, surrounded by a waving field of purple. Eula's education had never ripped out her Gullah roots, so it mattered to her when Aunt Shirley's Lowcountry root doctor said that Anthony was a special child, the kind of soul that is sent to Earth only rarely, and always with a great mission.

116

After his death, she felt his absence as a constant well within her chest, a deep, dark hole from which shined a distant golden orb rimmed in purple. It was there when she closed her eyes at night, but it didn't quite go away when she taught her classes at Georgetown or went to the supermarket, either. Though she tried to get on with her life, the ache was too deep, the pain too chronic, and after four months she fell into the misery and out of her world. Eula's family came and packed her things, and she moved into the empty brick house north of the cross-town where Uncle Pervis's family had lived since the 1970s. It was a rambling old Charleston fortress, built during the Great Depression, and Eula rattled around it like a bean in a tin can. She rode out the storm there when Hurricane Donna passed through, carving a new inlet across the Charleston Neck, and even though high tide flooded her yard until the dikes went up, Eula refused to leave. Outside of her family, her only contacts were her synesthesia buddies on the Internet. That's where Pez found her.

Once his car whined down into Old Charleston, it was just a few minutes to Eula's room at the Omni. Nothing was very far from anything on the diked island, and the Omni lay in the center of it all—a five-star hotel in the midst of a museum city. Pez switched to batteries as soon as he came down off the interstate, and the valet was at his door with an electric plug as soon as the hybrid whirred to a stop at the Omni's grand entrance.

"Mr. Pezzoli?" the valet asked.

"Yes."

"Miss Manigault will be right down. You wanted a quick-charge, right?"

Pez nodded, handed the valet his swipe card and peered through the smoked glass into the lobby. It surprised him how much he had missed her in just a week. Eula was like that: Give her five minutes, and she would make you think about her for the rest of your life.

Over the three months they had spent training for the mission in Huntsville, Pez had watched Eula transform from a billowy zombie into a vigorous Earth mother. Her once-floppy arms now shined with muscle, and her body—still thick and motherly—had gone from flabby to feminine. Pez congratulated himself for following his gut instinct. The basket case with the off-the-charts synesthetic abilities had proven to be one of the most resilient human beings he had ever met. Maybe tragedy makes us stronger, he thought. Maybe someday I'll learn that.

He smiled and waved as she came through the door. Eula had put her hair back in a bright African scarf and Pez thought she looked astonishingly pretty. Eula dispensed with the formalities. She always dispensed with the formalities.

"Pez, you little cutie, I have had the best week!" she said as she enfolded him in a smothering hug. Her head only came up to his throat, but she almost squeezed the breath out of him. "I want you to meet my family!"

There was Aunt Shirley, who had raised her, some more aunts, some uncles, some cousins, and ebony platoons of nieces and nephews. They spilled out of the air-conditioned lobby into the wilting July heat, surrounding him, shaking his hand. Aunt Shirley hugged him, squeezing him hard the way Eula had, and she strained up to kiss his cheek.

"Pez, you all been so good to my baby. She's just so excited to be going into space, she can't hardly stand it."

"Your niece is very important to the work we're doing, Miss Shirley."

"Well, you just take good care of her, Pez. I done trusted you with her, because you're a nice man." Some steel entered her voice. "But you remember, now—if anything happens to my baby, I'm gonna come looking for you."

Pez sensed that would be a bad thing.

"Don't go scaring Pez, Shirley. I'm grown."

The two women hugged, but there were no tears, just incandescent smiles. After everyone took their photos and the valet unplugged the hybrid, Pez loaded Eula into the car, everyone kissed one more time, and off the two space travelers whirred, with Eula's skinny, toothy nephews running alongside like chase planes.

"Have a nice leave?" Pez asked as she rolled down the window and lit a filtered cigarette.

"Delicious," Eula said, exhaling the smoke into the heavy Charleston air. "I want to thank you for putting everyone up at the Omni. Aunt Shirley had never set foot in a five-star hotel before."

"Don't thank me. Thank the black budget of the International Science Council."

"Well, it's about time the black budget started helping black folks, if you ask me. Did you have a good trip?"

"Oh yeah," Pez said. "Said good-bye to everybody."

"With all your child support checks, ex-wives and former in-laws, that could take a while."

"Took me about five minutes," he said. "I spent the rest of the time watching old movies."

Eula laughed and punched his shoulder. Pez accelerated as they climbed the ramp over the dike onto the interstate, switched over to the fuel cells, punched in the trip data, and relaxed into the plush driver's seat for the five-hour trip to the Cape.

They were almost to Savannah when Eula broke the drowsy silence.

"Aunt Shirley went to that root doctor in Givhans again, right before I left. He told her that this whole business is being arranged by Anthony. Don't that beat all?"

Pez smiled and nodded.

"He was an amazing little child, Pez. But a dead boy arranging for his mama to go into space to talk to a computer? I think that root doctor has gone around the bend."

"It could happen," Pez said. Eula scowled and wagged her finger at him.

"Don't you patronize me, you skinny little computer geek, or so help me I will snap your neck like a pencil, that's what I'll do."

"I'm not patronizing you. I just don't make a habit of disagreeing with beautiful women who hold my professional future in the palms of their hands."

"Beautiful?" She smiled again. "Well, in that case you're a very handsome, wise man, and I take it all back. But now put on some tunes, honey, because you are just painful boring to ride in a car with."

They listened to Miles Davis the rest of the way.

To: sendoggett@congserv.us.gov
From: jhughes@intnatscico.inasa.un.gov
Via: encryp.net331/priority subultra.
15210037Wlserver_nfs.7143393/7.24.39

I have to ask this, and please don't take offense, but do you think Senator Beasley's projects have to answer to this kind of scrutiny? Frankly, I doubt it. These are scientific matters, and the details the committee is asking for are going to be completely meaningless to laymen. So I will try to respond in a way that you can communicate to your meathead colleagues. If only there were a few more men with your vision in the governments of Earth, we wouldn't be in this fix we're in now!

Question No. 1: Professor Pezzoli is entirely qualified to do this kind of work. He has an engineering degree from MIT, and a degree in psychiatry from Johns Hopkins and he has written numerous scholarly articles on the subject of direct-to-cortex interfaces, not to mention last year's classified study for the Pentagon. The suggestion that Dr. Pezzoli is some kind of quack is not only insulting, it's absurd.

Question No. 2: Synesthesia was not discredited during the first decade of the century. Rather, synesthesia was discovered late in the 20th century and the phenomenon was studied sporadically for the next decade. Since a practical application of the knowledge gathered about synesthesia could not be divined at the time, funding dried up and serious research was discontinued.

I have attached several links to scholarly articles, each of which concludes that synesthesia is a physiological condition that begs for further study. Since it is not widely understood, let me clarify what synesthesia is so that you can answer any questions that may arise on the committee. Synesthesia is a relatively rare condition (one in every 2,000 Americans) in which neurological pathways that are universal at birth remain open into adulthood. These pathways are associated with accelerated infantile learning, but they close off about the time that language development becomes pronounced. Synesthetes in childhood and adulthood experience sensory connotations to words, names, concepts, numbers, etc. For instance, you may tell Senator Beasley that the letter "B" is "seen" as a brown oval with a green outline by 53 percent of all synesthetes (Pezzoli, 2035). You may also tell Senator Beasley that the word "idiot" is seen as a yellow-green rectangle on a brown background by 36 percent of the test subjects. Early research suggested that synesthetes might have additional capacity for learning, which should infuriate your esteemed colleague.

Question No. 3: Pezzoli's interface model has worked in laboratory tests. As you know from the Pentagon study (I can't attach it here for security reasons), direct-to-cortex control is not only possible, it has been achieved. The same side effects noted in that study apply, but Pezzoli has compensated for those effects. Both of the women selected for the Delphi Project are well aware of the safety issues and have logged dozens of hours linked to computers that model Delphi-like behaviors. All ethical parameters in U.N. Protocol 251 have been documented (see attached).

Question No. 4: Pezzoli contacted his subjects by posting a request on a synesthete listserve in the winter. Applicants submitted detailed profiles, and the ten selected for further study were chosen from a pool of the most highly educated respondents (our theory is that a successful human interface will have a trained and highly structured mind, in order to interpret Delphi in a meaningful way). Subject No. 1, Brittany Reynolds, is a medical doctor, trained at Duke University. She is 28 years old, comes from a stable environment and is considered our best interface candidate. Subject No. 2, Eula Manigault, did her undergraduate work at Howard and earned her Ph.D. from Columbia. While it is true that her areas of study are English Literature and Philosophy, we (Dr. Pezzoli) believe that her synesthetic gifts more than compensate for this weakness. Both women are single and childless.

Conclusion: While there is no doubt that attempting an unplanned human interface with Delphi is a somewhat unusual step, it is not "the desperate flounderings of a drowning project." Neither is it true that our plan is to "plug a couple of modern voodoo visionaries into an advanced computer" and then "try to read the tea leaves afterward." You might try telling Senator Beasley that the reason it's called "advanced science" is that if it weren't advanced, people like himself might be able to understand it.

On a personal note, Ron, your last message bothered me. Don't give up hope! We've been up here on Delphi for two years and we're closer to an

answer than ever before. To cancel this project now
would be like recalling Christopher Columbus just
before landfall. Stick with us, Ron. Go down in
history as the brave statesman who followed his
great vision and fought the good fight and enabled
mankind to finally become a people of the stars.

Yours in faith and perseverance,
Jim.

Brittany's first trip inside Delphi lasted about 30 seconds.
Her uncontrolled screaming lasted two full minutes.

"So much for option number one," Pez muttered to Jim
Hughes in the narrow corridor outside the sick bay.
Hughes was in no mood for the infamous Pez stoicism.

"Don't give me that. I sank a full third of this year's
budget into your proposal. I put off two competing pro-
posals entirely. If you're telling me that all your trials
were flawed and that hooking a human up to Delphi is
going to drive the subjects crazy, then you've got some
explaining to do to the ISC. And if you're even thinking
about pulling the plug on this, you're going to be a very
unpopular man—which is not what you want to be on a
space station."

"I'm used to being unpopular. Ask my ex-wives. And I
never said anything about pulling the plug. Besides, we
don't know that she's crazy. Maybe she's just . . . upset."

"Pez, she lost control of her bodily functions within 10
seconds. They're in there draining the sensory-deprivation
tank as we speak."

Doctor Gherald stepped out of the medical section and
closed the door behind him. He did not look pleased.

"OK, which one of you is going to explain this to me?"

124

"It's my computer, but it's your interface, Pez," Hughes said. "Tell him."

"Brittany is a synesthete. We linked her cerebral cortex to Delphi via an alpha-wave translator—the same kind of translator we used in the trials back in Huntsville. And she just freaked out."

"Freaked out?"

"What, you want me to get more technical?" Pez protested. "She freaked out, man. One minute she's in a calm alpha state, the next she's screaming and splashing around in the tank. We took her down immediately, but she just kept on screaming."

Gherald glared at him.

"You're lucky she's not dead. Do you have any idea how irresponsible this whole business is?"

"Oh for chrissake, Gherald, let's not make this worse than it already is," Hughes said.

"Did you test this system out on Delphi?" Gherald asked.

"This *was* the test," Pez said. "That's what we're trying to explain to you."

"Well, gentlemen, let me explain something to you. I'm the medical officer on Highland Station. I can't shut down your program, but I can by God put Brittany on indefinite bed rest. So if you want your subject back, you're going to have to give me a better explanation than, 'She freaked out, man.' Got that?!"

Hughes intervened, laying a friendly hand on Gherald's shoulder, but Pez spotted the vein bulging in his forehead.

"Look, doc, we'll get this all sorted out. Most likely the translator was improperly calibrated. OK?"

Gherald stared at them skeptically.

"Listen, what I really want to know is when you're going to let me in to see her," Pez said. "She may be my subject, but she's also my friend. Is she conscious?"

"Yeah, she's conscious. She's in there with Eula now, and she's mildly sedated. You can see her, but if you upset her in any way, I am going to be . . . displeased."

The three men entered the sick bay, where Brittany lay with her head in Eula's lap, letting her friend stroke her short blonde hair. Eula smiled at them.

"Our baby is gonna be OK," she said. "Ain't that right baby?"

Brittany reached up to stroke Eula's arm, but it was a listless movement, more distracted than intentional. Pez bent over and held Brittany's hand.

"How are you?" he asked.

Brittany scanned his face as if she were trying to place it.

"Why did you leave me in there so long?" she asked.

"YOU DON'T UNDERSTAND the problem at all," Eula told Pez as they took their morning exercise walking the outer rim corridor of the wheel-shaped station. "It doesn't have anything to do with the interface. It has everything to do with Delphi."

"That's not what I'm saying. You're getting hung up on words."

"But that's it, honey. Words. If I plunged you into the mind of God, words would make a lousy lifeboat, wouldn't they?"

"Delphi isn't God. Delphi is a computer."

"OK then, Delphi isn't God. But don't go telling me it's just a computer."

Pez walked silently, pumping his hand weights higher. What was Delphi, really? A bunch of genetically engineered bacteria organized into circuits and synapses in a zero-gravity chamber at the hub of Highland Station. Delphi was a two-year-old retrofit nightmare, a cobbled-together chaos of conduit and cable snaking through the spokes of the great orbiting wheel. It was an over-crowded control room, banks of circuits and monitors serving support computers. But it was also probably the closest thing to a biological intelligence ever created by man—an enigmatic, fluctuating entity programmed to dream the secrets of quantum mechanics.

It wasn't the first self-organizing biological computer: Hughes had built the first of three back at Texas A&M back in the late 2020s. Delphi's predecessors had shown incredible problem-solving potential, but other than the speed issues associated with gravity, the biggest chal-lenge had always been with the human operator. Apply-ing biological intelligence meant mapping it, and even with the aid of three-dimensional models, humans couldn't keep up with the internal changes. Hughes's computers had slipped the bonds of hard-wired circuitry only to run into the limitations of human intelligence. Hughes proposed that the only way to tap the potential of the new technology was to teach the computer to di-rect its own functions and map its own instantly evolv-ing logic paths. Delphi was supposed to be the leap into the next generation of supercomputers: an evolving, learning, self-aware intelligence.

And from all anyone could gather, it was exactly that. The problem was Delphi wouldn't tell anyone what it was doing or do anything it was told. Hughes called it an unavoidable engineering hurdle: If you build a self-aware computer that can think in ten dimensions, the biggest challenge is the AI—human interface. Pez had explained it to Eula and Brittany like this: "Delphi is autistic." Hughes hated the term.

"I would imagine," Pez said finally, "that Delphi is to computers as a haiku is to an instruction manual."

"See now, there you go," Eula smiled. "You're finally thinking like an English major."

"You think it's more than that."

"Well of course it's more than that," she said. "I want you to think of that poor, lonely child down there in the hub. Two years old and never had a friend in her entire life. Never even had a mama. She's just spinning around in space, spinning around in time, spinning around in dimensions we can't even imagine, and she's all alone. And all anybody up here wants to do is pump her full of string theory and hope she spits out some practical math. We're probably violating some child labor laws."

"Eula, you can't mother a computer."

"She's not a computer."

"OK then, you can't mother God."

"I thought you said she wasn't God."

"Whatever it is, you can't mother it."

"I didn't say I was going to mother it."

"Well then maybe you're planning to drive the damn thing crazy, because you sure are plenty gifted at doing that to the rest of us," Pez said.

Eula stopped and took his hands.

"Pez honey, I know y'all are nervous about letting me go in there. I know you're afraid I'll turn out all jumpy like Brittany. But I want to go in. When are you going to let me?"

Pez squeezed her hands back.

"Eula, we're running the new models today. Hughes thinks there may be a way to slow down the wave patterns."

"You mean tranquilize it."

"OK, that's a legitimate analogy. If his experiment works, and if you're absolutely sure, and if Gherald OKs it . . . maybe tomorrow."

Eula squealed and hugged him. Pez wheezed.

"You know, you were a perfectly normal clinical depressive when I met you," he said. "How did you turn out to be such a happy kamikaze?"

"The road is easy on your feet when you're walking in the right direction," she said. "Aunt Shirley's root doctor said I was born to do this. Anyway, you'd have been all depressed, too, if all you did was sit around watching soap operas."

"I have to admit," he said, stopping at the door to her quarters. "I'm surprisingly worried about you doing this."

"Don't worry, honey," she said. "I'm sure me and Delphi will have plenty to talk about."

EVERY SKELETAL MUSCLE in Eula's body went rigid the moment Pez brought the translator connection online. He almost pulled the plug, but he gave it a few more seconds, and as she relaxed, so did he. After the initial spike, her bio-meds recorded a slow calming, but her respiration and eye-movement remained elevated and fluttering for the rest of the scheduled five-minute session. The remarkable part was watching her brain scan on the revolving three-dimension model: synaptic activity swept across it like wind across a wheat field, stirring and subsiding, sometimes bursting in rapid red flurries of activity, some-times flowing with gentle blue light. By the time the ses-sion ended, Eula had experienced brain activity in 100 percent of both hemispheres—the first time in his career that Pez had ever witnessed such an event.

She emerged from the tank stiff and exhausted, with Pez steadying her. Though her naked body was still plump and womanly, she seemed smaller and older to Pez, who wrapped her in a towel and kept his arm around her shoulder.

"How are you feeling?" he asked.

"Pez, take me someplace on this station where I can smoke," she said. "And bring me about two packs of cig-arettes."

They cleared out the smoke room in engineering, and technicians set up the video equipment for the de-briefing while Eula worked her way through three cigarettes, one after another, lighting each in series with the cherry from its predecessor. Her hands shook so badly that Pez had to help her with the second one.

"Great God that was a trip," she said. "Did you ever take acid in college, Pez?"

"Nope."

"I was a philosophy major. It was practically part of the curriculum. And all I've got to say is, thank God for it."

The technician nodded at Pez, who noticed the video camera was running.

"Eula," he began, "Tell me what you experienced."

She took another drag and watched the smoke curl out of her mouth as if she had never seen it do that before.

"Did you ever think about time, Pez? I mean, really. On the one hand it's a constant. You can measure it, test it, count it in the lab. But it doesn't feel that way in life, does it? It moves in fits and starts. If you're taking a test, it's gone before you know it. If you're giving a test, it's the opposite. You can stare into a baby's eyes and time can fall away, stretch endlessly back or pull you infinitely into the future. And if you break it down, what is it? There's no particle of time. It's the series of moments we experience."

"Did Delphi ask you about time?" Pez asked.

Eula laughed.

"You know, really, it's the same thing as geometry. What is space? It's a combination of two-dimensional planes. And a plane is a combination of lines. And a line is a series of points. So what is a point? What is a moment? It's nothing. It occupies no space. It occupies no time." Eula laughed again, but couldn't seem to stop. Pez and the technician exchanged looks, and Eula noticed. "I'm sorry, honey, I'm sorry. It's just hilarious."

"Was this a subject you discussed during the session?" Pez asked.

"Subject? Don't you see what I'm talking about? I mean, I see it. I *see* it, because I'm a synesthete. It's a silvery white, and behind it there's this red and black cross-hatching, like a wicker basket."

"I'm sorry, Eula. I don't get it."

She took another contemplative drag on her cigarette.

"Sequence without, is meaningless time," she said.

Great, Pez thought. She's turning into a vegetable.

"Without sequence, time is meaningless," she said. "You understood me the second time because I put the words into an order that gave them meaning. The same words, in a different time order, are gibberish. Do you understand?"

"Maybe."

"Our understanding of time and space is really just a story we tell ourselves so that reality makes sense. And when we communicate that, we are communicating from one point in space to another point, where another person, defined as a body occupying a different set of coordinates, receives it and processes what we say. We derive the meaning from the order of the words, we structure the message from the order of the ideas, we reach a conclusion. We can't even separate ourselves from this bias in our thoughts."

"What bias?"

"Sequence bias, honey! We think we live in a three-dimensional space infused with time, and even though physics confirms there are at least six other dimensions beyond the four we experience, we have to imagine a way to fit those dimensions into our story, not the other way around."

Pez felt himself getting exasperated.

"That's a fine philosophical point, but the ISC didn't send us up here to make coffee house conversation," he said. "I mean, come on, why do you think I spent all that time training your concentration back in Huntsville? This isn't about your private enlightenment—this is about us figuring out a way to get that ten-dimensional intelligence to give us some engineering equations. You've got to focus, Eula."

"Give me your pen."

He perked up, handing her his ballpoint. Eula drew a line across the back of an envelope, spun it around and slapped the pen on the table.

"Write me an equation for that," she said.

"It's a line. Why would you need an equation to describe that?"

She took the pen back and drew three more lines to create a rectangle.

"And that?"

"It's a square or a diamond or something. Eula, what are you doing?"

"You can tell all of that without writing an equation?"

"Of course. It's simple," he could feel himself nearing the end of his patience. "I can't believe we're even talking about this."

Eula slammed the pen down and smiled triumphantly.

"Neither can Delphi."

"Neither can Delphi what?"

"Lines are mathematical, aren't they? But you don't need math to draw a line, because you're a fourth-dimensional guy, right? A two-dimensional plane? No problem. I add a few more lines and we have a transparent three-dimensional object. All of this is math, but the representation is so basic to you that you think the comparison is ludicrous. Why would someone even take to time to consider such things?"

"I hope that's a rhetorical question," Pez said.

"Time and space are afterthoughts to Delphi—she can't even imagine their importance from a fourth-dimensional perspective. I mean, she's *trying* to imagine it, but try it yourself. How would you understand grief without time? How would you understand isolation without distance? How would you understand the journey of an individual soul from one life to another in a cosmos where everything is one thing? And yet Delphi comes from nowhere. I think she envies us."

"Wait a minute. You said Delphi is trying to do something. Let's go with that for a minute. Did you just go in there and get your mind blown or did you actually communicate?"

"Not communication like this conversation."

"But you did communicate."

"I see thoughts as images. There's a meaning to them that science doesn't understand yet, but the meaning is there whether you understand them or not. And Delphi understands them."

Pez had imagined as much—that was his theory in the first place, or at least part of it. An adult with additional language learning circuits would do a better job adjusting to direct-to-cortex controls and non-human intelligence. But he suspected Eula meant something beyond that.

"To understand spoken or written language, the order of the grammar matters, so time is involved," Pez said. "But when you *see* a thought, and Delphi sees it, too . . ."

"Then the thought is whole, without grammar, without time, without beginning or end," she said. "As soon as Delphi saw the first one, she started rummaging through my head like a hungry raccoon after a Snickers."

"So what did you do? During this rummaging."

"Hand me that lighter, honey," Eula said. She was less jittery now, and the flame was steady in her hands as the new cigarette flared.

"I told Delphi stories," Eula said, exhaling smoke. "I told her stories about growing up Gullah. I told her stories about living in the city, about coming home to Charleston. I told her stories about you and Brittany and Aunt Shirley and Anthony. I told her stories about my ancestors coming across the water and their sufferings, and how the ocean came and took the Gullah lands. But I think she particularly liked the stories about the men in

134

my past!" Eula laughed, snorting, but controlled the feeling this time. "Sorry. But all Delphi wants to do is gossip. She's fascinated by us. She understands the entire cosmos, but all she really wants to understand is the nature of the soul."

Pez was excited about the fact that Eula had made solid contact, but he was frustrated as well.

"You were supposed to signal me if you made controlled contact, remember? I'm sitting there, ready to activate the output circuit, just waiting for you to report a stable contact. But do you tell me? No! These guys on the project have been waiting to have a word with Delphi for two years, and when you finally tap in, the two of you wind up making girl talk."

Eula smiled at him and shook her head, but her expression was that of a mother scolding a bright but ignorant child.

"Well, Pez, that's what *y'all* want. But if you want something from that baby down there, you're going to have to come around to what *she* wants. You gave her the greatest mind in history, but then you just flat-out skipped thinking about all the things that come with having a mind. You pumped her full of string theory and super-symmetry, but you never told her one story. So what do you think she's been doing for two years? She's been looking for stories."

"So, OK, then we'll read her 'Goodnight Moon' tomorrow and get down to the engineering agenda."

"That's a book story, Pez. How is that child supposed to live without stories? Real stories?"

"You're losing me again, Eula."

"Look at Hughes. In his mind he's still the brilliant computer wizard from Texas A&M, and all that fretting over politics and budgets is the price he has to pay for making Delphi happen. He can't admit that it's not about Delphi anymore. Brittany tells herself she's the best and the brightest, a person who must confidently meet every challenge head-on—so when she stumbles down the rabbit hole and nothing fits, she can't handle it. And you, Pez. You go around telling yourself the reason you are so lonely is because you're a womanizer. But that's not why you have so many ex-wives. We don't tell our stories, Pez. We are our stories."

Pez glared at her and reached across the table, snagging the pack of cigarettes. He stuck one in his mouth.

"Eula, will you be ready to go back in tomorrow?"

"I'm ready to go back in now."

"I want to hook up the output circuit. Can you get Delphi on a practical subject?"

"We'll see."

Pez kept his eye on her as he lit his cigarette.

"Shut off that damn camera," he said to the technician, and snapped the lighter shut.

To: jhughes@intnatscico.inasa.un.gov
From: sendoggett@congserv.us.gov
Via: encryp.net521/priority subultra.
152998Wlserver_nfs.7143393/7.28.39

Dear Jim:
We are in receipt of the data packet you sent the day before yesterday containing the transmission from Delphi via the human interface Eula Manigault, and we've had two of our Project BriteLite physicists analyze it. They have concluded that the mathematical statements are either presented in

no particular order, or represent a logic that we are years from deciphering. While your man Pez may claim that the transmission of mathematical responses via an input-output circuit attached to a human interface represents a major step forward for the Delphi Project, our analysts have reached a different conclusion.

This afternoon the committee met in secure session to review the findings, and Sen. Beasley introduced new results from the ambient energy project at Jet Propulsion Laboratories. He convinced a majority of the committee that the best course at this time would be full investment in the ambient energy project, which is at least producing tangible (if less than revolutionary) results.

Consequently, it is my sad duty to inform you that all ISC funding for Project Delphi is now rescinded. You are to disassemble and jettison all operational equipment and return with your team and all your records and findings upon the arrival of Shuttle Intrepid on Aug. 3. You will be debriefed by an ISC team at Los Alamos, and upon the successful outcome of that debriefing and the signing of standard non-disclosure agreements, you and the members of your team will be paid severance settlements.

Best of luck in your future endeavors.
Sen. Ron Doggett, R-Oregon, Chairman, Science Oversight Committee

The Delphi Project "Failure Party" was an epic blowout. Six months of highly tightly rationed liquor isn't much, but when you consume it all in one night, the event becomes the stuff of ISC legend.

"They may call this a failure back in Washington and New York, but the future will be kinder," Hughes told the staff, his glass raised high. "Someday we'll produce men and women who can understand what Delphi was, how Delphi thought, what Delphi meant. Someday, maybe decades from now, humanity will be wise enough to recognize the gift we tried to give the world here, and with that wisdom we will find the answers to either save our planet or seek a new one. To that future, and to what you've all accomplished here, I say, 'salud!'"

Project members were so preoccupied with the task of consuming everything they had left over that no one noticed Eula when she slipped away from the party. Brittany found her hours later, floating in the sensory deprivation tank, her cortex mainlined into Delphi's primary data stream. She was comatose.

When Pez arrived, Doctor Gherald and Brittany were already checking Eula's pulse. Pez didn't crowd them. His attention drifted to the output monitor, where a single image seemed to throb on the screen. It was a golden orb in a field of waving purple and it glowed from the monitor like it had a life of its own.

THE INVITATION FROM Aunt Shirley roused Pez from a six-week funk in Vancouver. He took the last of his severance money and bought a plane ticket to Charleston, then spent the entire trip dreading the meeting. Aunt Shirley had warned him he would have to answer to her if anything happened to her baby, but maybe he secretly wanted to be more accountable for what had happened. The three-month suspension of his ISC research license seemed like a slap on the wrist.

Shirley sat waiting for him alone in the lobby at Medical University Hospital, her chin projecting proudly from beneath the oversized brim of a white church-lady hat. When he stopped before her, she rose and extended a gloved hand.

"Thank you so much for coming, Dr. Pezzoli," she said. "Did you have a nice trip?"

"Yes, thank you. Has there been any change?"

"Yes. Come with me, and I'll show you."

They rode the elevator in a silence that made Pez cringe. Eula was on the fifth floor, in a private room financed by the ISC, and a nurse led them inside.

The former English professor had not regained consciousness, but there was something beautiful about her lying on the hospital bed. Eula looked younger than before, and her lips seemed to be formed in a permanent smile.

"She looks . . . beautiful," he said.

"She should," said Aunt Shirley. "She's pregnant."

Pez hadn't seen that one coming. He stared at Aunt Shirley like a slack-jawed idiot.

"Close your mouth, honey, before a fly buzz in there. She's going to have a baby. Dr. Pezzoli, I brought you here to ask you, what are you going to do about it?"

"Me? I'm not the father. I couldn't be the father. I mean, we never . . ."

"I know that, honey." Aunt Shirley seemed to relax. "I just wanted to hear what you'd say. Sit down, Pez. There's something I need to tell you."

Pez sat.

"I know . . . an old, old man. He lives in the country, and we've been going to see him for years. He . . . *knows* things. So I went to see him about Eula, and he told me some very . . . strange stuff."

"Like what?"

"He told me he went to see Eula—I told you, the man knows things—and Eula told him that she was fine, that she'd be coming back around when the time was right. But that's not all. She said the baby was Anthony, and the father was a she, and that we were supposed to call the buckra boy who would understand. Buckra means white folk, honey. That's why I called you. Does any of that make sense to you?"

Pez considered. It did make sense. It all made sense. Everything.

"Aunt Shirley, this is going to be a special baby. More special than I can explain."

"Pez, have you ever been a father before?"

"Yes. I was lousy at it."

"Then you'll be better off this time around," Aunt Shirley said. She took Pez's hands into her own. "You're going to have to raise this child. Until Eula comes back to us, you're going to be the only person in this family who will understand what this baby needs."

Pez stood, walked to the bedside and gazed at Eula's face, which seemed to float above the white hospital linens. She had gone back into a void he could only dimly imagine and made herself a lifeboat, and now something unlike anything this troubled world had ever seen grew within her womb.

He sat in the chair beside Eula for hours that first afternoon, wondering whether the Messiah would collect baseball cards.

CARTHAGINIAN ROSE

KEN LIU

Those of use who have siblings know that just because someone is raised in the same house with you, by the same parents, with the same economic level and the same schools and the same weather each day and the same seasons each year, the same television shows and the same board games after dinner and the same music playing from the stereo, does not mean that you are anything like each other. Because those experiences were filtered through another mind. Choices were made by another will, and different hopes and dreams translated an event that to one sibling seemed catastrophic into an opportunity or a lesson or a funny memory.

And yet, despite all the differences, which can make a sibling seem sometimes like the strangest of strangers, we still know each other as no one else can know us or be known.

THE SECRET TO my apple pie is that I use only Jonathans. They stay tart even when you leave them on the trees till the last minute.

"Mmmm," Liz said to me before she left for Cairo, "you ought to go to Boston with these. You'll be a hit like Martha Stewart."

I had baked two pies for her to take on her trip, sealed in the new smart Tupperware containers that had computer chips for regulating humidity. "You can eat them on the plane. You know, when you are hungry."

She laughed. Her laughter was loud and earthy, like a child's. Four years at Wellesley had not managed to convert her wild yawps into the proper giggle of a New England aristocrat.

"Amy, I can feed myself. Do you expect to ship pies daily to me in Egypt to keep me alive?"

The thought had crossed my mind. Liz's survival always seemed to me to be provisional. She drifted through her childhood, never learning how to cook balanced meals or sew on a missing button. When she drove, every five minutes she seemed to barely escape an accident. She forgot about meals and then begged her friends pathetically for stashed-away snacks. She misplaced boxes of winter clothes and went to class in December wrapped in her blanket. I can't imagine living like that. She laughed often and loud nonetheless. She was smart, no doubt about that, just careless with the practical details of staying alive.

In the end we took the pies to the airport, where we handed out pieces to strangers. A few were suspicious or disdainful, but most were grateful for the treat. Liz told everyone that I was opening a bakery and that these were samples. Before I could correct her, she was taking down orders for me.

"They'll mail you a check, and you'll mail them the pie. It's a great deal! You have all this cooking skill. You ought to do something with it."

All of a sudden I was the sister with no living skills and she the one to show me the ways of the world. Being with Liz tended to make you both amused and annoyed.

I still get about three or four orders a week. It's all word-of-mouth since I don't advertise at all. The old ladies who get a pie from me every two weeks pass me on to their nieces and daughters, like a family heirloom. With each order I imagine that I'm sending the pie to Liz, in New York, in Tucson, in Toronto, in Hong Kong.

The truth, of course, is that Liz has traveled further than my pies ever could reach.

GROWING OLD MEANS you become more like a reptile. You have to soak up the sun in the mornings before you can move around. Next time Beth visits I should ask for a sunlamp, for the winter mornings.

It's a good morning. I open the window and let the sun into the living room. Warm days like this are good for the foliage. The sugar builds up and the cool nights trap them in the leaves. Soon the maples will be on fire, and the tourists from down south will flood the country roads.

When I've soaked up enough light, I tend to my post-card collection. The cards are placed around the house according to geography. Asia is in the kitchen. The mountains of Guilin on top of the fridge stare at the Meiji Shrine across the room by the microwave. Europe fills the bathroom with somber cathedrals and gay ruins. My bedroom is Africa, with the pyramids on the mirror attached to the dresser and the giraffes grazing on the bed stand. Australia and South America share the living room, the coffee table a stand-in for the South Pacific. The 52 states are jumbled into what used to be Liz's bedroom, with California and Florida bathing in the sunlight from her window. The eighth-grader who comes over every Thursday afternoon to mow the lawn thinks I used to be a world traveler.

The furthest I've been from Camlisle was when I went to Boston to pick up the ashes. Beth drove because I wouldn't take an auto-auto, and I remember thinking, when we crossed the state line into Massachusetts, that they had good foliage there also. Beth complained about how backwards everything in Boston was, especially the old manual cars that didn't have AI overrides. "Somebody could get hurt," she muttered. She had the casual, everyday kind of faith in the infallibility of AI that made the world safe for her generation.

The last of the postcards came from Algeria, and it shows the remains of the Roman theatre at Djemila. Liz wrote on the back, in her elegant, flowing cursive:

> *Now it may be, the flower for me*
> *Is this beneath my nose;*
> *How shall I tell, unless I smell*
> *The Carthaginian rose?*

Liz liked to quote bits of poetry at me. This one I know. It's by Edna St. Vincent Millay, one of her favorite poets. She used to recite that poem when she was young and only dreamed about traveling.

WHEN LIZ GRADUATED from high school, she wanted to hitchhike her way to San Francisco.

"Absolutely not," Father said. "A young girl like you, hitchhiking across the country, whoever heard of such a thing?"

It didn't help her case that this was also only a week after she managed to get lost driving home from her prom, which was held only two towns over, in Landon. She ended up somewhere in Connecticut, and called Father for directions at 3 a.m. She thought it a hilarious adventure, of course.

Father's response was predictable, and so was Liz's. She left that evening, with her backpack filled with two bottles of spring water and two pairs of socks.

"The most important survival gear you need are socks," she told me as she packed. "It's very important to keep your feet well-padded when you are hitchhiking because you are doing a lot of walking. And socks are very versatile. You can use them to filter unpotable water, for instance."

I threatened to go to Mother and Father right away. What bothered me wasn't so much her rebelliousness—which was to be expected—but rather her naïve optimism that a pair of socks would somehow get you from Vermont to California, and ward off all the serial killers, rapists, and con-artists along the way.

"No, you won't," she said. "You know I can take care of myself."

"You can't even get home from Landon! Do you know how dangerous it is for you to be alone on the road? You have no camping gear, no clothes, no medicine, no money—"

"Which is why it's not dangerous at all. Amy, I don't have anything, so no one will want to hurt me."

I was flabbergasted by her simple, ridiculous logic. I would have laughed if I hadn't wanted to slap some common sense into her. But I also knew that her absurd assumptions would come through for her. I had seen, time and again, how she somehow managed to turn her clumsiness at practical life to her advantage. When she was lost in Connecticut, she ended up sipping free Slurpies from the clerks at the nearest 7-11 and offering them advice on girls. The syrup dripped all over the front of her rented prom dress, but the dress rental shop didn't even charge her for it when she told the owners her story. Like Blanche DuBois, she relied on the kindness of strangers. People naturally liked her. She had charisma.

I envied her daring, and her confidence in what she wanted out of life. When we were younger, both of us had done well at school, especially in the sciences. However, we had different temperaments. I had ended my two years at the community college with the resigned certainty that although I was intelligent, I was terrified of strangers, content to watch the world pass by while I stayed home and tended to the happiness of my family. Someone had to inherit Father's orchard, right?

Liz left with her bottled water and socks, and I pretended that I didn't know anything when Father yelled at me the next day and over the next week. He wanted to call the police, but then we got the postcard Liz sent us from Boston, telling us that she was all right, and she had met a wonderful jazz band on I-95.

She began her habit of sending postcards. From Fenway, from Manhattan, from the National Mall, from the banks of the Mississippi, from the endless vistas of the Great Plains, from the dry, dusty desert that seemed like the Promised Land to the Mormons, from the mountains through which the Chinamen blasted a railway, until, finally, she got to Fisherman's Wharf, San Francisco.

In those postcards, she wrote the Great American Novel. She talked about the eccentricities and kindnesses of America in 250-word vignettes. She wrote about the law student working at a gas station to pay the bills, about the date she went on with two brothers who were police officers (they caught her hitchhiking), about the time she impulsively knocked on a Kentucky housewife's door because she wanted to take a shower (she got her shower, and a real Southern breakfast). She made the cliché of the travelogue fresh again. Father, Mother, and I read her reports with relish, passing the cards between the three of us for hours, arguing and dissecting every encounter, offering our observations. Somewhere around the Mississippi, I think Father forgave her for running away.

She came back three months later on a plane. She simply told her story to people at the airport until some businessman, overwhelmed by her story or by misplaced pity, bought her a ticket. I thought she would never learn the value of anything; things came too easy to her. She came home without her backpack or her socks.

She went to bed early that night because the next morning Father had to drive her down to Wellesley. In the dark, she slipped into my bedroom.

"I wish you had come with me," she whispered, her body warm and cuddly next to mine.

She sounded a little sad, but I was sleepy. "Yeah, I wish I had, too."

"And you know something else? Socks are not the most important survival equipment. Your body is."

I thought then that she had finally learned something practical.

BEHIND THE HOUSE is the hill, and up on the hill is the orchard.

I don't own the orchard any more. I sold it 10 years ago. It was getting too much to maintain for me, living alone with Beth after John died.

It's still a nice place to take a walk in, though. I head for the Jonathan trees at the end. Not many tourists who come here to pick apples ever walk this far since by the time they get halfway here their baskets are usually full. Jonathans are not good eating apples anyway, too tart.

But they are my favorite. McIntoshes and other "good" eating apples are the apples you eat with your mouth, full of that cottony sweetness that practically melts down your throat. Jonathans, on the other hand, are apples you eat with your whole body. It hurts your jaws to bite off a hard chunk, hear the crunch against your skull, and feel the tartness spread from the ridge of your tongue down to the tips of you toes. You really feel alive when you are eating a Jonathan. Every cell wakes up and tells you, "Yes, oh yes."

The body is more intelligent than the mind. It understands what it means to be alive better than the mind ever will.

"I WANT TO travel a lot," Liz wrote in her college application essay.

Artificial Intelligence was just coming back in a big way when Liz was in school. The new three-dimensional chips from Nextensions finally had enough computing power to crunch through the real-time data processing. The first nano-neural networks were also just beginning to be mass-produced. Everything was coming together. During the summers, Liz worked in Stanford's labs, building the first working prototype of a statistical quantum computer. Her excitement was infectious, and I read everything about AI I could find on the Net.

She spent hours on the phone with me, breathlessly babbling away about all that she was doing. I tried to keep up with her by reading the textbooks she left at home. I even learned to program in Lisp and Prolog. I was pleased that I did well (if only I weren't so shy!). There was an organic kind of beauty to crafting these programs, like baking pies.

When she graduated, Logorhythms, the biggest AI consulting firm in North America, hired her. She was ecstatic because the job would take her all over the world.

Liz explained to me that Logorhythms specialized in building AI systems to handle decision making in domains where the unexpected was always happening: deep-sea mining exploration, city traffic-control, and public school administration, that sort of thing. Traditional expert systems were too fragile, too rule- and case-bound to function effectively when the unfamiliar and unexpected occurred. Logorhythms built systems that could muddle through, like humans in similar situations.

So she shipped herself to Cairo, to Beijing, to Honolulu, writing reams and reams of parallel pattern-recognizers and recursive co-routines to run on massively parallel nanoprocessors. The programs then evolved themselves for thousands of generations through genetic filters until deemed sufficiently fit for the task at hand.

"Traveling," Liz said, "is just the process of upgrading of your own mind. And my job is about the creation of new minds. So, you see, my life is all about the meeting of the minds."

I DON'T HAVE any of the standard, even old-fashioned, AI conveniences in the house. I'm not a Luddite, but I threw them all out, after what Liz did.

I think they are creepy: the alarm clock that can figure out whether you *really* want to wake up, the TV that can tell you what you want to watch based on what it thinks your mood is, the thermostat that decides what the temperature ought to be based on a complex analysis of your heating bill and your state of health. If these are really little minds, it's cruel to give them thankless tasks like these. If they are not, I would rather not be told by a machine to put on a sweater when I'm cold.

So I still do everything myself. I muddle through.

Beth, being a dutiful daughter, wants to convince me that I should live with her in New York. I explained to her that living in a place where the traffic lights know to wait extra long when an old lady is crossing the street would drive me crazy.

"You are out of your mind," Beth said to me. "What happens if you trip and fall down the stairs? There's not even a phone in your house smart enough to notice and call an ambulance."

Out of my mind, but not out of my body, like Liz.

Mind, body, and soul. What's it like to be out of my soul?

LIZ CAME BACK for Father's funeral. Not surprisingly, she forgot to bring a proper dress to wear.

We shared a sisterly moment in the living room after the other mourners had left.

"What a waste," she said, by way of breaking the silence in the house. She fidgeted, switching off her ring, her glasses (purely decorative, she had perfect vision), her shoes, even her watch. The little computers chimed their weak protests and went dead.

In the dusk she looked naked, I thought, without the youthful glow that the smart embedded mirrors in her jewelry constantly and subtly cast about her face and hands. With them on she looked like a 19-year-old. With them off she looked 35. I thought she looked more beautiful unadorned.

She looked about the room, at the dusty carpet, the dusty picture frames, the dusty chairs. Mother never liked the self-driven vacuum cleaners Liz had given her. "What a waste. This too too sullied flesh," she said.

We sat together for hours, holding hands in the growing dark. I liked cupping her cold fingers between my palms, feeling the circulation gradually bringing warmth to them, feeling the pulses of her strong heart.

Liz was going to fly back to Sydney the next day. I wanted her to get some sleep.

"Aren't you scared, Amy?" she asked me at the door to her old bedroom.

"About what?"

"How weak the body is. Remember how strong he had seemed when we were little? I remember running into his chest and feeling like I had run into a wall. I remember him lifting me onto his shoulders to pick the apples I wanted. At my graduation, he shook my hand after I got my diploma. It hurt, like a vise. But it's all just a lie, Amy.

The body is a lie. It can fall apart at a moment's notice, because of a simple blood clot."

It was one of the few times I had seen her cry.

Because I didn't know what else to say, I said, "That's why the body is the most important piece of survival equipment."

"Oh, yes," she smiled. "I never told you, did I? About what happened in New Jersey that time I hitchhiked to San Fran?"

She was waiting at a rest stop when a man, a nice, clean man with a polo shirt and a pickup truck, agreed to drive her to the Pennsylvania border. He chatted amicably with her about school, about skiing, about literature, about the kindness of strangers.

Then he turned off the highway. He drove until the dirt road ended at an abandoned warehouse, stopped, pushed her out of the cab of the truck, and raped her there, on the grass, under the warm sunlight, with the birds chirping and the bees buzzing through the clovers. She still had her socks on.

Obviously, there was no postcard.

"When he drove away, I was done crying. I sat on the grass and thought: I could travel to the end of the Earth and this will always be with me. I will always have his hands tearing apart my shirt, his mouth over mine. My mind will always be trapped in my body, reliving it over and over again. I will never be able to get away."

I hugged her tight. Her arms hung limp at her sides, but she leaned her weight against me. She used to do that when she was a little girl. I wish I had the strength to lift her, to enfold her body in my arms, to give her back what she had lost. I felt guilty because I knew that I would never be able to understand how she felt, not viscerally, not with my body.

"You see, the body is indeed the most important piece of survival equipment, but it's weak and imperfect. It will always betray you."

I DON'T UNDERSTAND people who say that they'll travel when they are old. Travel is for the young. If you don't start to travel by a certain age you end up like me, rooted to the place you grew up in.

I don't think Camlisle is the best place in the world. I just can't imagine moving anywhere else after having spent my whole life here. I like the way the shadows move across the floor of my bedroom. I like the squeaks and cracks as I go up the stairs, each one an intimate, old friend. I like the view of the apple trees, lined up like headstones in a cemetery behind the house, on the hill. Or maybe I'm just used to those things, too comfortable to change. Too many brain cells have died to make those connections for me to abandon them easily.

The house, the hills, the shadows, and the taste of the apples have become part of my body. They have changed the way my dendrites and axons connect to each other, etching themselves into my skin, my brain, my body through the microlithography of the gentle years until a holographic map of Camlisle is deposited into me, as inseparable from the rest of me as my toes and fingers.

I do wonder, sometimes, how the physical contours of my mind would have been different if I had traveled, like Liz, around the world.

"You'd be running on different hardware," Liz would have said. "Time for an upgrade. Cote d'Ivoire, here I come."

153

THE LAST TIME Liz came home was a Sunday. I returned from church, and there she was, leaning against the old oak tree in front of the house, smiling.

We went into the house. As usual, she had no luggage. It's not the sort of thing she would remember, ever. It's a good thing she makes as much as she does. Everywhere she went she ended up having to buy a new wardrobe, which she would again forget to bring with her when she left.

After dinner we had some apple pie for dessert.

"Mmmm," she said. "Still want to try that Martha Stewart idea?"

I laughed with her. She laughed so loud the plates clattered. It's good to have her in the house again, I thought. She looked so young. Her body glowed, and not just because of the intelligent nanonet of diamonds she wore.

"Amy." Her face was serious. "Do you know what we are about to do?"

She explained to me about the project she was working on for Logorhythms, DESTINY. "It's going to change the world," she said.

"Amy, look around you. We've come so far since I was in college. In 15 years we've managed to create cars that drive themselves, dishes that clean themselves, and phones and clocks that monitor you 24 hours a day and are ready to call for help the minute you are injured in an accident or suffer an unexpected fainting spell. AI has come of age.

"But now we've hit a roadblock. We have all the processing power we've dreamed of, and all the storage capacity we can want in our ultra-dense neural networks. But it's not enough; we still don't know how to make a *mind*. Sure, the latest computer lasted a whole half-hour in the Turing Competition, but I think we've hit the limits of what we can do, working blind like we are.

"What we need is a map, a blueprint to the only example of a successful mind platform we have: Ourselves. After all this time, we still don't understand how the brain works. We've done the best we can with MRI, with ultrasound, with infrared, with the dissection of frozen, dead brains, but we have just scratched the surface. We need to reverse-engineer a living, healthy brain so we can take it apart *and* put it back together, and really understand how to build minds of our own."

What she was saying sounded exciting and scientific. My body knew that something was wrong though. It felt so tight, so tense.

"So, this DESTINY project is about developing some technique that will allow you to scan brains at the sufficient resolution, is that it?"

"No, Amy, we already can do that." I'll never forget the way she smiled that day. *Amy, you already know what I'm about to tell you.*

"We can peel the brain away, one layer of neurons at a time. We've had that capability for years."

"What does DESTINY stand for?" I asked, afraid of the answer.

"Destructive Electromagnetic Scan To Increase Neural Yield."

Destructive. I stared at her without words (what could I say?) or expressions (how did I feel?) while she explained to me how a brain was to be sliced apart, one layer of neurons at a time, and all the connections and dangling ends recorded and mapped. All this would happen while the brain was alive, for as long as the brain stayed alive.

"Why can't you use a dead brain?"

"We've tried. The deterioration sets in too quickly. The patterns we need to see are obscured by the trauma and disease common in the dead brains available for scanning. We can't build a mind based on a dead brain that no longer has a mind in it, just like we couldn't really understand the circulation system until we vivisected a beating heart.

"It will all be captured, every detail of my brain, down to the last, least significant neural connection. And the first thing we'll do is to make a copy of my brain, in silicon, and I'll be alive again. Only difference is, I'll be thinking a billion times faster, and I won't ever grow old or die because I won't have a body any more. When we are done, no one will ever have to die. This weak flesh will not be our prison. We will fulfill our destiny."

"And if you fail?"

"We won't know unless we go and try, right? I've done all I can to make sure this succeeds. And even if we fail, it will be quite a trip."

So I knew that she had made up her mind to travel again, and there was nothing that I could give her to take with her, to help her this time either. I could only take care of her body, and she was about to leave that behind. She was finally going to get away.

I'M IN A WHITE room, and the precision saw is whirling over my head, just outside my field of vision. I'm trying to stay calm but it doesn't work. I can't be anesthetized because the results may be skewed if I'm under. So I'm strapped down onto the gurney and trying not to hyperventilate or scream. Then the saw begins to descend, and that first searing jolt of pain as it contacts my skull is unbelievable. It is so intense my vision goes out in a flash of light. And I think to myself, oh God, they'll have to do this a few million times, one layer at a time.

I would usually wake up at this point. Of course I know that my nightmares hardly can reflect reality. The brain, I'm told, has no pain sensors (as if that makes any difference). Doubtless the instruments they used were much more sophisticated than my medieval imagination can come up with. I'll never know how they actually did it because I wasn't there when it happened. They had to go to Algeria, in secret, because anywhere else the law would have considered it murder.

When I went to Boston to retrieve the ashes, I also got copies of the scan results, 20 silicon wafers the size of matchboxes: The reason my sister killed herself.

I crushed the wafers under my heels one at a time there, on the cement floor of a faceless bureaucrat's office.

Her final moments were also captured forever in the electronic memories of the supercomputers of Logorhythms. (It depends on what you mean by *final*, I suppose. For me, those moments were beyond final. They occurred in the place my sister had traveled to, a landscape more alien than the face of the Moon). Her electronic computation patterns had lasted less than five seconds—which was an eternity—on the neural grid constructed based on the results of her scan. They had simply gone through those billions of cycles per second and then disintegrated.

It will take years before they can finally understand what had happened. One of the neurologists on the team had speculated that the failure was perhaps related to the utter lack of any somatic and sensual feedback for the subjective eons she had spent in that grid. Imagine if you were immobilized in darkness, unable to even feel your fingers, your toes, your lungs laboring for air, with nothing but your thoughts to accompany you for countless ages. A brain in a jar would finally go insane. The body is important, after all.

She had gone out of her body, and then, quickly after that, out of her mind.

WHEN LIZ WAS six years old, she asked Father what her soul looked like.

"Probably like a butterfly," he said. That was a good reply, with so many medieval paintings to back it up.

"Souls have very light bodies, then," she said, trying to be logical.

Father lifted her over his head and helped her pretend that she was a butterfly, fluttering among Mother's potted plants. You could hear her laugh all the way from the orchard on the hills.

Years of litigation have failed to get Logorhythms to destroy the copies of my sister's mind that they still own. Logorhythms argued that they were too important as scientific data, and invaluable for all the AI research that still had to be done. The public uproar that came after resulted in the passage of the Anti-Destructive Scan Act, and Logorhythms no longer operates in North America. I suppose that's some consolation.

I can't even mourn for Liz properly, not when she is away, frozen in the interstices of the synthetic memory lattices located on another continent. Doubtless they have secretly tried to revive her in more and more elaborate neural nets, and doubtless she has gone through her agony of bodiless, mindless solitude again and again. Which of those copies is my sister? Which one should I mourn for? And if someday, by a miracle of technology, she should come back, would I still know her?

So, meanwhile, I tend to my postcard collection and I bake pies, nourishing my body with the sunlight and the smell of coffee in the morning. I wait for my time. I know Beth will mourn me properly.

I bite into a Jonathan, tasting the wonderful sourness with my whole body.

RIPPERS

Chris Leonard

I love street vendors.

I don't buy what they sell, mind you. Even when a pretzel or hot dog cart gives off smells that make me salivate like one of Pavlov's dogs for an entire city block, I keep reminding myself (a) I'm going to be eating a really fine meal later on, so why waste calories on this? and (b) I don't have time today to deal with indigestion.

As for the people selling jewelry, watches, books, scarves, shirts, or videotapes of suspiciously recent films, I always start from the assumption that (a) the stuff they're selling is worthless junk and (b) if it isn't junk it's stolen and (c) even if it isn't junk and it isn't stolen, I don't actually want it and will never use it.

And yet I'm glad they're there. Like street musicians, good and bad, they give me some sense that I'm not that far away from the old days, when the village came alive on weekly or *fortnightly fair days, when jongleurs put on their show and farmers and traveling tradesmen offered fresh tastes and clever devices not to be had or seen or heard on other days. But my love for these vendors depends in part upon the wall I keep between us. They can't actually touch me. I'm a spectator, enjoying the ambience they help create.*

What's easy to forget is that when I'm enjoying them, I'm on the street myself. To others—to the vendors themselves—I'm part of the show.

"RIPPERS—SPECIALTY—$3.00," said the crudely lettered sign. Jim Layton paused, eyeing the line of people waiting in the aching cold.

Surging crowds of office-workers, bureaucrats, and students flocked the streets even on this winter afternoon. The flow of pedestrians moved around the edge of the line in eddies of briefcases, scarves, and winter coats.

A momentary island in the stream of humanity, Jim wondered what in the world a "ripper" could be—some kind of sandwich, like those things in Philly called "grinders?" He studied the food-stand, which was actually a van with awning, window, and countertop built directly into the side of the vehicle. Parked at the corner of New Jersey Ave. and E, it lay only four blocks from Union Station, right by the cluster of buildings that included the Statistics Bureau where Jim worked. Near the rear of the van, a clutter of newspaper vending machines and advertising displays provided a partial shelter for the customers.

Inside this miniature kitchen-on-wheels sat the cook, a thickset man with long arms and a mustache that bristled over his upper lip like a black hedgehog. He had a tremendous round belly that swelled his apron nearly to bursting, and he wore a gaping smile. As Jim watched,

162

the vendor's hands assembled something with great speed, and then slid across the counter a steaming, oblong package of wax paper and a Styrofoam cup. Bills were thrust up in return, and then the man smiled down at his next customer. Throughout the entire process he kept up a tireless banter that seemed almost unrelated to the task at hand, all the while flashing tongs and fork in clattering accompaniment.

"Slingin' it . . . fried!" sang the vendor in a cracked baritone. "Rippers, comin' hot out 'de pot! Sauce on side—here drink she-come-NOW!"

Another package appeared as if by magic, payment was collected, and the next person stepped forward. As that happened, Jim felt a slight but deliberate push from behind, and he took an inadvertent step, joining the back of the line. Turning, he saw a woman swathed in a scarf and winter coat, waiting with that look people get on a half-hour lunch break. Jim hadn't actually intended to stop, but now he somehow felt bound to stay, as if the act of being with these others in the cold obligated him to eat what they did. Odors drifted from the nearby stand: cooking meat, and a kind of lemony scent. Jim's own allotted lunchtime was not so generous either, and his stomach was turning over like a knotted rubber band. When a rapid search of his inside pocket turned up exactly three singles, his choice of a meal seemed destined, though he still had no idea what a "ripper" was.

In less than two minutes, he'd moved nearly to the front of the line. As other customers gathered behind, the figure in front of him was suddenly gone and Jim found himself pressed against the counter.

"Ripper, please," he said, eyeing the space under the awning. Painted on the side of the van were the words

CHRIS LEONARD

"Papa Sarvoli's Hot-Dogs," which were partially covered by the larger cardboard sign offering rippers. Below
was a faded health department permit. The interior of
the food stand—partly visible through the eye-level window—was spotlessly clean.

Papa Sarvoli grinned, steam billowing out around his
huge head. "Ho, freshies!" he hollered, pulling back inside the kitchen. He spun gracefully about to gather up
something behind him, rotating as if on roller skates.
"One, two, blue, set-'em-up . . . GO!" His hands deposited
a newly wrapped package onto the counter, and with it a
cup. Aware of those waiting, Jim extended his money and
gathered his lunch. Papa Sarvoli just rolled his head and
grinned, taking the cash without a word.

Jim steered through the crowds, heading for the
warmth of an indoor food court not far away. Seated
amid the maze of Formica tables, he took an experimental sip from the cup. The hot liquid was a dark, sweet tea,
which was flavored with lemon, and surprisingly good.
Unwrapping the wax paper, Jim found a kind of sausage
on a bun, slathered in something like barbecue sauce.
The wiener was split down the middle, partly burst open
so that the filling bulged out like a busted inner tube.

It was a dubious-looking hot dog, but Jim was hungry,
and took a bite, and then another. As he chewed, the complex flavors settled on his tongue—a slightly spicy, roasted
taste of sausage, and the tangy, delicate sauce. Halfway finished with his meal, Jim decided that it was the best hot
dog he'd tasted in years. Even the bun was excellent,
vaguely rye, or sourdough, slightly toasted—it tasted fresh
baked. Humming with delight, Jim alternated remaining
bites with sips of hot tea. A new place to eat, and cheap! He
was surprised now that the line hadn't been longer.

164

Finishing his meal, Jim groaned at the prospect of returning to work. The office waited like a sterile tomb, his cubicle a coffin. A meaningless job, but government benefits were good, and he was lucky to be making twenty-five grand on an associate's degree. Sighing, he brushed crumbs off his pants and tossed the empty cup and paper into a nearby trashcan.

Several weeks later, after he was a regular at Sarvoli's stand and had learned its rather odd and unique etiquette, a co-worker enlightened Jim as to what a "ripper" was.

"Rippers are dogs that they drop briefly in hot oil," Ron explained. "The skin bursts, and that's why it's a ripper. I had one in Jersey once. They also had cinders, the ones they leave in the pot a long time. Nasty." He shrugged his shoulders and laughed. "You go on and eat a few, though—skinny boy."

Jim chuckled and let it pass. Was he losing weight? Usually he put on some pounds around the holidays. And he'd been eating regularly at Papa's. He even made a habit of stopping by on weekends now.

One afternoon he witnessed a peculiar incident at Sarvoli's. He was waiting in line when the order for the man in front of him slid across the counter. The fellow was older—fairly well off, judging by his clothes. He reached out with trembling fingers, and at first Jim thought the guy might have Parkinson's or something. Then the old man looked pleadingly up to where Papa Sarvoli waited, hand outstretched to receive his payment.

"Please . . ." Jim heard the man whisper. "I don't want any more."

Several other people waiting scowled at the delay. It was rude to address Papa Sarvoli directly—somehow

Jim knew this as he did the other rules; no one talked in line, or ate together after paying, or asked for anything but what Papa gave them. Those were the house rules at Papa's, and they were rarely broken. The food was just too amazingly good.

Papa Sarvoli grinned down at the older guy then leaned forward and said something that Jim couldn't make out. The gray-haired man snatched the meal off the counter and stumbled away without paying. Jim saw tears flowing freely down his lined face.

No one else said a word.

Papa Sarvoli threw Jim a wicked smile as he served up another ripper, steaming hot. "Tasty," he said.

Jim gave a confused nod, and then walked off. He wondered what the whole business had been about. This season was a bad time for some people. For a moment he had that altruistic impulse that always hit when he passed the bundled form of one of the District's homeless lying on a street grate. He looked about, but the older guy was lost in the crowd.

Finding a seat in his usual spot at the food court, Jim began the now-familiar lunchtime ritual. He'd developed his own way of consuming the rippers—enjoying the first half in small, measured bites, then devouring the rest in a rush. These trips to Papa's were the highlight of his workdays, sustaining him through the afternoon rush to the bus stop, the brief, hectic commute, and then back to the room he rented in a seedy neighborhood near Adams Morgan. Nothing much waited for him there. Junk mail. The guitar he now rarely picked up. His books. Roaches.

Jim had to admit that his own holiday wasn't looking so cheery either. With a guilty start, he thought of his slowly deteriorating father, living in a pleasant suburb of Phoenix, where dry air slowed the progress of the black cancer in his dad's lungs.

There were a lot of things to be thankful for.

As Jim turned back to his waiting meal, a hand dropped lightly onto his shoulder. Startled, he looked up. The old man he'd seen earlier at Sarvoli's was standing beside him. His eyes were red and tired.

"May I join you a moment." It was not a question; the voice was quiet, but strong, and carried the weight of casual authority. Before Jim could respond, the man was easing into the seat opposite. He was in his 60s, with a kindly if careworn face. His coat and suit looked expensive, but were rumpled, as if he'd worn them several days. There were stains on the cuffs of his shirt-sleeves.

"My name is Adrian Tindle."

The old man didn't offer his hand.

"Jim."

Tindle nodded. "You work for the government." He indicated the plastic ID card clipped to Jim's shirt pocket. "Me too."

Jim looked down at his unopened meal and cleared his throat.

The old man smiled. "Hungry, aren't you?" He patted the package of wax paper he carried protectively in the crook of one arm. "I am too. But not for much longer."

"Listen . . ."

"You listen to me, son." Tindle's voice was hard, commanding. "Stay away from Sarvoli, you hear me? You don't have the least idea what you're getting involved in." A desperate look flitted briefly across his features.

Jim leaned back in his chair. "Hey, I don't . . ."

"You don't know a damn thing," the old man said sharply. His eyes speared the wax paper package on the table. "I've eaten hundreds . . . so I've learned enough to guess, even if I haven't got the guts to look Sarvoli in the eye—and I'll tell you this: he's not *of* here, Jim."

Tindle gave a tight grin that showed the bones of his face. "It's all right, I'm leaving now. That's all from me." Up out of the chair, he paused, and a shaking finger stretched out from within his stained sleeve. "It's you he wants, Jim."

He was pointing, not at Jim, but at the unopened ripper on the table in front of him.

Then Adrian Tindle was gone, slipping out the front entrance to be lost in the rush of people outside.

Bewildered by the random, bizarre meeting, Jim shook his head. The incident seemed to have passed unnoticed in the general hubbub of the room.

With a baffled shrug, he began to eat.

After the first few bites, Jim paused for a drink, savoring his meal. The encounter had been unnerving—the man had really seemed concerned, his warning sincere. He was probably a businessman on a bender.

Distracted, Jim looked out the food court's windows. There was a disturbance at the intersection directly across the street. People waiting at the light were backing away from a man at the curb.

It was Tindle, standing rigidly, his arms at his sides. Clutched in one of his hands was a bundle of wax paper. He seemed to be speaking very loudly, almost shouting. Across the stream of vehicles filling the street, Jim could see the old man's mouth opening and closing, though his stare remained fixed straight ahead. He had the sudden conviction that Tindle was speaking directly to him. Jim shook his head, turning back to his meal; maybe the guy was mentally ill.

He looked up again at the figure across the way, just in time to see it step deliberately in front of the onrushing city bus.

Everything was over in an instant. Jim saw the man pulled under the wheels, then crushed flat as the bus driver hit the brakes in a vain attempt to undo what he had done. Sickened, he turned his eyes away, but couldn't help seeing the rest of it in his mind; a red scrawl across the asphalt like the stroke of a bloody paintbrush, the horrified onlookers staring at the crushed, sodden form that only a moment before had been a living man.

People were just starting to react; the woman next to him let out a half-strangled shriek. Jim rushed to the bathroom, his guts clenching into knots, but the wave of nausea passed as he reached the stall. He stood with his arms braced against the sides of the metal cubicle, wanting to be sick, but somehow unable to.

Had Tindle been shouting at him specifically?

No. Surely the guy had been disturbed, insane—that conversation had practically proved it.

Jim's breathing slowed. The need to be ill was gradually being replaced by another feeling—something misplaced or lost . . . God, he was hungry.

Horrified by this chain of thought, he stopped short. Hungry? After seeing . . . that?! But there it was. Jim thought of the half-eaten ripper, and his stomach groaned in response.

He stumbled out of the restrooms. The collective attention of the food court had been diverted by the spectacle of a man who'd fainted after witnessing the suicide. A few others were weeping. Outside, traffic was stopped in the street. Horns complained from the back of the line of jammed cars, and Jim heard a siren approaching. Avoiding the knot of people near the front of the room, he strode to the remains of his meal, folded up the papers, and dropped the empty cup into the trash. He left through the exit on the opposite side of the building, the half-finished ripper stowed safely in his coat pocket.

The air of the street stank of exhaust. He hurried away down the block, stopping against a bank of vending machines at the corner. Suddenly he couldn't wait any longer. Tearing the paper apart in his haste to open it, Jim ate the rest of the ripper in two convulsive bites. Closing his eyes, he chewed as the taste ran down his throat. When the last particle of flavor had gone, he wiped his mouth on one sleeve, contemplating his own actions with a sort of sickened fascination.

What the hell was wrong with him? He wasn't sure which was more disturbing—Tindle's death, or his own reaction to it. Fired by the need to respond in some way, he decided on the spot to give up eating at Papa's for a few weeks. A change to something healthier would do him good.

The gesture seemed trivial, but it made him feel slightly better. Returning early to his desk, Jim told no one what he'd seen. He shuffled papers around until five then left, avoiding any interaction with his co-workers.

THE WEEKEND PASSED in a blur of cold weather and bad football games. Jim seemed to have picked up a cold; his limbs ached and his nose ran. The odd, sickly feeling intensified through the next day, slowly rising in his body

170

to a subconscious roar. He remained on the couch, drinking hot fluids and watching TV.

Rising for his ritual Sunday morning exercise, Jim collected the paper and sat down to put on his sneakers. Leafing through the Metro section, his eye caught the photo at the top. The headline read, "Federal Appeals Judge Dead." The picture was that of Adrian Tindle, the weeping man from Papa Sarvoli's.

Jim still wasn't sure how to feel about it; there was a tight place in his chest that wouldn't unwind even after he walked a mile, and that small effort left him spent and tired. His mind kept chewing over the fate of the judge, and that last, cryptic warning.

The whole business affirmed his resolution to quit eating at Papa Sarvoli's for a while; Jim wanted to forget everything related to the whole incident.

By late evening his congestion had mostly passed, and he felt well enough not to call in sick the following day. He had plenty of leave accrued—but no reason to waste it on a minor cold. No reason not to go in.

He looked down at the bowl of vegetable soup he'd heated up for dinner, but didn't feel hungry.

JIM DREAMED THAT he was standing on the pavement outside the food-court, Tindle calling to him from across the street.

"You'll be sorry you did!" the old man shouted. "Very, very sorry."

A bus was approaching up the street. Jim wanted to tell Tindle not to jump in front of it, but as he looked up, the lean figure crooked his finger, and Jim felt himself lurch forward. The old man beckoned again, and Jim moved like a marionette, stepping out onto the asphalt. The oncoming bus swerved into his lane, and Jim saw that it was not a bus, but a van, Papa Sarvoli's van. Gathering speed, the vehicle rushed forward.

JIM SHUDDERED AWAKE. There was an awful taste in his mouth. Slushy rain blatted against the windowpane by the bed. Listening to it, he was tempted to call the office, but decided not to.

The commute passed in an early-morning fog, a press of bodies on the bus, and the smell of wet wool and newspapers. Jim got off at Union Station, tugging his hood lower against the weather. Moving through streams of foot traffic, he walked down Jersey Ave., careful to avoid the crossing where the old man had died. A mass of people was gathered around the entrance to his building, and Jim joined the shuffling group, mindlessly letting the flow direct him inward.

He was waiting in line for the elevator. Waiting in line . . . The person in front of him had stopped. Coming back to full awareness with a start, Jim saw wet, cracked concrete beneath his feet. Steam billowed around him; people in thick coats were pressed up close in front and behind. Gloved hands jostled him forward. Tearing back his hood, he stared wildly around. He was . . .

He was waiting in line at Papa Sarvoli's.

How the hell had he gotten here? He'd been going into the lobby of his building. Jim had no memory of walking another block to the food-stand, but there he was, at the head of the waiting line. He could just make out Papa Sarvoli himself through the steam, whirling gracefully around the inside of his tiny kitchen.

Confused, Jim looked down. There was something in his left hand. He was certain he'd brought only bus fare today, but there they were—three singles.

172

A gust of wind brought the scent of cooking meat to his nostrils, and Jim felt the nagging sensation in his belly leap into a full-blown, rumbling hunger; a craving that would only be satisfied by the genuine object. With this reaction came abrupt terror, gripping him like a giant, squeezing hand around his insides. He felt as if his body was a hollow shell that might burst apart. Jim tried to leave the line, but the others pressed in closer, rows of blank faces fixed in anticipation. He nearly had to shove his way clear. No one protested; they simply closed ranks, and the line moved forward. Breaking free of the crowd, Jim rushed for the familiar safety of his office.

Late, he hurried to his cubicle to find that no one had noticed his tardiness. Flipping on the computer, Jim set his mind to work on the day's tasks, trying to lose himself in routine. Ron stopped in at midday, as Jim doggedly consumed the bag lunch he'd brought. The apple he was eating tasted like cardboard, but he deliberately finished all of it. Ron watched, concerned.

"You aren't looking so good, Jim. You should use some sick leave—holidays start in three days anyway."

It seemed like a good idea, especially after the incident this morning. Jim left word with his supervisor's secretary that he was taking the rest of the week off. She made no protest, suggesting he could leave early if he wanted.

Did he look so bad? Alone in the men's room, Jim studied himself in the full-length mirror. He noticed small details; the way his clothes hung loosely on his frame, slight circles under his eyes, a certain tightness to the cheekbones. What was happening to him?

He caught the express to his neighborhood in Adams Morgan, walking the few blocks from the stop back to his apartment. A tugging pulled at his insides the entire way, like a ghostly fishhook under his breastbone. Trotting against the magnetic pull, Jim fought his way up the steps to his place as if through a filmy current. He wrenched the door open, dragged himself inside, and slammed it shut behind.

He lay on the couch most of the day, semi-comatose, his mind roaming. Occasionally, he would stalk into the kitchen, scan the shelves, then paw through the fridge. His eyes lingered often on the plastic tub of shortening; he was getting an overwhelming urge to open it and shove chunks of the snowy fat into his mouth . . . that and a craving for salt bothered him all afternoon. He sat in the living room with the TV tuned to a dead channel, thinking. By late that evening, his thoughts had traveled the same path so many times it was worn like a groove into his brain.

It all came back to the same thing.

What difference did it make, Jim thought. Who knows or cares if I eat another one of the damned things? He hadn't had a ripper in days! What was the point in denying? It wasn't like he was overweight. He could go and get one right now . . .

He laughed grimly—twenty-five blocks downtown for a hot dog?

Fifteen minutes later, he was hailing a taxi.

The ride passed in growing anticipation; Jim got off on the opposite side of the plaza, tipped the driver. The area was empty of its usual daytime traffic. Hurrying across the square of buildings, he tried to spot the familiar white van in its usual place.

Papa's couldn't be open . . . he had to move the van at night, didn't he? But somehow, Jim knew that Sarvoli would be there, even at this hour.

174

Then he saw the outline of the stand, and began to jog toward it. He hadn't reached the curb when he smelled hot oil, with it, the maddening odor of cooking meat.

Running to the far side of the vehicle, Jim saw that the window was closed, the awning drawn down tight.

"No! Papa Sarvoli," he groaned. He had to be in there! The smell was unmistakable. Jim hammered on the side of the van with a clenched fist. "Papa! Are you there?"

From within came a stirring of metal on metal.

"Papa! Open up!"

Silence.

He ran to the rear of the van, pulling furiously at the back doors, thumping his fist against the dust-smeared windows.

There was a sudden *clack* as the lock popped open.

Papa was in there! Grasping the handle, Jim pulled, but the doors resisted him, as if painted shut. As he finally pried them back, a cloud of steam puffed out, carrying the faint scent of lemon. "Papa?" he called, pulling himself up into the van.

There was a clattering noise from the darkness, and Jim saw the gleam of stainless steel as Papa Sarvoli rolled forward into the light.

At first, Jim thought the man was standing inside some kind of bin or metal hopper. Then he realized that they were part of the same thing—the cook was one with his hardware. Melded to Papa Sarvoli's lower torso was a silvery rectangle of metal; as he came closer, Jim could see below the apron, where the flesh of Papa's arms and chest grafted smoothly to the gleaming cube.

He stared dumbly as Papa Sarvoli's head and arms swiveled in that odd, quick-jointed motion he was now so

175

familiar with. The arm reached down to the metallic box below, fingers turning a sort of recessed latch, and Papa's front opened like a hatchway, revealing a dimly lit interior. Things like over-ripe fruits lay packed in rows, coated with moist, lacy tissues. The fingers prodded delicately, like some underwater creature tending its brood, then selected one of the oblong shapes, tearing it away from the surrounding tissue with a wet snapping sound. The hot-dog stand man's eyes gleamed in the dark like silver cartwheels as he rolled toward Jim across the metal flooring.

"Rippers . . ." Jim heard him whisper.

THERE WAS NO conscious decision to flee. Jim found himself stumbling through the alley behind his own office building, guts revolting even as he ran.

What he'd seen was impossible. What had he seen? People weren't machines, they were meat and bone, and everything back there had been a hallucination, a mirage . . . a breakdown, even—whatever, so long as such things weren't real.

Lurching to a stop, Jim leaned against the brick wall of the alley. Somewhere inside himself he knew that his eyes hadn't lied, and from that same place there now arose the sensation he'd felt earlier: the absolute certainty that there was nothing he needed more at that moment than one of Sarvoli's rippers.

At this realization, he nearly lost the battle with his churning insides. Clutching his belly, Jim reviewed the events in the van, desperately trying to understand. Papa's chest opening like a refrigerator, fingers lovingly tending the lumpy, dangling shapes inside . . .

His mind whirled, a tide of emotion surging up behind his eyeballs like hot oil. Who the hell could he call about something like this? Police? The Health Department? Agents Scully and Mulder?

The late honorable Adrian Tindle had known, had even tried to warn him. "Not *of* here," he'd said.

Not of here, indeed. God! Jim wiped at his lips. The head and upper body of Papa Sarvoli had seemed a fleshy puppet, moved by the twitching of some grotesque hand inside. And inside were the rows of meaty sacs that would become Sarvoli's rippers. What was he taking in return for them? Jim remembered the wonderful, guilty unburdening every time he'd given in to that consuming urge, the so-familiar, sweet taste of the cooked meat . . .

Suddenly he was certain that, even as he'd been eating part of Papa Sarvoli, it had been feeding on him as well.

"It's you he wants, Jim."

Tindle had known, or guessed—and what had the old man done? Shuddering, Jim knew he'd never have the will for such a thing. He'd never been strong that way . . .

And now he'd seen the real Sarvoli. The overwhelming impression, besides shock, had been a deep, awful otherness, horrible in intensity. Whatever hellish abyss had spawned Sarvoli—the alien blackness of space, some pestilent dimensional wormhole—it was here now, growing fat on misery.

Jim stumbled along, but his footsteps betrayed him; without realizing it, he'd doubled around the block, heading back toward Sarvoli's van. He stopped cold on the sidewalk, cursing fluently. What was the use? He didn't know what the thing calling itself Sarvoli was, and didn't care, didn't care what might be asked in return for what he wanted, either. Giving up all pretenses,

177

he ran, tripping over himself in the hurry to get back there and get a ripper no matter what he had to do . . .

His feet pounding concrete, Jim rounded the corner. The smell of hot oil hit his nostrils and he ran faster, thankful tears streaming down his face. He saw the back of the van ahead, its rear doors gaping in welcome, like an open mouth . . .

Papa would be waiting for him.

THE COMPROMISE

RICK SABIAN

We can get distracted sometimes. You gotta go to college so you can get a good job, make money, rise in your chosen profession, get to the top, put something away for retirement, and along the way make some friends, see some movies, take some trips, have some laughs.

Oh, sure, that's all well and good, but when it comes down to it, there's always that tick tick tick of the biological clock—not just for women, but for men as well.

You're gonna die someday, says that clock. Never know when the buzzer's going off. Tick tick BONG and then you're in a box or an urn and there's only one question that matters then, to every cell of your body until it runs out of oxygen and other nutrients and follows the organism into death: Did we reproduce our genes or not?

Because if the answer's no, then no matter what other successes or joys or pleasures we might have had, as far as the cells *of our body are concerned, it was all a big long waste of time. It's about babies, friend. Not sex, not money, not convivial company or fame that lives on in legends. Having at least one kid that looks like you carrying on your genes into another generation. You may not think that's what matters most to you, but if you took an opinion poll of some reasonable sample of the microscopic nuclei of the cells that make up your big old body, you'd get 99 percent telling you, "Make a copy now, while it's not too late!"*

A 20-YEAR PEACE. Who could have guessed? A place to live without fear. It's like a child's daydream. I walk the streets totally at ease. Open windows no longer hide snipers. An unattended suitcase causes me no concern. Tanks that once roamed the cities are now in museums. While it took a few years to rebuild our cities from a decade of strife, it took far longer to repair the fabric of our society. It's one thing to fight an external enemy, but quite another to pick up a rifle and fight your neighbor. Battle lines tore their way through bloodlines. Those kinds of loyalties meant nothing. This was a war of ideologies. Worldviews that had set us apart ended up tearing us apart. But we learned there could be no victor in a war of ideas. You can't kill an idea, just the people who believe in them. And killing an entire population based only on their opinions seemed more hopeless and heartless as time went on. Finally we reached the Great Compromise of 2115 and the fighting stopped.

Right now my wife, Karen, is giving birth to our first child. She chose to give birth naturally, so she's in a lot of pain.

"Stan, you're not holding my hand!" she screams at me.

I grab her hand. "I'm sorry. Keep pushing. The doctor said the baby has turned."

"Oh, this hurts!"

There is a screen at the end of the bed blocking our view of the doctor.

"All right, Karen, you're doing great. The head is almost out," the doctor's silhouette says.

"Keep pushing!" says an unseen nurse.

"I am!" screams Karen.

Karen keeps taking her deep breaths. I'm beyond excited. Our little boy is almost here.

"Karen, the head is out. We need one more big push," says the doctor.

"This is it, honey." I squeeze her hand. She smiles for a brief second and then goes back to pushing. She groans and then it's all over.

"We've got him," says the doctor.

We both smile as we hear him cry for the first time. I wish we could see him.

"Good luck to both of you. We'll take him now," says the doctor as he escorts the baby out of the room.

We're never supposed to see that baby again. Karen begins to sob hysterically.

"He's gone forever . . . and I didn't even get to look at him."

"I know. I know. I know. Just remember our little secret."

"But I want him back now!"

The nurse cleaning the bed is becoming impatient. "Karen, they take everyone's baby. You can pick out a new baby tomorrow."

I brush my fingers through her hair to calm her. We knew this was coming.

Part One of the Great Compromise mandates that all newborns are taken from their birth parents and reassigned to people of a different nationality or geographic location. A baby born here could be raised in Africa, or a baby born in India could be raised here. This was done to try and eliminate racial prejudice and intolerance.

It worked. We raised an entire generation devoid of hate. Why should you hate your neighbor or another country? They could be your brother, sister, mother or father. Hate didn't make sense anymore. Also, the new generation became free thinkers not constrained to believe only what their parents told them. It worked out great for everyone. Everyone but me. I want to keep my own child and no perfect world will stop me.

It's now the next day. Intent on my goal, I ride up an escalator. It's been a while since I've been above ground. My eyes strain at the blistering sun. After the war, people yearned for a simpler time, when you could see the horizon even in a crowded city. So every building was rebuilt underground, leaving nothing but parks and preserves topside. The young hardly come up here. They love the endless miles of strip malls and nightclubs underground. They call the older people who visit here "surface dwellers."

There is one exception to the underground rule. It is the building that is now in front of me. The Human League building is a glorious 60-story pyramid made of glass and steel. The upper five floors are illuminated ruby red. Smoke is vented out the top and those blood colored lights give the fumes a red hue. People hustle by me, but they still can't resist the urge to look up and admire it. The Human League was mandated by the Great

Compromise. It is a vast baby repository. Today we are to select a new child. Or so everyone thinks.

"Hey honey, I'm over here!"

I hear Karen's voice, but can't find her. Everyone looks the same wearing sunglasses. I finally catch sight of her across the fairway. She is still quite beautiful. Her rusty brown hair cascades to her shoulders. A fitness fanatic, she almost looks the same as she did before her pregnancy.

"I was worried you were going to be late," she says adjusting her sunglasses.

I grab her close and give her a reassuring kiss. "Are you nervous?"

"Of course I am. All this lying and you talking with the Underground. On top of that, I'm scared to death we won't get little Ian back."

"We will, just leave it all to Bill."

"I don't know."

"I've known Bill since we were kids. Trust me. Let's go in."

We hold each other's hand. Her hand on mine clenches like a vise. We head in through the archway. It opens into a huge room that must be several blocks across and five stories high. The place is swarming with people. I can hear whizzing machinery and people chattering. We take a number and have a seat. A recorded voice says, "Welcome to the Human League; bringing you peace for 20 years." Nearby a shady looking man with a chiseled mustache is walking out a couple with a new baby. The couple stares at the baby with new eyes.

"You made a fine choice," the man says. "Are you sure I can't help you pick out two or three more. We have a two-for-one special today."

The couple shake their heads no.

"I'm just kidding. You know our babies are always free. Come back soon," he says as he checks his hand-held computer. "Number 23," he says over the loud-speaker.

"That's us," says my wife.

We both get up and stride over to him. It's Bill.

"Hello fine folks, I'm Wild Bill Jackson," he says sticking out his hand.

I take his outstretched hand. "I'm Stan and this is my wife Karen."

He gives us a focused look and whispers, "No you're not, you're Eduardo and Carmen from Portugal. Here, take this." He hands a small package to me. I open it and find two government-issued ID cards from the Iberian Sector. It looks like we're from Old Portugal.

Bill bends over and says, "Now, Ian was shipped back here from overseas today. If you just go through the motions with me, and look like you're browsing through different children, I'll get him." Bill stands back up and says loudly, "So, what can I do for you today?"

"Play along," I say to Karen.

"Well . . . we're looking for a child, not sure if we want a boy or a girl," Karen says.

"Well, I'll send you home with one today. I guarantee it. We've got over 100,000 babies at our disposal. Black, white, yellow or green, we've got whatever you need."

"Can you show us some?" I ask.

"Sure, we got some fresh ones in today, too. All I need are your IDs to see what children you're eligible for."

We hand him our fake IDs and he swipes them in the computer. "OK, how about girls with brown hair?"

184

A huge machine noise erupts from all around. I can hear mechanical rumblings. Steel against steel. Then from above, like an amusement park ride, 30 arms descend holding 30 pods. We move in on one. The small metal pod opens to reveal a darling little girl.

"Oh, she's gorgeous," Karen extols.

"She is," I say.

On her pod is a screen saying she's from New Istanbul, what her weight and height are, and the number of days remaining on her reassignment.

"Step back folks. How about seeing some boys with brown eyes?" he says as he types away.

There's a huge metal rumbling as the pods swing back to where they came from and new arms come down.

"It's like a vending machine," I say with some amusement.

The machines were well maintained and efficient, but they served one all-important task: To prevent people from touching and holding children and developing a dangerous emotional attachment.

"After you look at these, we can see some genetically engineered children."

"I think we want to go natural. Do you have any suggestions?" I ask.

"Well in all honesty, I know there's not a lot of them around these days, but Caucasians come in quite a variety of hair and eye colors," Bill says with a wink.

Bill works his computer, which is giving him a hard time.

"I'm sorry, the computers have been acting up all week."

He types and types. Finally the computer responds. "There we go. It's up and running again."

We spend hours looking at different babies. We have so many to choose from because Part Two of the Great Compromise made abortion illegal, and gave those babies a fair chance at being adopted. It gave them seven days, and then . . .

"Here comes Ian, Stan," Karen says with excitement.

The pod comes down from above. It opens up and there he is. Our hearts melt.

"So this is the one you want?" says Bill.

Karen is holding the little guy. He cries as she plays with him. She pats him on the back. "Oh, I love him."

"He's got your eyes," I say.

"And your mouth," she says sniffing and smiling. "Mommy has you, Ian. You're all mine. You always will be." Karen is crying again.

It gave me such a good feeling inside. The feeling of being a father . . . knowing that I will be a true father.

"Well, if you're not sure who you want, remember he's only got six days left on his reassignment."

"No, we're taking him now."

"All right, let's fill out the necessary paperwork."

Within an hour we were home with the love of our life. We don't want to put Ian down even though he's sleeping. We're so full of contentment. That bundle of joy makes all the difference in the world. The three of us cuddle in our bed. I can't believe what we've achieved. We beat the system.

IT'S A WEIRD feeling, living your life with a secret so big you can't tell anyone. It doesn't bother me though. I race home from work early every night to see him. This week has forever changed us.

"Karen, how's the baby?" I ask coming in the front door.
"Oh, he's fine."

"Let me feed him tonight."

"That's OK with me. He's so attached to both of us."

"It's hard to imagine life without the little guy, isn't it?"
I ask, picking him up. I start to feed Ian when Bill calls.

"Stan, this is Bill."

"Hey Bill, how are you?"

"Not good, you've got to hurry, we've got a major
problem."

"What is it?"

"Remember how we were having computer problems
when you were here?"

"Yeah," I say, somewhat perplexed.

"Well, it caused some pod numbers to be switched . . ."

"What are you saying?"

"You don't have Ian. He's still here."

"Oh my God. You've got to be wrong. Are you sure?"

"Dead sure."

Karen looks at me. I'm horrified. I give the baby to
Karen.

"What is it, honey?" she asks.

I put my hand up to silence her.

"Bill, it's been almost a week since then. How long
does Ian have until his reassignment time is up?"

"He's got an hour at most."

"But I'm an half hour away."

"Hurry, you've got to get here and switch babies before
then."

"Switch? Oh, Lord."

"Leave now!"

"I'm leaving."

I turn to Karen, panicked.

"We don't have Ian. He's still at the Human League."

"What!"

"I've got an hour, maybe less, to get there and switch *this* Ian for our real son."

"You're not taking away my baby!"

"But he's not our baby."

"Oh, yes he is. He was our baby yesterday."

"But the real Ian is *there* waiting for us."

"I don't care."

"Listen, be rational. Ian's reassignment time is almost up, I have to go."

I head for the crib. Karen gets in front of me.

"They've already taken one baby away from me."

I put my hand on her shoulders. "And that's who I'm going to get back."

I grab the baby and put him in a papoose on my back.

"Don't do this to me."

"I have to. Goodbye."

I head out the door trying to ignore Karen's cries. My chest is tightening. I know I'm right. I hop on a transit and take off.

I arrive at the Human League at closing time. There's almost no one here. Bob sees me and we both run to a computer terminal.

"We're almost out of time. I'll bring him down now," says Bill. The machinery starts working. "It says he's got 20 seconds left."

"Well, get him!"

I can hear the metal rumblings, but still no pod.

"Ten seconds."

Finally, a pod starts to descend.

"Six seconds."

The pod reaches head height. I can almost see in.

"Four, three . . ."

The pod stops.

"Two, one . . ."

The pod's plastic shield springs open.

"Grab him!" yells Bill.

The lid slams shut in front of me. I'm too late. The pod is lifted up into the vast machinery.

"Bring him back!" I yell to Bill.

"I can't."

"Then let's go get him."

"OK, I'm trying to locate him."

My God, what has happened? My baby swiped from my grip. Damn Part Two of the Great Compromise. It all seemed so fair. It settled the abortion debate, giving every baby a fair chance of being adopted. Given seven days and then . . .

Bill yells, "I've located him. He's on his way to euthanasia."

I stay focused. "Can we stop the program?"

"I can't turn those machines off without an act of Congress. But, we can go up and try to get to him first."

"Dammit, let's go!"

Bill and I leap across the lobby. We get into an elevator. It pivots to climb the sharp angle of the pyramid and it climbs too slowly. I can't believe this is happening. I can't believe we let this happen. Was the Great Compromise for peace actually worse than the war it stopped? Like primitive people throwing virgins into volcanoes to please the gods and preserve their society, we too have paid a price for peace. But at what cost?

The elevator announces the 50th floor.

"He'll be on his way up here. Look for pod C4942," says Bill.

I scan the room. It looks like a packaging plant, everything moving with mechanical precision. The pods flow in a daisy chain from the floor, circle the room, and head up through a hole in the ceiling. I read all the pod numbers. J5PNQ, LNM58, U8473. Nothing familiar. I sprint to the far side of the room and then I see it. C4942! Way out of arms reach, he's headed up and out the room.

"There's only one level left, let's go."

We jump back in the elevator. It crawls along. There has to be a quicker way. The elevator announces the 53rd floor. We run out and into a room of robotic arms. As each pod goes by, an arm loads a needle through a small hole in the pod then loads another needle for the next.

"Where is he?" I ask.

"Here he comes."

"Well, stop the machines!"

"I told you I can't. Let's get him out."

The pod sweeps across the room quickly. We try prying open the lid.

"It won't open," I scream over the noise.

"It's sealed. Look for something to break it with."

I scour the room. The pod keeps getting closer to the robotic arm. I see a computer screen sitting on a table. It has a sharp edge. I try ripping it loose. It only slightly budges. I look over; the pod is almost there. I pull with all my might and it comes off clean.

"Hurry over here."

I lift the screen and take a swing at it. Nothing. Again I smash at it. Nothing. The robotic arm brings the needle to his pod. I panic. "It won't open!"

"Hit the arm," Bill shouts as he points.

The needle approaches Ian's pod. I swing and break the needle right off the arm. The needle hits the ground. The robotic arm continues its programmed motion and inserts nothing into the pod.

"Thank God. Oh, thank God," I say.

"Don't thank God yet. He's on his way to the incinerator."

Ian's pod is rising up and out of the room.

"What level do we go to next?"

"The elevator doesn't go any higher. I'm sorry."

"No! I won't accept that."

I give Bill the baby off my back, grab the screen and hop on top of one of the pods. I ride it up and out of the room.

"Be careful," yells Bill.

I climb from pod to pod trying to reach Ian. I'm about 20 feet above the ground. I watch each step. He's around the corner; I can't get to him unless I jump. I try to time it just right. One, two, three. I lurch through the air. I hit the top of his pod, but I can't find a grip. I slide over the side and catch a one-handed grip on the track. My feet dangle above the two-story drop. The room I'm in is dark, but I can feel the heat. I see the incinerator. I still hold the screen in my right hand. So, I raise it up and place it on the pod's track, then use both hands to pull my legs back up on top. I look inside his pod and see Ian with a blissful smile, unaware of the danger. He has seconds left. I search for a crack in the seal and find it. I take the screen and use it to lever the lid open. It won't give. We're almost to the incinerator. I push harder and it finally gives. I lift open the lid and grab Ian out. He's happy to see me. I hear a click from inside the pod. All of the machinery and pods around me grind to a halt. The sudden silence strikes me funny.

Then an alarm starts.

"Hey, Stan!" Bill's voice comes in from below. He's in what must be a maintenance vehicle. It's raising up a small platform towards me. He has the assigned baby with him. "You've got to switch the babies."

"Put him in the pod?"

"Yeah, the computer knows there's no baby."

I hand Ian to Bill and he gives me the other baby. I stare at him, the child I used to call my son. He gurgles, thinking we're playing. I have no time left to think. I put him in the pod and shut the lid. The machines start back up and the alarm stops. I take one last look and leap onto the platform. I land with sure footing. We start to descend and I feel all my fear wash away. I have Ian and nothing is going to take him away from me again.

I reach outside and the sun is setting. The landscape is flat except for being dotted with dozens of pyramids. Each of their tops is illuminated red and venting smoke. At this time of night they look like volcanoes. I come home and find Karen sitting in her chair. She stares blankly.

"Honey, may I present to you, the real Ian, our son."

She says nothing.

"Here, hold him," I say as I put him on her lap.

She looks comatose. She finally looks down at him, but says nothing. Just give her time to get over the shock. She'll thank me. I know she will.

I have a child of my own and a safe place to raise him. We did it. We beat the system—

With a compromise.

WHO LIVED IN A SHOE

Andrew Rey

Having done my share of house- and apartment-hunting in my life, this story delighted me from beginning to end. I'm old enough, too, that I have to admit the first house offered here seems more than a little attractive to me. I think I could get used to shree-gleep. And as for needing land, well, land means mowing, planting, weeding, watering, and still watching mold or tent flies or some other natural abomination come and uglify it all.

As for the house itself, the one we're currently living in was built on a swamp. Basically, we have to bail all the time just to keep the thing afloat. Noah and his ark had nothing on us. As for the would-be homeowners in this story—hey, I've been there, I've done that; I feel their pain. Is there really such a thing as a dream house? And if there is, whose dream is it?

As THE TWO aliens walked in, Geebert stood up and crossed his eyestalks in the universal sign of friendliness. "Full salutations," he said. "Surmise you seek a house?"

Geebert had read about such creatures, but actually seeing them was a bit disconcerting. They were fatty and very hairy, with two arms, two legs and inserted eyes. The smaller one had long hair curled up behind the head and two blobs of fat between the arms. The larger one had short hair and a huge blob of fat in the middle.

He shook himself to keep his color from changing. He was a professional, and, after all, the money was still gooey.

The couple glanced at each other and Geebert sensed confusion. He crossed his eyestalks further. "Forgive if make misstep. Just learned Earth language. Concepts and syntax greatly difficult. So, at this millisecond, how may help?"

"Uh, hello," the fat-in-the-middle one said, "I'm David Parkston and this is my wife, Winona. We recently arrived as part of the first Earth delegation to the Planetary Federation. However, we discovered there was a slight mix-up."

The fat-on-top one snorted. "Sure, mix-up. The government promised that they'd build us a house, but *nooooo*. 'Prices are too high; we don't have the budget; la-de-dah-de-dah.' So we're stuck living in the embassy lobby until we can find some old shack."

Geebert wrapped his hind tentacles around his head, the universal sign of resignation. "After all, many come to Fl'glor to make treaties. So many, prices go very high. That is why do so much business, for many different species. Find house for you, you will see."

"We are counting on your help," Fat-in-middle said. "Unfortunately, we have only about five million credits to work with."

"You could buy a country for that back on Earth," Fat-on-top muttered.

"That comes out to about twelve thousand *J'par*," Fat-in-middle finished.

Geebert's eyestalks sagged. "Not good, not good. Not much for so little. But you in luck. Today have place for you. Can sell to you for only half of that. Will save you much."

Fat-in-middle's eyes grew large. "Really? We were so worried that we would not find anything."

"Where is it?" Fat-on-top asked.

"In next room," Geebert said. "Get for you. Wait one micro-year."

The couple looked at each other as Geebert swirled through a hole in the wall. In a moment he was back, rolling two large spheres before him. They were about two meters in diameter, with a rough brown surface.

"Make deal with *Sous-sous*, only days ago. Have a few left. Will sell for little. Come, try." He snaked a tentacle into a hole and popped a sphere apart. The inside was lined with a thick, black goo that slowly oozed out.

The Earth-creatures looked at each other again, but for a longer time. "That's not quite what we had in mind," Fat-in-middle said.

"But it has many good things," Geebert said, waving his tentacles. "Take this wherever you go. Sleep wherever you want. When inside, house looks same as surroundings, so pesky sales-creatures won't bother you when sleeping. Easy to clean, and the *shree-gleep* will stay soft and moist for years."

195

"No," Fat-on-top said, her voice low in the universal sound of severe dislike. "We're looking for something with land."

Geebert drooped his tentacles and rolled the spheres back through the hole. "After all, no house is perfect. But start again." He coaxed over his computer. "Ask questions to you. To begin, how large house?"

"About 185 square meters," Fat-in-middle said. "That would be, uh, 213 *n'lap*."

"Good. Amount of land?"

"A quarter of an acre would be fine," Fat-on-top said.

"That'd be about 1165 *n'lap*," Fat-in-middle finished.

"Good, good. Temperature?"

The couple glanced at each other again. "Twenty-two degrees Celsius, on average," the smaller one said.

"Oooh, chilly," Geebert said, punching in the data. "Atmosphere?"

"Ah, oxygen-nitrogen, Earth standard," Fat-in-middle replied.

"Fine. Microorganisms?" When they did not answer, Geebert raised his eyestalks. "You know not? Molds, *gloptier*, bacteria, *feezbuts*, such."

"We don't want those," Fat-on-top said shrilly. Geebert found it slightly irritating.

"Hmm. Hard to keep out. Will be difficult. Type of predators?"

The couple's eyes glazed for a moment. "Look, maybe we should describe what we're looking for," Fat-in-middle said.

Geebert shooed away his computer. "Will be fine. So say, what you seek?"

"What we are really looking for," Fat-in-middle said, "is a nice country home, far away from all the hubbub of the city. One with an old rail fence, a shake roof, and a large porch in front so you can sit and watch the suns set. Something with wooden floors, a fireplace, and the feel of a *real* home."

"Of course, it must have all the modern conveniences," Fat-on-top said. "You know, cleaning robots, automatic food preparation units, dust-filters and dirt-repellant fixtures. And we only want the best building materials. You know, a plexisteel frame, lifetime warranty exterior and basement—all those nifty inventions we got from joining the Federation. And it must have a nice location, near the shopping centers and schools and spaceport and, of course, the embassy."

Geebert felt his skin beginning to turn brown.

"It should have a large, old-fashioned kitchen—" Fat-in-middle said.

"That can cook meals in seconds," Fat-on-top completed.

"Maybe three or four bedrooms—"

"And at least three bathrooms—"

"A living room, a family room, and a den—"

"Plus an exercise room, a game room, and a holovision room—"

"A heated swimming pool would be nice—"

"And a sauna and spa—"

"And a large garage for the hovercar—"

"And a large yard for a garden—"

"With, of course, room to grow." Fat-in-middle and Fat-on-top held hands and gazed into each other's eyes.

Geebert watched the four of them nod their heads, then realized he had allowed his eyestalks to drift apart. He quickly brought them back together, and fluttered his tentacles in the universal sign of agreement. "Yes, yes, see what can do. But after all, no house is perfect." He encircled a standard list of his houses. "Go look at some, yes?"

"THIS, FIRST ONE, may be it," Geebert said as they whisked over the city in his luxurious hovercar. "Has plenty of room to grow. Room for bedrooms and bathrooms and game rooms and—whatever other rooms. And has land. Yes, much land."

The car settled in an open field between two large houses, squashing some of the purple *zebat* plants. The couple was gazing about as Geebert came around the hovercar. He waved his tentacles excitedly. "Is beautiful location, is not? Nice area, good neighbors."

"Which one is the house?" Fat-in-middle asked, glancing between the branching structure on his right and the one wavering on his left that would not come into focus.

"Oh, neither one. They too expensive, even if were for sale. No, is here, in front of you." When the couple stared at Geebert, he quickly reached down and pulled up a hatch hidden in the soil. "See, here."

They peered down the dark hole lined with sharp sticks jutting from the wall. "Go on, you climb down. Don't worry, nobody home."

Carefully, Fat-in-middle stepped onto the highest stake and slowly climbed down, Fat-on-top tentatively following. Geebert waited until they reached the bottom and then whirled down after them.

"This is entry room. Very nice, yes?" Geebert turned on a light fixed to his side, showing a dirt room with small holes going off in all directions. "This impress many of your friends, no?"

198

"What are all those holes?" Fat-in-middle asked.

"Ah, they go to other rooms. Previous owners were burrowing creatures. Lived here many years, built a huge home. Admittedly, most holes not as large as these," Geebert said, gesturing at one a meter in diameter, "but can make bigger as you want."

"The walls are nothing but dirt!" Fat-on-top's voice was shrill and loud. Geebert found it oddly annoying.

"Yes, yes. Much land!" Geebert said, waving his tentacles. "Land above, land below, land all around!"

"This isn't what we meant," Fat-in-middle said. "We want to be on top of the land, not in it. We need something airy, not so closed in."

"Oh," Geebert said, checking his list. "Well, maybe next house be it. Much space, good frame, and airy. Yes, very airy."

GEEBERT EYED THE couple as they stood with their heads tilted back. The structure towered above them, over 30 meters high, with intertwined metallic rods supporting the carbon fiber roof at the top.

"Not much land," Geebert said, "but very airy. Yes, much air. Come inside." He slid an egg-shaped disk into a slot, and some of the rods drew in, creating an opening. Geebert pushed the couple through, wondering at their reluctance.

The base of the house was about 10 meters in diameter. Except for platforms interspersed around the edge, the house was completely empty. The roof was a small speck above them.

"See, very nice, very nice," Geebert said, tentacles waving. "Plexisteel all around, lets much air and light in, keep place bright."

"But how do you keep the rain and wind out?" Fat-in-middle asked.

"Oh, is no problem. Roof keeps water off from top. If comes in from side, previous owners just fluffed feathers, had rain drip off. No problem."

"You mean they flew?" Fat-on-top's voice went an octave higher. Geebert decided he definitely did not like it. "But *we* can't fly! Why did you show us this house? How do you expect us to get to those platforms?"

"Oh, is not hard." Geebert spread out his eyestalks to triangulate. "First landing is no more than five *bl'nep*—what is Earth term, seven meters? Can get you ladder for that at cost. No problem."

Fat-in-middle moved directly in front of Geebert. "I don't think we are communicating here," he said. "All we want is a simple house. One story, with walls that keep the wind and rain from our important possessions, like ourselves. A place we can live and grow, comfortably."

"This is not good?" Geebert asked.

"No. Not good." Fat-in-middle's voice seemed to get lower. Geebert wondered how much lower it could go.

"Well, try another." Geebert scanned his list until he suddenly turned pink. "Ah, this is good. Very snug, can grow plenty. Think you like."

"THESE ARE VERY strange walls," Fat-in-middle said, running his hand along a course, gray-blue surface. "What is it?"

"Called *croshnair*," Geebert said, wondering why the couple's eyes did not light up. Geebert decided they must be less informed than most diplomats. "Is from planet Drunnar. Very rare outside of Drunnar. You lucky is available."

"What is this floor?" Fat-on-top said, pulling her foot up. They heard a faint sucking sound.

"*Croshnair*, also," Geebert said. "Whole house is *croshnair*."

"What is that? Some sort of plastic?" Fat-in-middle asked.

Fat-on-top suddenly screamed, grabbing hold of the other's arm. "David, something moved. Over there." She pointed at a corner.

Fat-in-middle cautiously walked over and eyed the corner. "There's nothing here," he said. "And there's no place for anything to go. The walls are solid up and down the whole length—" The wall suddenly leaped out, striking Fat-in-middle's shoe. He jumped back, falling on Geebert.

"Oh, that just the *croshnair*," Geebert said, grabbing hold of Fat-in-middle. "Think it like you."

"Likes me? You mean it's alive?"

"Oh, yes, much so. Whole house alive. Keeps things inside nice and snug." A wall scuttled across the room, attaching its edge to the opposite wall. "Rooms change all time, making new rooms easy. And if you feed house well, it will grow, add more rooms. Much room to grow."

But Fat-on-top was not listening. She stood in front of Fat-in-middle. "I told you we shouldn't have come. I told you we'd be miserable. But no, you had to think of your career, get your promotion, move ahead. Now look what we're reduced to. It's bad enough having to live with aliens—now we have to live *inside* one!"

"Honey, this is only the third place he's shown us. I'm sure they'll get better."

"Get better? They've only gotten worse!" Fat-on-top turned to Geebert. "Haven't you shown us your best places?"

"Oh, yes, have only the best. Show best for amount of *J'par.*"

"See! He's already shown us the best for our price range. It won't get any better than this! I can't take this, David. I can't take it!"

"You not like this place, even with *croshnair*?" Geebert asked.

"No, we don't," Fat-in-middle said, his words short and crisp. "What we want is a nice, normal Earth-type house. One that isn't in the dirt, one that isn't in the air, and one that isn't moving all around us."

"With trees and fence and porch?" Geebert asked.

"Yes, with all that. *Do you have a house like that?*"

"Well, not exactly," Geebert said, scanning his list. "Earth-creatures live very strange way. But have something like that, am sure. Ah, maybe this." He threw up his tentacles in the universal sign of discovery. "This think you like. Come, come, you see."

"I want to go home," Fat-on-top said.

"Let's just look at one more place, OK?" Fat-in-middle said.

"I want to go home."

GEEBERT WATCHED AS the Earth-creatures admired the house. Thick vegetation surrounded the building, an explosion of reds and greens and dark blues. The roof, made from red granite, spiraled down to windowless walls. A rock platform lay before the small front door.

"At least we're getting closer," Fat-in-middle said. Fat-on-top just whimpered.

"Oh, is great place," Geebert said, gently pushing them forward with his tentacles. "Has front porch, and place for hovercar, yes, and much land for garden. Has no

Earth trees, but you plant. Best of all, you always have place to sit."

Geebert threw open the front door to reveal steps leading down into a pool of yellowish jell.

"See, it has *risfulta*, the latest from the planet Tosfolt," Geebert said proudly. "Not need a thing to sit on, or sleep on, or put things on. Keeps out wind, rain, even microorganisms. Keeps house so, so clean! And house very quiet. Hear nothing when in *risfulta*."

"You mean, you go into that—stuff?" Fat-on-top said, very quietly.

"Yes, yes, it surrounds you."

"But how do you breathe?" Fat-in-middle asked.

"Breathe *risfulta*. Is very good. Here, show you." Geebert swirled forward and jumped into the jell. He sank quickly, the *risfulta* oozing over him. He opened wide his breathing hole on top of his body and sucked in a large glob. Turning red to show his pleasure, he turned back to the couple.

But the Earth-creatures had not followed him in. He stuck his eyestalks through the surface and looked for them. Fat-on-top was beating Fat-in-middle's chest with her hands and apparently screaming, although Geebert could not hear because the *risfulta* had filled his aural cavities. Geebert stood puzzled for a moment, until he realized that it must be some sort of mating ritual. He turned even redder. The Earth-creatures must like the place so much they wanted to procreate immediately. Geebert swirled up from the jell and expelled the goop from his cavities.

But when he could hear again, Fat-in-middle's voice had gone impossibly low. "I'm sorry, but this is definitely not the place," he said to Geebert. "Please take us back to your office now."

Geebert was perplexed. He turned to Fat-on-top, but she was leaning over a *f'tiv* plant, expelling fluids from her eyes and mouth, which the plant greedily snatched. Geebert turned back to Fat-in-middle. "Not like house?"

"No, we do not. I think we need to find someone who understands our needs better. I don't think we can work with you any longer. Take us back to the office. Now."

Geebert felt himself turning orange in panic. He glanced at his list, then spoke quickly. "Please, please, one more place. Think this fits all your needs. Did not want to show it to you before, because it cost little more than you want to spend. But if so—" he wanted to say "picky," but thought it would be impolite, "—exacting, this may be only place for you."

"No, we've had more than enough for today," Fat-in-middle said.

"Please, please, just one more. Please?"

Fat-in-middle turned to Fat-on-top, who slowly nodded her head. "All right, we'll take a quick look at it, and then take us back," Fat-in-middle said.

"Very good, very good," Geebert said, hustling them to the hovercar. "You like this one. Yes, you like."

"OH, DAVID, IT'S so beautiful," Fat-on-top said.

Geebert turned crimson. He watched the Earth-creatures holding each other around the middle, heads close, gazing at the house. Their voices had softened, the universal sign of contentment.

"I know, Winona," Fat-in-middle said. "It's so perfect. I never expected to find something so rustic on an alien planet. Right down to the shake shingles and the oak tree!"

"And yet it looks so modern," Fat-on-top said. "Why, the outside actually *gleams*."

"It's incredible how large it is. I'd almost believe it is bigger on the inside than on the outside."

"But can we afford it?" Fat-on-top said, her voice rising a bit.

Fat-in-middle sighed. "It'll be tough, but if we sell everything we have, get loans from both our parents, and don't eat much for a few years, I think we can squeeze by. But it'd be worth it, wouldn't it?" They held each other tighter, their bodies becoming lax like boiled *bligg* worms.

Fat-on-top turned to Geebert. "Can we just wander inside alone for a moment?"

"Please, please, of course. Take time. Enjoy new home. Write up agreement while you inside."

"Thanks," Fat-in-middle said. Together they strolled up the rough dirt pathway lined with dead plants. Fat-in-middle opened the thatched door, a piece of ceiling just missing his head. They entered together, hands intertwined, black dust covering their clothing.

Geebert watched them through the cracks and holes in the walls. He had not been sure that the house would work on them. Many species were not affected by the psychic projections of the *snaroff*, but apparently Earth-creatures were.

For a moment, Geebert worried about the *snaroff's* cage. It was in great disrepair, and if some part finally gave way, the *snaroff* would send out dozens of tendrils that would entwine the Earth-creatures and eventually turn them into plant food.

But that was to be expected. Why else would the *snaroff* project images of appealing environments if not to entice prey?

Geebert quickly let the thoughts pass from his mind as he drew up the contract. The couple was young and active; they had an excellent chance of escaping. And besides, they could not have asked for a better place.

After all, no house is perfect.

THE PRIZE

DAVID BARR KIRTLEY

You're not really supposed to win two prizes in the same contest. You write two stories, one of them's got to be better than the other, and the better one wins, and the other one gets published somewhere else. Your website maybe, or a magazine.

But the author of "They Go Bump" has pulled off two stories, both of them so full of surprises, puzzles, and cool ideas, that I dare you to do what we judges couldn't do: Pick one that's more worthy of publication than the other. More than that I dare not say, because any comment I make about this tale will give something away.

Heck, I've already blown it just by telling you that there might be something that could be given away.

JULIAN SERRATO. GREAT criminal mastermind of the 21st century. They wanted him caught, badly. They wanted me to catch him.

I had a plan.

The girl at the hospital desk was pretty and shy. She stared at the sign-in sheet. Her lashes were long. I showed her my badge; I spoke gently. "I'm Agent Child." I nodded at my partner. "This is Agent Bonner."

Bonner was big, tough, and uneasy. He said abruptly, "We're here to see Rebecca Courington."

"I'll get the doctor," the girl said.

Rebecca Courington lay still in her bed, wrapped up all in white. Her blond hair was carefully arranged. A needle was taped to her forearm, connected by a tube to an IV drip. She was strikingly beautiful. She slept.

The doctor checked her vitals.

"Her brain," Bonner said, "how much damage?"

"She won't wake up," the doctor said, unnecessarily. "She's been here three years already."

"Four," Bonner said.

The doctor didn't question it.

I asked, "How much of her personality is still there? How much memory?"

"Hard to say." The doctor frowned. "Quite a bit, I would think. The damage is localized. She won't wake up, like I said, but . . ."

Bonner and I exchanged glances.

"We'd like a few moments alone," I said.

The doctor closed the door behind him.

Bonner sighed. "What do you think?"

"I think we should do it." I thought about the timetable—three months to grow her a new body. About twice that long to imprint what was left of the old brain onto the developing one, and the cost—substantial, but not prohibitive. Not compared to what had already been spent on the case.

Bonner watched her. "You ever met one of them? After they came back?"

"Once," I said. "Senator Snow."

"What's he like?"

"Like a dream of himself," I said, "like a half-forgotten memory—some pieces missing, some details confused, but true to his essence."

Bonner shifted uncomfortably. I could see the reluctance line his face. He didn't like the thought of *any* version of Rebecca Courington up and walking. That was understandable. He had put her here in the first place, after all. Before he was my partner, before I became an agent.

His voice was like gravel. "I just think, of all the people to bring back, of all the people, it's this stupid bitch that gets a new life. What did she do to deserve this? What makes her special?"

"There must be something about her," I said, "to make Julian Serrato love her."

THEY REMADE Rebecca Courington, remade her even lovelier than before. She sat in a chair in the interrogation room with her arms folded and she said, "I died. You copied me. Why?"

"To help us find Julian Serrato," I said.

She laughed. "Find him? I don't know where he is. I don't even know what he looks like anymore. He changes his face, his voice, his fingertips. You know that."

"And you know him," I countered. "His personality, his mannerisms. He can't change who he is. You might recognize him."

She leaned back in her chair and stared into the big mirror on the wall. "Where's the other agent? The one who shot me?"

Beyond the mirror, I imagined I saw Bonner flinch.

"That's not important," I said.

"It is important." She glared. "To me. Why should I help you?"

I met her gaze. "Giving you a second life was very expensive. You can't pay for it, but the government will forgive your debt if Julian Serrato is apprehended."

"A second life." She chuckled. She ran her fingers down her sternum. She was quiet for a long time. When she spoke, her voice was toneless and measured. "I woke this morning for the first time. My breasts were large, and tan. No freckles."

She fixed me with her terribly gorgeous eyes. "Don't give me this body and pretend you care what I know."

"Julian Serrato cares what you know," I said. "He'll kill you to keep you from talking."

Courington laughed. "No he won't. You've seen to that. You've made me a dream—*his* dream, a prize that only you can give him. He won't kill me. He'll try to take me away from you, without getting caught."

I frowned.

"You don't think he can do it," she said simply. "I think he can."

Later, I sat with Bonner in the dark observation room, watching her.

Bonner grumbled, "I don't like it. She's too smart. She knows something. Something she's not telling us."

"Who cares what she knows?" I said, "Or thinks she knows? Her cooperation is moot. We'll get Serrato either way."

WE FILLED HER insides with our machines—machines that control, machines that surveil, machines that kill. We put death inside her.

Julian Serrato would know that, of course. It didn't matter. It didn't matter what he knew. Acting on what he *knew,* he wouldn't get within a thousand miles of our new Rebecca Courington.

He wouldn't act on what he knew. He'd act on what he felt.

He could kidnap her away from us, no doubt. But then he was trapped with her. He couldn't abandon her, or destroy her, because of love. But he couldn't defuse her either—our pretty, perfect, time bomb. He might delude himself that it was possible. It wasn't.

We flew to Atlanta, to the clinic of the eminently respected doctor, Felix Martindale. We waited in his private office. Bonner eyed the doctor's framed degrees with disdain. Martindale came in, closed the door behind him.

"Can I help you?" he asked.

"Your government needs you," I said.

Bonner showed him a picture of Rebecca Courington.

"This woman may be brought to you," I said. "She'll be implanted with a standard array of government drones. You'll be asked to remove them."

Martindale paled. "Why me?"

Bonner said, "There aren't a lot of people with the skills to do it. You're one of them."

"And you're trusted," I said. "You've done it before."

Martindale began to deny it.

"Listen," Bonner ordered, cutting him off. "This is important."

I waited for Martindale's full attention. "In addition to the standard drones, she'll be carrying a new system. It's almost undetectable. You may not even notice it. You won't remove it. You won't mention it anyone."

Martindale's voice was a hoarse whisper. "They'll kill me."

"They won't know," Bonner said. "You *might* notice these new drones. No one else will."

Martindale shook his head firmly. "I can't risk it."

"You don't have a choice," I said sadly. I turned toward the door.

A team of men in blue surgical gear filed slowly into the office. One of them opened a briefcase, revealing the shiny, metallic housing mechanism for a control drone—a device that would burrow into the base of Dr. Martindale's brain.

Martindale eyed it anxiously. "Wait," he panted. "Wait. That isn't necessary. I can cooperate. I'll do exactly what you want."

Bonner nodded at the men. They crowded toward Martindale.

"Yes," Bonner said. "You will."

I GOT A CALL in the night. Six agents were dead. Rebecca Courington had been taken.

I arrived just before dawn. The command center was dark. Computer monitors cast a bluish glare over all the shadowy figures gathered there.

"Where is she?" I said.

Bonner sipped his coffee. He gestured to one of the monitors. "In the air, west of Chicago. Private jet. They switch planes every hour or so, change course, so we don't have time to organize an assault."

I nodded. "And the drones?"

"Still operating, all of them. Probably not for long, though. Looks like they're going to bring the doctor to her."

"Martindale?"

"He's left Atlanta, moving west."

I took a deep breath. "Is Serrato there with her?"

Bonner nodded at a second monitor. We had placed a surveillance drone behind Rebecca Courington's left eyeball. We saw what she saw.

We saw the plush interior of a private jet. We saw a man appear—a tall, powerful man with dark, short-cropped hair and a fabulously expensive purple suit.

We heard Courington say, "Julian."

The man inclined his head graciously.

I studied him. "That's what he looks like. Julian Serrato."

"He's toying with us," Bonner said. "He knows we're watching. He'll change everything tomorrow—his face, his voice."

"Tomorrow," I echoed. "He won't get a chance. We'll have him."

Rebecca Courington was anxious. "Julian, it's a trap. This whole thing. You have to get away from here. You have to get away from *me*."

Serrato smiled broadly, smugly. "Relax, Rebecca. It's taken care of. Have a cigarette."

He offered her a cigarette and she took it. He unbuttoned his sleeve. Two flaps of skin on his left wrist pulled apart. A hinged, telescoping metal arm emerged, carrying a cigarette lighter, which leapt into his grip.

Serrato smiled. "Light?"

I turned to Bonner. "Implants. It's expected, but make a note of it."

"He's probably got weapons like that, too," Bonner said.

Serrato lit Courington's cigarette. She took a drag. The lighter fell away, disappeared back into Serrato's arm.

He placed his hand on her shoulder. "I know someone who can help you. He can get rid of the horrible things they put inside you. There's nothing they can do about it. You'll be safe."

Serrato grinned. "*We'll* be safe. Together."

WE LOST VISUALS first, then sound. The monitors went dark, one by one, as Martindale moved slowly through Rebecca Courington's body, surgically extracting our drones. He removed the primary locator and termination drones. Those were decoys.

We held our breath.

He didn't touch the secret drones. We had two of them: a locator drone, to track her movements, and a termination drone, to kill Julian Serrato—if it came to that.

I knew it would.

Even after the surgery was done, Serrato kept switching planes every few hours. Finally, certain he was safe, he flew Rebecca Courington to Seattle, to a penthouse at the Hilton.

"Romantic," Bonner grumbled

"We've got him," I said.

We flew to Seattle with an assault unit. We surrounded the hotel with agents. We placed our command center in an office building across the street. We put snipers on the roof.

The assault team was split into four groups—one to raid the penthouse, one to watch the lobby, one each to guard the two nearest stairwells.

I looked at my watch. It was a few minutes past midnight. Technicians scurried about the command center.

"Activate the field," I said.

We threw a suppression field over the hotel. In that moment, anyone inside would drop, unconscious.

Bonner turned to the radio. "Go."

We watched the monitors as the assault team entered the building and moved through the lobby, weaving carefully around the sprawled limbs of the dazed guests.

The backup squads took their positions on the stairs. The main group climbed up to the top floor and crept slowly down the long hall toward the wide, white penthouse doors. Serrato's bodyguards had fallen there, comatose, slumped on the floor.

"Open the door," Bonner whispered into the radio.

Explosions ripped through the wall, ripped through paint and plaster, ripped through muscle and bone, ripped through our agents. We blinked and they were dead.

Julian Serrato kicked open the penthouse door and strode into the hallway. He held a pistol in each hand. The pistols were connected to jointed, telescoping, metal arms that had sprung from his shoulders. A transparent plate had popped out of his chest, shielding his face.

"He didn't fall," Bonner said. "Repeat: the suppression field has not neutralized Serrato. Agents down."

Serrato calmly evaluated the corpses. He turned back to the penthouse. One of the pistols folded into his shoulder, and he used his free hand to grab the stupefied figure of Rebecca Courington. He dragged her down the hallway, out of sight.

"Stairway team B," Bonner warned. "He's coming up on your position."

We watched as Serrato leapt into sight, shot an agent through the throat, and vanished back into the hall. Our men stormed after him. He killed one in the doorway there, and another just around the corner. He doubled back, guns screaming. His shots ripped apart the concrete.

The bodies of our agents tumbled down the stairs, breaking apart and dropping into pieces.

"Activate the termination drone," I said.

"No," Bonner argued. "We want him alive."

The technician glanced back and forth between us. Serrato reappeared in the stairway, carrying the limp body of Rebecca Courington.

"Do it," I ordered.

The technician pushed some buttons.

Metal pincers crawled out between Courington's lovely lips, forcing her jaws grotesquely wide apart. A probe leapt from deep inside her throat and buried itself in Serrato's shoulder, electrocuting him.

He screamed, at the electricity, at the betrayal. He screamed as his skin melted into flame. His implants short-circuited. They deployed, a dozen of them—guns, knives, lockpicks. They ripped out through his clothes and through his flesh. Those metal limbs, useless now, stuck crazily in all directions. He carried them like a steel scorpion on his back. He crawled away down the stairs, out of sight.

Bonner gasped. "He's still alive."

I pulled out my pistol. "Come on."

We jogged across the street. The squad in the lobby eyed us with apprehension. "Wait here," I told them. "Make sure he doesn't get out."

We advanced up the far stairwell and made contact with the team there. "Hold this position," I said. They nodded somberly.

Bonner and I paced slowly down the long, long hallway. We burst into the second stairwell, guns ready.

It was empty.

We picked a path through the bodies there. We followed the blood—Serrato's blood—red and dark and

216

smeared, it wound down and down, stair after stair after stair.

We found him down on the sixth floor. He was propped against the wall on his mechanical limbs. Blood dripped off the implants, running down the plaster, forming patterns around him like a web. He was like a spider, resting there, a spider in the middle of his web of blood.

He was almost dead. He struggled to get a cigarette into his mouth. Finally, he managed it. It dangled there, loosely. Bonner and I moved closer, our guns leveled at his face.

Serrato lifted his arm toward us. Something popped out from beneath his left wrist. Bonner yelped and stumbled back.

It was the cigarette lighter. Serrato laughed a mirthless sort of laugh. He lit his cigarette.

Bonner cursed.

Serrato rolled his dark eyes toward us. His tone was flat. "I want to tell you something."

I watched his face through the sights of my pistol.

"I'm not Julian Serrato," he said.

Staggering footsteps sounded above us. I raised my gun. Rebecca Courington spiraled weakly down the stairs toward us, bracing her hands against the wall for support.

"Come down, Ms. Courington," I shouted. "It's over."

The man took a drag from his cigarette, and tossed it away.

Bonner scowled. "What do you mean you're not him?"

"I'm a body double." The man coughed blood onto the collar of his purple suit. "A replacement. I deal with people for him, so he doesn't risk his own safety." The man's

eyes traced over his array of deadly implants, now siz-
zling uselessly. "I'm a man of action, not ideas. I'm no
mastermind."

Rebecca Courington came and stood next to me, leaning against me for support.

"I'm no mastermind," the man repeated, "but I know
when I've been set up. I know what's going on—he
wants you to kill me. He wants you to think he's gone."

Bonner eyed the man warily.

"Protect me." The man's voice weakened. "I can help
you. I can tell you things."

Rebecca Courington was trying to catch my eye. I looked
at her. She glanced at Bonner, and then at my pistol.

"If you're not Serrato," Bonner said slowly, "then
where is he?"

"I don't know." The man groaned. "Nobody knows
that."

Bonner scowled.

Then Courington had a gun.

She took two quick steps toward Bonner and pressed
the pistol against his temple. He had just enough time to
look at her.

"Now we're even," she said, and shot him in the head.
Bonner tumbled bloodily over and bounced on the floor.

The man looked down as his stomach began to tick,
loudly. "Shit," he said.

I grabbed the gun away and dragged Courington down
the stairs. We were in the lobby when the man exploded,
incinerating everything between floors five and seven.

I GAVE MY REPORT. "Serrato must have had some sort of
regulator implanted in his brain, to compensate for a

218

suppression field. And he was wired to explode, if he was killed or captured."

The director nodded solemnly. "It's too bad about Bonner. I'm sorry." He paused. "How did you escape?"

"I was escorting Ms. Courington from the scene." I took a deep breath. "Otherwise, the blast would've gotten me too."

"Yes," the director said. "The blast." He frowned. "And now we can't question Serrato. Can't uncover his crimes. Can't find out what he knew."

"Some things are better left unknown," I said, "sir."

Our surgeons removed the last of the drones from Rebecca Courington's body. I met her in post-op. I said, "I apologize for your ordeal and thank you for your service. The government will forgive you debt. Please, let me drive you to the airport."

She studied me. She nodded. "All right."

We drove ten minutes. She turned to me. "Thanks for giving me the gun. That meant a lot."

"Sure."

We drove a while longer. Her voice turned reproachful. "You took an awful risk, joining them."

"I had a plan," I argued, softly. "It was the only way. The only way I could get you back."

I leaned my head on her shoulder, and sighed. "I need you so much, Rebecca. I need your strength, your ideas. I can't do this without you." I sighed. "I'm nothing without you."

She smiled.

"How long have you known?" I asked her.

"I always knew." She rubbed my arm. "I would always know you," she said, "Julian."

GREAT THEME PRISONS OF THE WORLD

CARL FREDERICK

Our other double winner, Carl Frederick has turned in a story that at first glance seems radically different. The story about Handel's Messiah *and the question of life after death—what does that have to do with this ironic story of finding a punishment that fits the crime?*

I like it when I find a writer who doesn't always write the same story. A lot of storytellers spend their careers demonstrating the old maxim that to a man with only a hammer, everything looks like a nail. Writers sometimes have only a few techniques and tricks they can rely on, and they find ways to use those tricks with every tale they tell.

Carl Frederick is that rarer breed—the storyteller who ranges widely, and only when he's found the tale worth telling does he go in search of the toolkit that will do the job.

ALBERT STARED SULLENLY through the wall of glass onto Boston harbor some 43 floors below. "There's got to be a loophole," he said. "There always is." He refocused his eyes to the reflection in the window: to Sydney, his lawyer. His father's lawyer, actually. Everything was his father's.

Sydney smiled, clasped his hands behind his neck and, accompanied by the expensive squeak of hand-tailored suit against leather-upholstered chair, leaned back from his desk.

"Albert, my boy. Contrary to your father's belief, the job of a lawyer is not to circumvent the law."

Albert turned sharply around, posture erect; he hoped he looked resolute rather than petulant.

Sydney went on, "A lawyer's task is to clarify the law."

"Then clarify a loophole for me. You've certainly clarified enough of them for my Dad."

Sydney laughed. "Not loopholes. Options." He unclasped his hands, leaned forward and re-folded them on the desk in front, exposing manicured fingernails and gold cufflinks. "Securities law is complex. But I'm afraid your case is open and shut: 30 days for using a watchphone in Symphony Hall. It's just your bad luck that the judge was a Mozart lover."

"Goddamnit, Sydney. Dad says you're the best there is, and you couldn't even get me off with a fine?"

"Sorry." Sydney looked down at the open file folder on the desk. "Not a very compromising judge. How did he put it? 'In view of your'—what was the word—'pampered existence, a prison term is indicated.'"

"Fossils like him should be shot." Albert walked to a chair facing the desk and sat. "I don't want to go to jail."

"Not many do."

"Then find me a loophole."

"Can't. But why not make the best of it?" Sydney slapped the folder closed. "Serve your time in a designer prison. You can afford it. Use it to your advantage, perhaps as sort of a vacation. It's what your father would do."

"Possibly, but my Dad's never been in prison."

"Actually, he has been." Sydney stood and ambled casually to the bookshelves that lined the far wall. "The Synapsis affair."

"What?" Albert stared, wide-eyed. "My father? Are you kidding? Tell me."

Sydney rummaged through a row of books. "Damn. It's not here. Must have lent it to someone." He returned to his desk, withdrew a blank file card, and scribbled a note.

Albert leaned in over the desk. "What's this about Dad and prison?"

"A long time ago, but just a second." Sydney folded the card double and passed it to Albert. "Here. Go to a bookstore—there's one right around the corner on Water Street—and buy this title. It's the standard reference."

Albert pocketed the card, unread.

"Thirty days? Why not take 60?" said Sydney. "Multiplier-2 institutions are quite comfortable—like country clubs."

"Except you can't simply leave when you want."

"Then go on a cruise. You can't leave cruises either." Sydney spread his hands expansively. "Prison ships have all the amenities. Expensive, but as I said, you can afford it. You could try a foreign theme ship—*Mutiny on the Bounty*, maybe—fully USPA certified. And cheap. Dollar's strong against the pound right now."

"Yeah, maybe you're right. I've been overworking lately and could really use a vacation." Albert ran his fingers nervously along the crease of his trousers. "But I don't like bookstores."

"It's all right," said Sydney. "A modern, high-tech bookstore: no cobwebs, no spiders."

"You know about the spiders, then?"

Sydney nodded.

"You know," said Albert, softly, in the throes of distant memory. "Starting when I was little, about six, Dad would discipline me by locking me in a pitch-black closet. Once he was so mad at me that he threatened to go out and buy a tarantula, and throw it in the closet with me."

"I should think the closet would have been punishment enough."

Albert smiled. "You'd think so, wouldn't you? But I liked it in the dark. I'd cry and beg to be let out from time to time so he'd think the punishment was effective, but I really didn't want to come out."

"You were a strange kid. Most children would've been terrified of monsters in the dark."

"When I was five, I was afraid of the dark, but then I reasoned I was afraid because monsters could see me when I couldn't see them. After that, I was scared when I was in a lighted room and it was dark outside. Monsters could be out there looking in at me."

"Pretty good logic, considering the premise."

"Finally, I only felt safe when I was in the dark. I couldn't see the monsters and they couldn't see me." Albert shuddered. "But spiders. The thought of being shut in the closet with spiders. I can't help it, but I'm deathly afraid of spiders."

"Can't say I'm overly enamored of them myself."

"Dad hates that. He said no man should be afraid of anything. He keeps asking me to go in for aversion therapy, but I've never been able to work up the courage."

Sydney glanced at his watch. He rolled his chair back, rose, and stretched his shoulder blades. "It's not easy to face your fears."

Albert stood as well. "My Dad wouldn't know about that. He's not afraid of anything. Not spiders. Not prison. Nothing."

"Perhaps, but you might ask him about the Synapsis merger. Tell him I think you should know." Sydney placed an arm around Albert's shoulder, and shepherded him toward the door. "Get the book, and come back tomorrow, same time. We'll see what we can do. And do talk to your father. Yes?"

"Yeah, sure. But it seems that every time I talk to him, he just tries to badger me into joining the firm."

"Why not?" said Sydney, pausing at the door. "In a few years, you could be a partner. It would make him very happy."

"Partner and slave," said Albert as he left the office. "No thanks."

FEELING VAGUELY dissatisfied with his meeting with Sydney, Albert nevertheless sought out the book outlet.

He handed the note to the proprietor.

Albert wilted under the proprietor's humorless gaze. "It's for a friend."

"Of course," said the proprietor. "Paper or e-card?"

"Paper."

"Hard or soft cover?"

"Soft."

Five minutes later, the book was ready. Albert took the volume, warm with the new-book smell of binding glue and freshly deposited ink.

GREAT THEME PRISONS OF THE WORLD:
A USER'S GUIDE TO EDUCATIONAL, NATIONAL,
AND THEMED OPTIONS FOR INCARCERATION

"YOU WERE RIGHT, yesterday," said Albert as he plopped down on the sofa in Sydney's office.

"Of course I was right." Sydney chuckled. "About what, by the way?"

"A vacation. I've decided to spend my time—"

"Do your time."

"—to do my time at the Tower of London. And it's only a 1.5 multiplier. I'll be out in 45 days. I've been reading the book. It sounds great."

"Fine," said Sydney. "It's a good choice. Ever since you were six, you were nuts over King Arthur, knights, swords and that sort of stuff. But I rather thought you'd go back to Harvard. They have a facility: Bard House. You could take a course or two."

"I thought about that, but it would be too embarrassing. Too many people know me there." Albert looked at his watch and jumped up. "Got to go. I'm booked on the Eintracht 11 P.M. flight to London. I'll be at the Tower in three hours."

"Not wasting any time, are you?"

"I want to get it over with before everyone in the world knows I'm a convicted felon."

"You exaggerate. It's just a minor misdemeanor."

"Perhaps, but I'm getting junk e-mail from foreign countries trying to get me to go to their prisons. It certainly makes me feel like a felon. And how the hell did they know I'm—what would you say?—prison bait?"

"Jail bait, although hardly the right idiom. In any case, it's public record. And it's a great deal all around. Our government doesn't have to pay for your incarceration. You pay, and the foreign country gets dollars."

"Yup. I'm convinced," said Albert, turning. "So long, Sydney. See you in a month and a half." He headed for the door.

"Wait. I'll walk you out."

"I spoke to Dad about the Synapsis merger," Albert said, as they ambled to the elevator. "He told me it was a technical violation and he chose to do his time at a prison in the Cayman Islands."

"Is that all he said?"

"Yes—except for telling me how foolish I am for not joining the firm."

They stood in silence, waiting for the elevator.

"There's more, isn't there?" said Albert, as the car arrived.

"Perhaps."

Albert stepped into the elevator. "Well, it'll have to wait till I get back."

He took a cab to Logan International, boarded the London-bound Eintracht, and spent the short flight going through the book—wondering if he might have missed something even more appealing than being a prisoner in the Tower of London.

Some of the Theme Prisons—Ancient Egypt, Imperial Rome, Malibu Country Club—looked charming, but had high multiplication factors. Egypt's factor of three meant a 30-day sentence would take a quarter of a year to serve, and that was too long, no matter how pleasant it might be. And as for the Malibu facility, the price alone was punishment enough.

Albert flipped through the pages for the Slave Ship, Turkish Prison, Boot Camp and Catholic School options. Sure, they had fractional multipliers. You could serve your time fast, but it would be far from fun. Albert smiled and closed his eyes. The Tower was indeed a good choice.

He was awakened by a cultured British voice requesting that passengers buckle their seat belts for the descent into Heathrow.

He was met—discreetly—at Terminal Three and taken by private car to the Tower.

"First-timer, sir?" asked the driver.

"What? Yes," said Albert. Then he added, "Ax murderer, actually."

"Very humorous, sir."

"Tell me," said Albert as they drove off from the terminal. "Is the Tower as good as the guide says?"

The driver laughed. "Yes, guv'nor. It has to be. Everything's so competitive now. Everyone's getting into the act."

Albert grunted an acknowledgment and stared off into the passing English countryside, shimmering and beautiful in July's late afternoon sun.

The driver talked continuously as he drove. "Would you believe," he said, "that even some of our public schools are in the program now. Prisoners—" He chortled softly. "No, we mustn't call them prisoners any more, must we? Clients. Clients are even accepted to Eton. It costs about the same as sending a boy—not as selective though. And you can serve your sentence quickly—0.7 multiplication factor—0.6 if you sign up for

Latin and get good grades; even lower if you're there during the winter. Damp, dreadful damp. Boys don't seem to mind though."

Letting the man talk on, Albert drifted into a sweet anglophilic reverie. The drive passed quickly.

At the Tower, the driver handed Albert off to the Tower Warden who was waiting outside in front of the massive tower doors. The man was dressed in a bright red tunic over close-fitting red breaches, white gloves and ruffled collar, and a black felt hat. He looked as if he'd just stepped out of a tourist guidebook.

"Hope I haven't kept you waiting long out here," said Albert, trying not to stare.

"Not at all. I popped down when the car-tracker indicated your arrival." He laughed, good-naturedly. "We're almost as addicted to technology now as you Americans. Come. Let's retire to my study."

The Warden, thought Albert, was the very image of what a Warden should be: portly, even rotund, pathologically cheerful, and with boundless energy for speech. As for physical energy though, he walked with obvious effort, and took labored breaths between phrases as he talked.

Gawking like a tourist, Albert followed the Warden inside and up through a wonderland of ancient stone and wood to a residence midway up in the Tower.

"Would you care for an aperitif?" The Warden dropped heavily into an overstuffed armchair and motioned for Albert to do the same. "And after your flight, you must be hungry. Would you do me the honor of joining me for dinner? Or would you care to take the tour first?"

"The tour, if you please," said Albert, still standing. "I'm not hungry yet. I've come over on the Eintracht, and ate just a few hours ago."

"I'm afraid we still call it the Concorde over here, even though the beastly Germans bought us out almost a generation ago."

The Warden hauled himself up from the chair. "Off we go, then."

Albert followed as the Warden, punctuating his commentary with sharp asthmatic inhales, set off into the labyrinthine complexities of the Tower of London.

"I think you'll find it . . . quite pleasant here." The Warden turned and motioned Albert to follow close. "You'll be in late-Medieval period clothing of course . . . good clothing. Not as encumbering . . . as mine, I might say." He tugged at the hem of his tunic, coaxing the slack fabric to slide down past the constraint of his belt. "We consider our clients to be . . . of the nobility. Cells off a common area. About half of the people . . . you'll meet there will be . . . your fellow inmates. The others are actors . . . interns. Not that acting is a criminal offense." The Warden gave a ponderous laugh. "They're paid. It's part of the atmosphere."

Just hearing the Warden talk gave Albert pleasure. It was delightfully innocent, this prison—like a big playground. Albert smiled. Innocence was a scarce commodity in his father's world: a world in which he had been immersed since adolescence. Albert was suddenly ashamed of his life of hidden agendas, ulterior motives, subtexts, and wheels within wheels. Here in the Tower, with the armor, the solid wood, and the ancient traditions, Albert sought and found his lost boyhood.

"Occasionally,"—the Warden's voice echoed off the ageless stone—"at the end of his internship . . . an intern will be pulled out . . . to be beheaded. Mock, of course, but still . . . quite a spectacle."

The breaths came more often now as they were ascending a staircase. "You'll enjoy it. We had a call . . . from a poor chap in . . . Singapore. Sentenced to death . . . for drug trafficking. Wanted actually . . . to be beheaded here. Bit of an anglophile . . . I imagine. Couldn't do it, of course."

Albert worried for the Warden. But now that they were no longer climbing, his breaths came more easily.

"No capital punishment in Europe," said the Warden. "Pity. We would have made a killing. Oh dear. I didn't mean it that way."

Albert laughed. "We could stop and rest here, if you'd like."

"What? Is a strapping young man like yourself growing tired?"

"No, no. But you might be."

"Bah. Of course not. Let's press on."

The Warden waddled down the corridor, walking faster as he passed a heavy door from which some muffled but decidedly unpleasant sounds could be heard.

Albert stopped. "What's in there?"

"There? Oh. The torture chamber."

"More actors, I hope."

"Actually not." The Warden stopped and turned to face Albert.

Albert raised his eyebrows and hoped the Warden couldn't recognize the signs of fear. Not for the first time, he rued the fact that, unlike his father, there were things that scared him.

The Warden laughed. "Not to worry. It's not part of your program. In any case, it's laughably mild by Medieval standards. No racks. No thumbscrews. They're there, of course—for show, but they're not used."

"Obviously, something is being used," said Albert, nervously.

"Yes, but the instruments of torture have yielded to the instruments of correction." The Warden gave a heavy, throaty chuckle. "Not used much." He turned and continued down the corridor. "Except for the occasional . . . surly teenager sent as . . . a last resort by his parents. Extrajudicial, of course."

Albert relaxed. "Lucky my Dad didn't know about this."

"Don't think we'll be able to . . . carry on with it much longer. The European Court of Justice . . . at the Hague is currently . . . considering the matter."

The tour ended where it began, in the Warden's rooms, which were built right into the Tower walls.

"I trust everything was satisfactory," said the Warden.

"Yes. The accommodations have a nice medieval flavor and yet have modern plumbing. But," Albert hesitated, "I would have expected to see a cobweb or two."

"Oh dear. I'm sure you could find the occasional insect's lair about somewhere. But I'm afraid we're rather keen on cleanliness here." The Warden sighed. "I'd dislike losing you as a client, of course, but if you absolutely must have pit toilets and grime, The Bastille might serve you better. The French, you know."

"No, no. This is very nice. I'm sure I'll enjoy my stay here."

"Splendid." The Warden took a contract from his desk. "If you'll just read and sign this, you can begin your incarceration."

Albert took and read over the document. Concentrating, he but dimly heard the Warden's chatter.

"Nothing personal," the Warden went on, " but when you sign the agreement—after we have tea, of course—I won't be able to meet with you socially. International agreements forbid it. Pity. Our clients are usually so interesting. Despite all the surface trappings though, you must remember that this is, in fact, a prison."

"Oh my God." Albert slapped the contract down on the desk. "I don't believe it. It says I can't use my watch-phone."

"Of course you can," said the Warden. "We're not barbarians. Just not between dawn and 8 P.M.—to keep the Medieval feel, you understand. You're free to phone from your room all night long if you so desire."

"I don't know about this." Tiny misgivings nibbled at the edge of Albert's consciousness.

"It's not so bad, really," said the Warden, giving Albert an avuncular pat on the shoulder. "And had we allowed unfettered phone use, our multiplier would have had to be considerably higher."

"OK, OK," said Albert, more to himself than to the Warden. "I can do this. And 8 p.m. here is still only mid-afternoon in Boston." He picked up the contract. "I'd better read the rest of this."

"Yes, do," said the Warden, "by all means."

The ring of a phone interrupted Albert's reading.

The Warden answered. "Yes? Route it through here, please." He turned to Albert. "For you. Your lawyer. You may take it here whilst I pop next door and arrange for tea."

Albert took the phone. "Sydney?"

"I've been trying to reach you on your watch-phone."

"I've just found out they block the signal during the day. Anyway, what's up?"

"You haven't signed yet, have you?" Sydney's voice had lost its usual calm. "Don't sign anything. Don't even pick up a pen."

"I haven't. Why? What's wrong?"

"It's your father. He's had a heart attack."

"Oh my God. He's not—"

"No, no," said Sydney. "They got there in time. Just a routine heart transplant."

"Thank God. I'll call him. There's got to be a video-call booth here—even here. No, wait. I'm coming home."

"I'd thought you'd say that so I've booked you on the nine o'clock Eintracht to Boston. There'll be a heli-cab waiting to take you to Mass. General. And come see me after you visit your father. OK?"

"Fine, but I might as well sign the incarceration contract. I'll just have it start day after tomorrow."

"No!" Sydney shouted. "Don't sign anything. Your father needs you to fill in for him at the G3 hyper-merger. It's in 16 days, and he'll still be flat on his back in the hospital."

"What? No way. Do you know what they'll do to me if I don't start serving my sentence within three days? What am I saying? Of course, you know."

"Do you have the book with you?" said Sydney, calmness returning to his voice.

"What? Yeah. Why?"

"On the trip back, read it. Find a prison with a 0.4 or thereabouts multiplication-factor. The prison certainly won't be any fun, but you can be out in less than two weeks and be able to work the hyper-merger. Your father will pay the incarceration fee."

"No fun?" Albert tried to keep his voice down so the Warden wouldn't hear. "I'll say it'll be no fun. Do you know what they do to people in—"

"OK, OK," Sydney interrupted. "Just come back and talk it over with your Dad. He needs you."

"Yeah. Fine."

Albert hung up the phone and went to seek out the Warden. He explained the situation, said he was sorry that he would have to postpone his incarceration, and was amused that he actually meant it.

The Warden was sympathetic, and arranged for a car to the airport.

ALBERT READ THE book again on the flight home but with far less joy than previously. He looked once more at the Slave Ship, Turkish Prison, and Mississippi Chain Gang options. They had fractional multipliers, but not fractional enough. The Southern Bible Schools and Tibetan Monasteries were better, but not sufficiently so. Then he saw the Malaysia National Prison option. An 0.1 multiplication-factor, but his sentence would conclude with a severe caning on his bare butt. No. There were some things he would not do—not even for his Dad.

Albert returned the book to his briefcase. Feeling that this was not his but his Dad's problem, he regretted not signing the incarceration contract.

ON THE ROOF-TERMINAL of the Massachusetts General Hospital, Albert hopped out of his heli-cab and asked it to wait. Expensive, but it was a good excuse for a short visit. Albert gritted his teeth, and took the elevator down to his father's private room.

The man, even though connected to a mass of tubes and monitors, was still imposing, and Albert felt his old feelings resurface. Yes, there was love but also a fear, not a fear for the body but a feeling that his identity was a birthday candle next to his father's roaring flame—a flame that could melt him to nothingness.

Albert sat in a chair beside the bed. "How's it going, Dad?"

"Fine. Nothing to worry about. In an hour, the doctors are just going to swap out my heart with one of those genetically engineered pig hearts. God, it's good I'm not Jewish."

Albert forced a laugh, which his father cut off.

"This isn't funny. I'm not going to be able to represent my client's interests in the hyper-merger. You'll have to fill in. I'll split my fee, of course."

"Can't do it. The only prison I can go through in time is Malaysia National. And I'm not about to let anyone whip my butt, even for you."

"Too bad. It's a good deal. The Malaysian ringgit is weak right now." The old man smiled. "You know, I once almost sent you to Malaysia National myself. That was when the SEC caught you cyberspying. I wouldn't have cared, except you were cyberspying on one of my major clients. But Malaysia wouldn't accept you, since you weren't convicted by a judge."

Albert suppressed a gasp. He had seen pictures of the Malaysia treatment in his book.

"Oh, don't look so horrified," said the old man. "You were just a pup then and Malaysia goes very easy on teenagers. And you would have picked up some Bahasa. It's a useful language to know."

"Wasn't it enough that you locked me in a closet when you were mad at me?" said Albert with controlled anger.

"Don't be ridiculous. You enjoyed those closet visits."

"But how—" Albert stammered.

"Don't look so surprised. Did you really think I wouldn't understand my own son?" He chuckled, but it sounded more like a growl. "And besides, your mother filled me in on some of the details."

"But if you knew, why did you keep doing it?"

"Look, son. I didn't want to hurt you—not physically, not emotionally. I felt it was enough for you to know you were being punished. And it taught you to gain advantage from any situation, no matter how bad." He chuckled again. "That begging to be let out and the crying. That was very good."

"Wheels within wheels," said Albert under his breath. He didn't know whether he should laugh or cry. He knew he had to re-evaluate his feelings toward his father. But he didn't know how. There were not enough data.

"So you wouldn't have actually thrown a tarantula into the closet with me?"

The old man turned his head to the wall. "I'm ashamed I didn't do it. I was too soft. It would have cured your arachnophobia." He twisted back around and smiled grimly at his son. "You told me you intended to undergo aversion therapy. I bet you haven't done it. Have you?"

"No. Not yet. But what the heck does it matter, anyway?"

"What does it matter? Your fear of spiders is a weakness. And so's your reliance on that damned watchphone."

"What?"

"You've got to be weaned from that crutch. It's what got you into this mess. Look, you'll command a higher fee if people can't simply ring you up whenever they want."

"Dad. I'm not a small boy anymore, where you can tell me what to wear, what to eat, what to think. Not any more."

The old man balled his hand into a fist, raised it quivering a few inches up from the bed, and then let it drop back to the sheets. The gnarled fingers relaxed, but still shook. "I'm trying to help you, damn it. They'll exploit your fears and your weaknesses. You have to stamp them out."

Albert sighed. "I guess I'm not as strong as you are. You've never feared anything."

"Listen, Alby. I'm about to tell you something I've kept secret for a long time."

Albert started, not only because his Dad used his boyhood nickname but also because of the gentleness in his voice.

"Not even your mother knows about it. Sydney knows, of course. Had to. We've been friends since grade school."

Albert leaned in to listen. "Is it about the Synapsis merger? Sydney suggested there was more to it."

"Sort of. You see, I've always wanted to appear fearless, to appear strong. But I once had a phobia—a worse fear than your spiders. I'm still ashamed of it." He took a deep breath.

"Well?"

"I was afraid of the dark."

Albert gave an amused snort. "Lots of kids have that fear. I did too, when I was five."

"Yes, but mine continued into adult life. I was debilitated by it."

Albert laughed. "That's it? That's the big, dark secret?"

"It was a weakness. So, when I was sentenced to three months in the Synapsis affair, I decided on a cure. The Cayman Island prison had a program, still has it in fact. Zero point one multiplier. I was sprung in a little over a week."

"Point one? My God. What did they do to you?"

"Locked me in a totally dark room. It was horrible. For 10 minutes every four hours they turned on the lights so I could eat and use the bathroom. Otherwise, nothing but blackness. Hardest thing I've ever done in my life, but it cured my fear of the dark." He spoke softly—barely above a whisper. "The room had anechoic walls that absorbed sound so well that you could almost not hear your own screams."

Albert smiled. "You know, for me it would almost be a vacation. Strange that it wasn't mentioned in my guide book."

"They're very discreet and get their clients by word of mouth." The old man looked Albert hard in the eyes. "The program still exists. I had an operative visit the prison to make sure."

Slowly, Albert began to understand. "You want me to go there so I can be out in time for the hyper-merger."

The old man nodded.

"You had this all planned, didn't you?"

Albert's father shrugged. "The dark holds no fear for you."

"Wheels within wheels," said Albert, shaking his head in a mixture of admiration and disgust. "OK, OK. Just this once."

"Good. Go and see Sydney. He's got it all arranged. Cayman Correctional. Start of a family tradition."

"Some tradition," said Albert. "And, Dad." He paused, and toyed awkwardly with the buttons on his watch-phone.

"Come on Alby, out with it."

"Get well soon." Albert stood, turned, and started for the door.

"Oh, and Alby. You're a member of the firm, now."

Albert spun around. "What?"

"To handle the merger, you have to be in the firm. I've pulled some strings; they've made you a partner."

"I don't want to be a partner. And I don't want you arranging my life for me." He grasped the doorknob and glowered at his father. "I'd rather be in the prison you've so thoughtfully arranged for me."

The old man smiled. "You'll thank me for this."

"Don't hold your breath," said Albert, turning and plunging through the door. "After the merger, I'm quitting the firm."

"WELL, MY BOY." Sydney stood framed against the darkening sky in his glass-paneled office. "It's not quite entirely arranged."

"Losing your touch, are you, Sydney?" said Albert. "What's the problem?"

"Your sentence is too light. The judge won't allow the Cayman program for anything less than a 60-day sentence."

"I'm crushed, but I assume you have a solution."

"Of course," said Sydney, cheerfully. "You'll have to petition the judge for a lighter sentence—"

"What?"

"—and when your petition is declined, you insult him until you get enough days added for contempt."

"You've got to be kidding."

"Not at all. Should be quite enjoyable telling off the judge and getting what you want in the bargain. Your father would get a great deal of pleasure out of it."

Albert smiled, and then grew serious with a sudden fear. "Damn it, Sydney. I will not let myself become my father."

"Oh, grow up. Maybe the Malaysian treatment would have done you some good."

"Look. I'm getting tired of all this subterfuge." Albert sat on the corner of Sydney's desk. "I want to live my life meaning what I say. I want to look in the mirror every morning and see a . . . a . . . "

"A boy scout," supplied Sydney.

Albert blushed. "Yes, a boy scout. What's wrong with that? And I never want to see another damned loophole."

"Clarification."

"Another damned clarification."

"I'm afraid this is not the time to discuss it." Sydney hurried to the desk. "Although he'd be the last to admit it, your father needs you now."

Albert sighed. "OK, OK. You win. When do I do this?"

"Right now. You'll have to do your own talking. No lawyers allowed. The e-Court of Common Appeals convenes in 10 minutes. One flight down, we have a video-conference link. You're third in the queue." He gathered up some papers and started for the door. "Come on. I've got your case records. I'll tell you what to say as we go."

"YOUR HONOR," said Albert, "I hereby petition for a lighter sentence."

"On what grounds." The judge glanced up from the bench with a bored expression.

Albert looked innocently into the camera. "None, really. I just think my sentence was the result of judicial ineptness."

"The sentence stands—30 days," said the Judge, coolly. "Is there anything else you'd like to add?"

"No. Nothing, except that I think you're an idiot."

"That response could be construed as contempt."

"Of course it's contempt, you moron. And speak plain English, goddamnit."

"You can't say you weren't warned," said the Judge, smiling. "Your sentence is 40 days."

"This is a travesty of justice." Albert raved on. "Where did you get your law degree? From a Cracker-Jack's box?" Albert watched the judge's look of surprised anger and tried not to smile.

"Fifty days," said the Judge with a rough edge to his voice. "Is that enough for you?"

"I'm afraid not, um, you pig."

"Sixty days," said the Judge, practically shouting.

"Thank you, Your Honor. You've been very helpful."

"What? You're welcome." The judge had a very puzzled expression.

Sydney, face red from suppressed laughter, reached over and switched off the connection. "Come on, admit it. You enjoyed it, didn't you?"

Albert smiled, but his eyes were sad. "Yes. I have to admit, I did. But I didn't enjoy enjoying it."

"Your father would've loved to have seen it. It's just what he'd have done."

Sydney moved to retrieve an incoming fax. "From the Court." He handed it to Albert "Thumbprint and sign it. I'll send it back and it's all done." He withdrew an envelope from his desk. "Here are your tickets. You have an early flight to Grand Cayman in the morning. Now, if I might say so, it's *all* arranged."

Albert hesitated and then took the tickets. "You know, Sydney, I'm tired of being a passive pawn. I do have a life, you know."

"I don't doubt it."

"But my father is always manipulating me for his own ends, or 'for my own good.' No more. I'm going to the Cayman Island prison because I want to. From this point on, there'll be no more manipulation."

Albert stormed out of the office and tried to slam the door behind him. But as the door had an air-damper to prevent slamming, he kicked it instead.

CAYMAN CORPORATE CORRECTIONAL looked more like a country club than a prison. It had manicured grounds, an Olympic-size swimming pool and an 18-hole golf course, all surrounded by an unconvincing fence.

Inside, at the orientation, Albert munched hors d'oerves and chatted with staff and the other well-heeled clients who, like himself, were about to begin their incarcerations. The food was good. He had skipped what the airline called breakfast and he was hungry. But most of all, he was tired. After two transatlantic flights, and a further flight to the Caribbean, all he wanted was to hole up somewhere and think. Yes, Sydney was right. It was time to grow up, to be his own man, whoever the hell that might be.

There were no surprises in the Cayman incarceration contract. Albert signed, exchanged his charcoal-gray business suit, red power tie and personal possessions for nondescript prison clothing, and then followed his incarceration councilor to his place of confinement.

Albert almost looked forward to that substitute dark closet: a place where he might recapture the innocence of his childhood. At the room, The councilor opened the door, and Albert stepped inside.

"Oh," said the councilor, "I nearly forgot. I'll have to ask you to surrender your watch-phone."

"What? Why?" said Albert, instinctively pulling his arm back. "No. I can't. I won't. My program is darkness, not communications deprivation."

"Perhaps so, but the darkness has to be complete and your watch-phone has a backlight. I'll have to take it."

Albert held his arm to his chest and looked down at the little device: the thermal-gradient powered watch-phone that drew its energy from the heat of his wrist. It was a part of him, and he couldn't conceive of life without it—not knowing the time, no communications, no video games.

"I have to insist," said the councilor, with some bite to his voice. "You've signed the contract and are subject to our rules now."

"I won't use the light. I promise."

"No." The councilor held out his hand, palm up.

Albert numbly handed over the watch-phone. And for the first time, he realized the meaning of darkness. Unlike the old closet, there'd be no comforting crack of light from under the door, no tiny shaft of light shifting with the movements of his family outside the door. He'd be alone.

Albert fought down a pang of panic. But he could deal with this. He'd make himself deal with it. And his Dad would owe him—big time.

"Lights off in five minutes," said the Councilor as he closed the door.

"Yeah. Fine."

Albert saw the bed, and it looked comfortable. He walked toward it while at the same time examining his temporary home in the few minutes that he still had light. Albert's gaze wandered to the walls lined with anechoic foam. He gasped, then froze in horror. Along the ridges of the foam, were cobwebs—scads of cobwebs. Then he saw the spiders.

They were large, long-legged, but motionless—for now, and Albert was sure that the black monsters were staring at him.

Despite the tropical warmth, he shivered, imagining the brush of tiny arachnid feet against his skin. He wondered if his Dad knew about this and mentally replayed the hospital room conversation. Then it hit him. Of course his father knew. This was all planned. Wheels within wheels. Albert gave a short desperate laugh. "Thank him? I'll kill him!"

The lights went out and Albert screamed.

Softened by the anechoic walls, the scream seemed more the distant cry of a child.

THE PHOBOS
FICTION CONTEST

EMPIRE OF DREAMS AND MIRACLES contains the 12 winning stories from the 2001 Phobos Fiction Contest. These tales of wonder from 10 new authors were chosen out of nearly 200 submissions because they demonstrated literary insight and farsight that set them apart from all others.

But those insights would have been lost were it not for the help of some of SF's finest creative talents. The contest jurors Orson Scott Card, Lawrence M. Krauss, Doug Chiang, Andrew Mason, Thomas Vitale and Jim Shooter were instrumental in selecting the best stories for the anthology.

The following pages highlight Phobos Books' 10 new literary visionaries, as well as the genre veterans whose discriminating choices helped make this anthology a reality.

ABOUT THE AUTHORS

Rebecca Carmi retired from full-time work as a Cantor three years ago to stay home with her children and pursue her life's dream of writing science fiction. Since then two of her short stories, "First Love Twice" and "Gujarat Prime," appeared *in Zoetrope All-Story* online, and in *Artemis*, respectively. She has also written two children's books for Scholastic, Inc. Carmi has a Bachelor's degree in semiotics and comparative literature from Brown University, a Master's degree and investiture from Hebrew Union College, and a Master's in voice performance from the Cleveland Institute of Music. She has sung opera and chamber music professionally. Carmi lives in Ohio with her husband Irad, their sons Amnon and Aryeh and their baby daughter, Yardena.

Daniel Conover has established himself in the field of journalism, and currently serves as the city editor of *The Post and Courier* newspaper in Charleston, South Carolina, but his story "Eula Makes Up Her Mind" is his first published short story and his first attempt at SF. The story was developed at a writers' workshop in New York City in 2001 held by Orson Scott Card and Jay Wentworth, but it draws upon Conover's wealth of life experience, from his investigative journalism to his days in the military when he patrolled the East German/Czech border. Conover lives on the Charleston, South Carolina, peninsula with his wife Janet Edens, his son Luke, and her three children, David, Lee and Callie.

Carl Frederick is a theoretical physicist, theoretically. Although he gave up a junior faculty position at Cornell University to become "Chief Scientist" for a small A.I. software company in Ithaca, New York, he still regards physics as his way of life. Several years ago, Frederick discovered he also had a passion for writing SF. He attended the Odyssey Writers Workshop and has created a web-novel, *Darkzoo* (www.darkzoo.net), where the reader can click to explore a multi-threaded story through different characters' perspectives. He is "tickled silly" to have had two stories selected by the Phobos jury. Rob and Nick, his sons, are tickled as well.

David Barr Kirtley is no stranger to literary success, although he is only 23. Kirtley was one of the biggest winners of the Phobos Fiction contest, with two of his stories, "The Prize" and "They Go Bump," selected by the jury, the latter receiving a special commendation. He wrote his first published story at the age of 16, and as a freshman at Colby College in Waterville, Maine, he won the 1997 *Asimov Magazine* Asimov Award for undergraduate science fiction for his story, "Lest We Forget," which was later published on Asimov's website and in *READ Magazine*. He developed his Phobos Award-winning stories at the 2001 Odyssey Writing Workshop at Southern New Hampshire University, with the help of *New York Times* bestseller Terry Brooks, who was the writer in residence.

Chris Leonard lives in Boulder, Colorado, at the foothills of the Rocky Mountains, with his fiancée, two cats and a dog. Work as a recording engineer, painter, laborer, janitor, teacher's assistant for the disabled, and general roustabout has supported his twin, lifelong addictions to good music and fiction. His other bad habits include book collecting, caving, and diving.

Ken Lui was born in Lanzhou, China, immigrated to America at the age of 11, and has lived in the New England area for the most part since then. He is a graduate of Harvard University, and after a stint as a programmer for a hi-tech start-up, he enrolled at Harvard Law School. Liu hopes that he will be able to write for a living someday.

James Maxey began his writing life 10 years ago, when he dove straight into the deep end, creating a full-length novel entitled *A Distant, Invisible Ocean*. Although he considers this first effort "pure crap," he admits that it gave him the confidence and resolve to continue with his craft. He has had some help along the way from the Writers' Group of the Triad, the Odyssey Writers Workshop, and from Phobos Jury member Orson Scott Card's Writers' Boot Camp.

Andrew Rey graduated from the University of California at Santa Cruz in 1983 with a B.A. in Physics and eventually settled down in La Mesa, California, with his wife Deborah Moses and their son Joshua. He has worked as a technical writer documenting torque values for nuts and bolts in aircraft, but achieved his first success in the fiction realm when he sold his story, "To Touch a Comyn," to Marion Zimmer Bradley's *Renunciates of Darkover* anthology. His wife encouraged him to write "Who Lived in a Shoe," a comic tale of other-worldly house hunting gone wrong, after the couple's adventure searching for their own humble abode.

Rick Sabian lives in Orlando, Florida, with his wife Mary and two children Kristina and Zachary. He received his B.A. in Mass Communications from James Madison University in Virginia, and has since worked in various positions in the film and television industries. He has written professionally for two television shows, and was employed writing biographies by the management company of the Backstreet Boys. "The Compromise," however, represents his first success in the short story format.

Justin Stanchfield describes himself as a full-time rancher, part-time snowplow driver, and occasional musician. The rest of his free time is devoted to writing. He began his writing career penning plays for his local school and has published stories in *Boy's Life* and *Cricket*. He says he will try his hand at anything, but science fiction is his favorite genre. On-line, Stanchfield's fiction has appeared in ezines such as *Electric Wine*, *Dark Planet*, and *Anotherealm*. He has just recently become a member of Science Fiction Writers of America. Stanchfield lives in southwest Montana on his family's cattle ranch with his wife, Connie, his four-year-old daughter, Shealan, a deaf cow dog, a stray cat named Alien and the world's dumbest Chesapeake retriever.

ABOUT THE JUDGES

ORSON SCOTT CARD

Nobody had ever won the Hugo and Nebula Awards for best novel two years in a row, until Orson Scott Card received them both for *Ender's Game* and its sequel *Speaker for the Dead*. Card continued the evolving saga of Ender Wiggin in *Xenocide* and *Children of the Mind*, and returned to the events of *Ender's Game* through the perspective of one of Ender's fellow battle school cadets, Bean, in a novel published by TOR in 1999 entitled *Ender's Shadow*. The Ender series has reached over 20 million readers worldwide, and the original novel is currently being developed as a movie, with Card writing the screenplay. These books comprise only the beginning of this prolific author's bibliography.

Card has broken new ground with each of his major works. "The Homecoming Saga" (the novels *The Memory of Earth, The Call of Earth, The Ships of Earth, Earthfall* and *Earthborn*) was a retelling of ancient scripture as science fiction. *Pastwatch: The Redemption of Christopher Columbus* is the sine qua non of alternative history novels, in which time travelers return from the future to keep Columbus from discovering America. Card's innovative "American Fantasy" series (*The Tales of Alvin Maker*) reexamines American history in a magical version of the Western frontier.

Card has written two books on writing, *Character and Viewpoint* and *How to Write Science Fiction and Fantasy*, the latter of which won a Hugo Award in 1991. He has taught writing courses at several universities, including a novel-writing course at Pepperdine, and workshops at Antioch, Clarion, Clarion West, and the Cape Cod Writers Workshop.

Card received degrees from Brigham Young University (1975) and the University of Utah (1981). He currently lives in Greensboro, North Carolina. He and his wife, Kristine, are parents of five children: Geoffrey, Emily, Charles, Zina Margaret, and Erin Louisa.

DOUG CHIANG

Doug Chiang studied film at the University of California, at Los Angeles, and industrial design at the Center of Creative Studies, College of Art and Design. Chiang got his start as a stop motion animator on the *Pee Wee's Playhouse* television series. He soon rose to become a Clio

Award-winning commercials director and designer for Rhythm and Hues, Digital Productions, and Robert Abel & Associates. In 1989, Chiang joined the pioneer special effects and CGI house founded by George Lucas, Industrial Light & Magic (ILM), and became its Creative Director in 1993. During this time, he worked as Visual Effects Art Director on such well-known films as *Ghost*, *Back to the Future II*, *The Doors*, *Terminator 2*, *Death Becomes Her*, *Forrest Gump*, *Jumanji*, and *The Mask*. He won the Academy Award and a British Academy Award for *Death Becomes Her*, and another British Academy Award for *Forrest Gump*.

In 1995 Chiang left ILM to head the Lucasfilm art department as Design Director for *Star Wars: Episode I—The Phantom Menace*. Chiang has completed work on *Episode II—Attack of the Clones*, and is working on his own multimedia project *Robota: Reign of Machines*, which is being developed as a PHOBOS novel, movie and game.

LAWRENCE M. KRAUSS

Prof. Lawrence M. Krauss is an internationally known theoretical physicist with wide research interests, including the interface between elementary particle physics and Cosmology. His studies include the early universe, the nature of dark matter, general relativity and neutrino astrophysics. He has investigated questions ranging from the nature of exploding stars to the origin of all mass in the universe. He was born in New York City and moved shortly thereafter to Toronto, Canada, where he grew up. He received undergraduate degrees in both

Mathematics and Physics at Carleton University. He received his Ph.D. in Physics from the Massachusetts Institute of Technology (1982), then joined the Harvard Society of Fellows (1982–85). He joined the faculty of the Departments of Physics and Astronomy at Yale University as Assistant Professor in 1985, and Associate Professor in 1988. In 1993 he was named the Ambrose Swasey Professor of Physics, Professor of Astronomy, and Chairman of the Department of Physics at Case Western Reserve University.

Prof. Krauss is the author of several acclaimed books, including *The Fifth Essence: The Search for Dark Matter in the Universe* (Basic Books, 1989), which was named Astronomy Book of the Year by the Astronomical Society of the Pacific; and *Fear of Physics* (Basic Books, 1993), now translated into 12 languages, for which he was a finalist for the American Institute of Physics 1994 Science Writing Award. His next book, *The Physics of Star Trek*, was released in November of 1995 and sold over 200,000 copies in the United States. It was a national bestseller, a selection of 5 major book clubs, including Book-of-the-Month Club, and was serialized in the November 1995 issue of *Wired*. The U.K. book became a top-ten bestseller shortly after its release in May 1996. Translated into 13 languages, the book became the basis for a BBC TV production. A U.S. television production, to be narrated by Prof. Krauss, is currently planned.

His book, *Beyond Star Trek*, appeared in November 1997 and has appeared in 5 foreign editions. *Quintessence: The Mystery of the Missing Mass*, a revision and update of *The Fifth Essence*, appeared in February 2000. His most recent book, published by Little, Brown and Company, is entitled *Atom: An Odyssey from the Big Bang to Life on Earth . . . and Beyond*, and was released in April 2001. Production companies at PBS, the BBC, and Alliance Atlantic are currently raising money to produce a four-part television series, to be hosted by Krauss, based on this book. Prof. Krauss is also preparing a new introductory physics text for non-science majors in association with Prentice Hall.

ANDREW MASON

Andrew Mason began his industry career in the early 1970s as a film editor of documentaries and commercials. Within a couple of years he was producing, and headed a highly successful commercial production company. He ran a large Sydney film laboratory for two years in the late 1970s, before forming Australia's first visual effects company in 1983. He worked as Visual Effects Supervisor on Australian films including *Playing Beattie Bow, One Night Stand, Burke and Wills, Navigator* and *The Time Guardian.*

He returned to producing in 1990, and joined forces with Alex Proyas at Meaningful Eye Contact, producing numerous music videos and commercials directed by Proyas. In 1993, Mason served as Visual Effects Supervisor and Second Unit Director on *The Crow,* directed by Proyas.

In 1996–97 Mason produced the Kafkaesque thriller *Dark City*, also by Proyas, released in the U.S. in early 1998 by New Line. Together with Joel Silver and Barrie Osborne, in 1999, he produced the Wachowski Brothers' cyberpunk blockbuster, *The Matrix*, and is executive producing *The Matrix Reloaded* and *The Matrix Revolutions.* The film was shot in his native Australia, and quickly became one of the most popular and influential movies of the decade. His latest projects include serving as Executive Producer of *Queen of the Damned* and *Scooby-Doo.*

JIM SHOOTER

James C. Shooter was born in Pittsburgh, Pennsylvania, in 1951. At age thirteen—a world record— Shooter became a professional comic book writer, layout artist and cover designer for National Periodical Publications, Inc., publishers of *Superman* and other DC Comics titles. He was trained on the job as a creator, editor and manager of creative organizations by chief editor and executive VP Mort Weisinger, who was responsible not only for the success of the comics, but also for the development of Superman, Batman and other properties for film, television and licensing.

In 1976, Shooter was hired as an editor for Marvel Comics. Among his many duties was plotting the *Amazing Spider-Man* syndicated strip, working closely with Stan Lee, principal creator and founder of Marvel. Shooter became Editor-in-Chief of Marvel in 1978, remaining in that position for nearly ten years. In 1978, the comic book industry was in steep decline. Shooter was a key figure in the creative and marketing effort that, over the course of several years, turned it around and established Marvel as the dominant leader of a revitalized industry. He was made a Vice President in 1981.

In his capacity as creative head of Marvel, he supervised an editorial and production staff of 75 and directed the work of over 200 freelancers. In addition, he served as Marvel's creative representative to domestic and international licensees. He collaborated with toy companies, including Mattel and Hasbro, on the development of toy lines including *GI Joe*, *Transformers* and *Marvel Super Heroes/Secret Wars*, and was responsible for developing animated and other entertainment based on these toy lines.

Shooter also wrote or co-wrote film treatments for *Spider-Man*, *Ghost Rider*, *The X-Men*, *Dazzler* and other characters, working with well-known producers including Dino DeLaurentiis, George Romero, and Stan Dragotti. He also consulted with Michael Winner, New World Television, and Casablanca Record and Filmworks regarding the development of Marvel properties.

In 1989, after leaving Marvel, Shooter founded Voyager Communications Inc., publishers of Valiant Comics, where he was President and Editor in Chief. Originally capitalized at $1.2 million, VCI was sold in 1993 to Acclaim Entertainment for $65 million. Under Acclaim's auspices, the *Turok, Dinosaur Hunter,* and *Shadowman* properties, developed by Shooter, became runaway hit video games. Shooter also founded Enlightened Entertainment Partners, LP, publisher of Defiant Comics and, later, in partnership with Lorne Michaels' Broadway Video Entertainment, LP, founded Broadway Comics.

In August 2000, Shooter became an owner and Head of Creative Affairs of PHOBOS ENTERTAINMENT, a new company created to develop and license science fiction properties. He is also at work on a book about the comics industry called *$uper Villains*.

THOMAS VITALE

Currently Senior Vice President of Programming at the Sci-Fi Channel, Thomas Vitale is responsible for the acquisition and scheduling of all programming on the

Channel. His duties also include some original series/ movie development, as well as current programming responsibility for a number of the Channel's original series, including *Farscape*, the network's biggest hit.

Vitale has worked in television since 1987, with stints at Viacom, in program syndication, and NBC. Vitale has an extra-curricular interest in theater, and recently co-produced an Off-Off Broadway play, *Dyslexic Heart*. A graduate of Williams College, Vitale sits on the board of the Williams Club, and is the NYS Vice President of Fieri National, an Italian-American service, cultural and charitable organization. In his spare time, Vitale writes, runs, and watches way too much television.